Train Dreams

Edited by

Roo B. Doo

and

H.K. Hillman

The Eighth Underdog Anthology from Leg Iron Books

Easter 2019

Disclaimer

These stories are works of fiction. Characters, names, places and incidents are either the product of the authors' imaginations or are used in a fictitious context. Any resemblance to any persons, living or dead, or to any events or locales is entirely coincidental. If any of the events described have really happened to you then I'm afraid that's your own problem.

Copyright notice

All stories are copyright of the original authors.

All rights reserved. No part of this book may be reproduced, scanned or distributed in any form, including digital and electronic or mechanical, including photocopying, recording or by any information storage and retrieval system, without the prior written consent of the relevant author, other than brief quotes used in reviews.

This collection © Leg Iron Books, 2019.

LEG IRON BOOKS

https://legironbooks.co.uk/

Cover art by H. K. Hillman.
UA8 logo design by cade F.O.N Apollyon

ISBN: 9781092636919

Contents

Foreword		5
BOGOF	*Roo B. Doo*	7
A Coelacanth in the Bathroom	*Martyn K. Jones*	19
A Moment in Time	*Mark Ellott*	31
Kevin's Grand Adventure	*Mark Ellott*	41
Danish Boy	*Daniel Royer*	51
New Fish	*Daniel Royer*	57
The Janitor	*Jeani Rector*	71
Under the House	*Jeani Rector*	75
Pandora's Lost Luggage	*H. K. Hillman*	81
A Little Knowledge…	*H. K. Hillman*	95
Claiming Number Eight	*H. K. Hillman*	103
Tears	*Justin Sanebridge*	109
The Mother of God	*Justin Sanebridge*	113
Exchange Students	*Cade F.O.N Apollyon*	115
She's In The Shower	*Cade F.O.N Apollyon*	123
Godjumenas	*Dirk J. J. Vleugels*	143
Cloaked Redemption	*Ginger Huff*	157
The Magician's Last Stand	*Justin Sunshine*	163
The Coming of Spring	*Justin Sunshine*	173
Hope	*Marsha Webb*	183
Six Months, One Week and Four Days	*Marsha Webb*	185
Poetry contents page		189
Afterword		213
About the Authors		215

Foreword

H. K. Hillman

Springtime, and this year the non-themed anthology is bigger than ever. Twelve authors, twenty-two stories and for the first time, a poetry section. I must confess that poetry is beyond my abilities, so it is fortunate indeed that Roo B. Doo was on hand to edit those.

Really though, it's twenty-one stories. Dirk J.J. Vleugels has written a story in Antwerpian and translated it into English and both versions are to be found here. Should the Antwerpian language disappear, this book contains a Rosetta stone to help future historians in their attempts to translate it.

This, the Eighth Underdog Anthology, contains pretty much any genre you can think of. Stories to make you laugh, some to make you shiver. Tales of humans and of aliens, in space and on Earth. Light romances and some very dark tales too. Absurdity and logic, merriment and gloom, anything you want is in here.

What do you see in the cover image? Is it the dawn of a bright new day, with the promise of hope and happiness? Or perhaps it's the onset of night, with all the dark things waiting to come out to play? Your perception of that image might change, depending on which story you happen to be reading.

In storytelling, the reader's imagination is as important as the author's. Often it is the things left unsaid that most affect the reader and, more importantly, in a very individual way for each reader. As with that cover image, what you take from a story depends on how you perceive it. Each person has an individual set of perceptions so no two people ever really read the same story. The same words, yes, but different understandings.

It has become somewhat customary for every successive anthology to include at least one new author. This time we have two: Jeani Rector, editor of the award-winning Horror Zine, and Ginger Huff, who presents the first story I have ever seen with a tense-switch that actually works. Since the point of these anthologies, indeed the very purpose of Leg Iron Books, is to bring new authors to the attention of readers, it is to be hoped that this trend continues.

Without further ado, then, I will leave you to enjoy the dreams of twelve different authors, writing in a very wide range of genres. Transgenre Dreams await your interpretation, using your own set of perceptions.

BOGOF

Roo B. Doo

The supermarket was already a hive of activity by the time Clive Ambrose squelched into the admin office of the Marchway Emporium. He removed his sodden jacket, shook his feet and inspected the wet hem of his trouser legs. "Good grief, Sylvie, the weather's absolutely filthy today."

His assistant looked up from the paperwork on her desk. Sylvie arched a quizzical eyebrow and clucked at the dripping store manager stood in front of her. "Morning, Clive. You're late."

It was barely fifty yards from his reserved parking space to the staff entrance, but the morning's unexpected squally shower had drenched Clive every step of the way. *The car park could do with resurfacing,* he thought glumly. *Some of those puddles were deep.*

"And today of all the days!" Clive exclaimed, pinching wet and steamy glasses off his nose. "Fiona's car wouldn't start, so I had to drop her off at the University first. She had an early lecture. Empowerment of women in a post-Brexit toxic wasteland, or something like that."

Sylvie widened her eyes and pursed her lips. She offered Clive the box of man-sized tissues from her desk. "Doesn't she know you voted to leave?"

"Lord no!" Clive snorted, patting away the rain and perspiration beads that studded his face. "That would kill her. A shock like that could cause an embolism."

"A heart attack..."

"Or at the very least induce a catatonic state."

"But they're all natural causes," Sylvie simpered slyly. "No court would convict you, surely."

Clive dried his glasses off with a fist full of tissues. "Probably not. I'll bear that in mind." As much as he enjoyed the banter with Sylvie, Clive was under no illusion that should his beloved wife Fiona ever find out that he'd voted for Brexit, *she* wouldn't be the spouse to die.

Sylvie pushed her ample frame away from her desk, stood up and slipped on her shoes. She straightened the seam on her skirt and tottered over to the office doorway. "I'll get you a coffee, Clive. A frothy one with sprinkles?"

Clive returned his now freshly dried glasses to his face and looked his assistant up and down. "You look different today, Sylvie. Are you taller?"

"I'm wearing heels."

"I've not seen you in stilettos before. And is that make up?"

Sylvie flicked her thick, blonde hair from her shoulders nonchalantly and plucked a non-existent piece of lint from her sleeve. "Well it's not every day the Emporium is graced by celeb chef royalty. Housewives favourite, Freddie Calender, here, giving a cookery demonstration? I thought I'd make the effort, Clive."

Clive was suddenly worried that he'd gone too far. He would hate to offend Sylvie; sometimes he thought she was his only friend. "No, you look very smart. That's smart thinking, Sylvie. Well done. Smart all round."

Sylvie smiled at her blushing boss and bobbed her head. "So, coffee. With froth and sprinkles?"

"Yes please," Clive said gratefully. He clapped his hands together and looked around his office. "So, big day ahead. I'll go and check out the Freddie Calendar books and DVDs promotion once my shoes have dried out a bit, but I do need to speak to Alan. With this weather, and the amount of customers we're likely to get in today, I suspect we'll need extra matting and mopping."

"I'll find him and send him through," Sylvie said with a smile and left the office with an unsteady wobble.

Clive grimaced and continued to worry about slips, trips and falls.

Kara Swinton pulled the sun visor down from above her head and checked her appearance in the tiny mirror fixed to the back of it. Despite the early hour, she didn't think she looked too bad; a little pale maybe, but better than she ought to considering what little sleep she'd managed to get the night before. As she turned her face from side to side she caught a glimpse of the figure slumped, sleeping in the back seat of the Uber cab they were taking to Marchway, and thought he looked considerably worse than her.

"There's a light if you want to fix your make-up," the driver next to her said helpfully. His eyes didn't waver from the dark road ahead as he reached up and flicked a switch next to the mirror.

Ugh! Kara thought at the dark rings under her eyes, now illuminated by the harsh, blue light that spilled over her. She quickly switched it off and pushed the sun visor up to its original position. She could kill for a cigarette. "No, that's okay. Thank you, I don't want to wake him."

"No problem," the driver replied. He flashed a bright smile at Kara before tilting his head back toward the sleeping figure. "Late night, was it?"

Kara considered telling him that they'd spent the evening in the bar at the House of Commons - how they'd drunk far too much in an effort to keep up with their very thirsty host, an MP of twenty years standing, in an attempt to solicit further backing – but decided against it. "Kinda," she replied with a shrug. "A work thing."

They travelled in silence that was intermittently broken by burbled snores from the back seat. Several times Kara noticed the driver's dark eyes flicking up to the rear view mirror, to stare inquiringly at the slack jawed, drooling face of her boss. *He can't place him*, she decided. *And no wonder, the public rarely sees Freddie Calender, TV chef and food activist, without his trademark grin and sparkling eyes.* Kara stifled a yawn, *I won't tell him unless he asks.*

Freddie turned in his seat and farted loudly.

"Oh Freddie," Kara groaned under her breath and pushed a button on her door. The window whined down and the raw sound of the motorway rushed in. "You'd better do the same," she advised the driver. "It's Dev, right?"

"Yeah and you're Kara," Dev chuckled and shook his head. "That's okay. I lived in India when I was little. Nothing pongs as bad as India. It's like being inoculated against bad smells."

Kara smiled as she allowed the cold air to stream over her face, letting it beat all traces of tiredness away. She breathed deeply; it smelt like rain. "Dev, would it be okay with you if I had a cigarette?"

"Freddie?" Dev started having caught the name. "Is that's Freddie Calender, the chef off the telly?"

Kara pulled a battered metal cigarette case from her coat pocket and waggled it at Dev. "I'll tell you if you'll let me smoke."

"Sure," Dev said, flashing Kara with another bright smile. "If you don't mind that I vape." He pulled a white plastic tube from his door well and twirled it between his fingers, waggling his eyebrows.

"Heh. Not at all." Kara returned his smile; Dev had a nice smile. "Thank you, you're a life saver. This is my first today." She reached into her other coat pocket and pulled out an equally battered lighter. "Of course, the first one always tastes better with coffee," she sighed, lighting up, careful to blow the first drag of smoke out of the window.

"So am I right?" Dev opened his window and took a pull on his vape stick. "I am aren't I? That's Freddie Calender."

"Yes he is," Kara said sweetly, turning back to look fondly over her comatose boss. Freddie shifted and farted again. "TV chef, mediocre businessman," she continued tartly, turning back to face forward, "and scourge of BOGOF." Kara inclined her head toward the open window and took another deep drag on her cigarette. "*That* Freddie Calender."

"And what's a BOGOF?" Dev asked.

Kara laughed softly to cover her surprise. She watched the orange sparks dance atop her cigarette and disappear into the morning air as the car's slipstream simultaneously whisked away its ashen hat. "You've never heard of BOGOF?"

Dev turned his head toward Kara and shook it, although his eyes remained fixed on the road ahead. "No, is it a toilet thing?"

"Eww, no." Kara studied the blank expression on Dev's face and concluded that he really didn't know. "It's short for *'Buy One Get One Free'*... bee-oh-gee-oh-eff. BOGOF." Still nothing. "Obviously you don't do the grocery shopping in your house," she teased.

Dev took another deep pull on his vape stick and blew a plume of steam out of his open window. "If you want to know if I'm in relationship, you can just ask me."

Cheeky sod, Kara thought, coughing to hide her embarrassment; she *had* noticed that the very good looking cab driver *wasn't* wearing a wedding ring. "Okay, I'll play. Do you have a girlfriend, Dev?"

"No," Dev stated seriously before flashing Kara with another winning smile. "But I take my mum to the supermarket and help with the food shop every week. I've just never actually heard anyone call it BOGOF before. Do people even say that?"

"BOGOF," Freddie slurred from the depths of sleep.

Kara and Dev burst into laughter. They tried suppressing their mirth so as not to wake him but their shoulders shook all the more. Kara threw the butt of her exhausted cigarette out of her window and let the rushing wind carry it away with a howl of laughter.

"Surreal," Dev said shaking his head slowly. "My first famous fare and it's completely surreal."

"Freddie has that effect sometimes," Kara sighed. "Have we got very much further to go?" she asked, arching her back. The cigarette and laughter had relaxed her somewhat, but Kara could do with stretching her legs.

"Marchway is about thirty minutes away," Dev replied, glancing up through the windscreen at the overcast sky. "If it doesn't rain." He tapped at the sat nav screen. "Actually, there's a service station coming up. Do you want to stop and get coffee?"

"That would be great, thanks. I'll wake his nibs up then, so he has enough time to come to." Kara knew Freddie would appreciate that, and a strong, black coffee would probably do him the world of good.

"There you go." Sylvie placed a bacon sandwich and cappuccino in front of Clive. "I thought you could do with something to eat as well. I doubt you had time this morning."

Clive was touched. He'd had to forgo his usual bowl of muesli because of Fiona's car troubles. Not that he minded missing Fiona's muesli, but he hadn't realised just how hungry he was until he smelt the aroma of bacon. Clive smacked his lips and beamed up at Sylvie. "Thank you very much indeed."

"You're welcome," Sylvie said, beaming a smile back. "Did you talk to Alan yet?"

Clive took a huge bite out of his sandwich and nodded enthusiastically.

Sylvie liked to see him eat and was quite convinced Clive's wife didn't feed him at all. "Good. I see Freddie Calender is in the newspaper today. We get a mention."

Clive stopped mid-chew and swallowed. "National or local?"

Sylvie pulled a folded newspaper from under her arm and passed it to Clive." Local, but he's in all the nationals as well. Page seven."

Clive wiped his fingers on the napkin Sylvie had thoughtfully tucked under his sandwich, and opened the newspaper. Freddie Calender stared out, all twinkling eyes and dimpled grin. Clive read the accompanying article in silence, while Sylvie watched his brow slowly furrow.

Eventually he looked up. "Here we are at the end, but what's this 'BOG OFF to BOGOF' business? What's he got against 'buy one get one free'?"

Sylvie had already returned to her desk and kicked off her shoes. "I'll look it up," she said, skittering painted nails over the keyboard. "Here we are. I've found the website."

Clive continued eating his sandwich, more slowly this time, and re-read the article.

"It's like it says in the newspaper," Sylvie murmured reading the words on screen. "He's heading up a national campaign to ban 'buy one get one free' deals. *'It's time to tell Big Retail that we don't want more of their junk products that we didn't need in the first place.'* Bloody cheek!"

Clive took a slurp of cappuccino and sucked the foam off his moustache. "Listen to this: *'It's all too easy to be lured into buying ready meals, thinking 'what a bargain', when the truth is, that second portion of processed crap languishing in your fridge, will be binned when it's past its sell-by date because the first tasted so bad.'*" Clive looked up at Sylvie and blinked. "He's very strident in his criticism."

"He's very rude is what he is," Sylvie huffed, bristling with indignation "And quite wrong. Our 'Authentic Dishes of the World' ranges are delicious and very popular. Especially the chicken Tikka Masala in 'Feasts from the East'. Do you think Head Office knows about this?"

"I doubt it, Sylvie." Clive rubbed his hands together to remove any sandwich crumbs from his fingers, and wiped his mouth. "They've been exceptionally buoyed ever since landing Calender's 'Time to Cook' demonstration tour of the UK. His name has a certain cachet, but you're right to ask. We should find out. Can you get me Megan at Head Office on the phone?"

"Of course." Sylvie picked up the receiver of her telephone console and jabbed at the keypad with a pen. "It won't stop with ready meals, Clive, you mark my words. We have BOGOF deals on wine, pet foods, toiletries... Oh good morning. Could I speak to Megan Prendergast, please. Clive Ambrose from the Marchway store would like to speak with her. Thank you, we'll hold." She kept the receiver to her ear but placed a hand over the mouthpiece. "And has he even considered the impact this could have on food banks? I bet he hasn't."

Clive drained his coffee cup and reached down to slip his mostly dried shoes back onto his feet. He appreciated his assistant's feistiness - finding Sylvie strangely attractive when she had her hackles up - but unintended consequences were a fact of life. The trick, in Clive's opinion, was to deal with them as best you can and to always look for the silver lining.

His thinking was interrupted when Sylvie nodded several times toward the phone on his desk. He picked up the receiver. "Good morning, Megan, Clive Ambrose from Marchway here. Tell me, have you seen the Freddie Calender articles in the press today?"

Sylvie leaned back in her chair and watched Clive's conversation. He didn't say much but from his facial expressions and body language, Sylvie could tell that Head Office was as shocked by the news as they were.

"No, of course you need to scrutinise his contract thoroughly. The issue I have is that we're expecting him to arrive in a little over an hour." Clive rolled his eyes at Sylvie at the response he was hearing before eventually saying "Goodbye" and ending the call.

"Well?" Sylvie asked expectantly. "Are we going to cancel?"

Clive stood up and pulled his jacket on. "No, the Legal department needs to study his contract properly. That takes time."

Sylvie gave a snort of disgust. "So we're going to have to be nice to him, all the while he's slagging us off in the press?"

"Well, not us *per se*, he's not stupid," Clive soothed, straightening his tie. "But Head Office seems a little bereft of ideas." He started for the office door, but stopped to pick at something stuck in his teeth. He pulled the irritant out; it was a piece of bacon. He studied it and thought about Fiona's muesli, the morning's deluge and his satisfied bacon-filled stomach, before popping it back into his mouth. *There's always a silver lining to be found.*

"Come along on, Sylvie," Clive said, holding the door open for her. "We should go and inspect the demonstration and promotional areas. I really hope this weather doesn't keep the customers away."

Dev leaned against the pillar in the coffee shop, watching Kara pay at the counter. He allowed his eyes a moment to rake over her slender form, though he quickly looked away when she glanced up and caught his stare. Kara was all smiles as she approached him with the coffees.

"Here you go," she said and handed Dev a cardboard cup, topped with a plastic adult teat. "A tall Flat White. That's on me."

"Thanks Kara, but there's no need."

They moved to the napkin station where Kara liberally applied brown sugar to her larger cup of white chocolate Mocha. "Oh don't worry about. I got it with my loyalty points." She pulled the wooden stirrer between her lips and sucked off the milky foam. "Consider it as part of your tip."

Dev sipped gingerly from the steaming hole in the lid of his cup. "I've had plenty of racing tips as tips but this is much nicer."

"Why? Weren't any of those tips any good?" Kara asked playfully.

"Nah, they were all nags," Dev said with a grin and tilted his cup toward Kara. "Thanks again."

They left the coffee shop and as they reached the entrance doors to the service station, were both surprised to find the rain that threatened earlier had actually arrived. A sheet of water fell from the roof covering the entrance like a second transparent door.

"Oh hell, we're gonna get soaked!" Dev declared as he gauged the strength of the rain and the distance to the car. "We'll have to make a run for it."

"No sodding way," Kara hollered over the sound of the falling rain. "I want to have a smoke before we go back. Freddie hates me smoking." She sauntered over to an empty table and chairs set back from the cascading rain, under the cover the overhanging roof.

Dev followed her and sat down. He patted his pockets. "Oh shit, I've left my vape stick in the car."

"You won't be able to vape when we get back either. Freddie hates that too." Kara said pulling the battered metal box from her pocket and extracted a cigarette. "Would you like one of mine?"

She watched Dev dithering as to whether to take one or not. *Oh you bad girl, Kara*, she chastised herself but felt no pangs of guilt. "You don't have to of course, but you should also consider this as part of your tip."

"No, it's okay," Dev laughed, "but I appreciate the offer." He took the battered Zippo lighter from Kara's hand and flicked it into life. "Here, let me."

Kara took a deep drag and blew the smoke out of the side of her mouth, away from Dev. She took the teated lid off her coffee and took a cautious slip. "Ahh, the second smoke of the day tastes equally as good with coffee."

Dev turned the Zippo lighter between his thumb and index finger. "Hey, the case and lighter match. That's neat."

Kara took another drag and plucked the lighter from Dev's fingers. She placed it on top of the cigarette case. "They were my granddad's. He swapped them with a Yank during the war."

"What did he swap them for?"

"Provisions. They were both POWs in World War Two. I got them when he died a couple of years back. Well, my sister doesn't smoke, so they came to me," Kara said with a shrug. "They're a useful memento."

"Of your granddad," Dev murmured solemnly.

"Well yes," Kara drawled and release a plume of smoke from her mouth. "And that neither smoking, nor bloody combat managed to see him off."

Dev eyed the steadily falling rain and lightly drummed his fingers on the table top. "Go on then, as it's part of my tip."

Kara chuckled and slid her cigarette box and lighter over to Dev. "Knock yourself out."

Dev lit up a cigarette. "So if Freddie Calender doesn't like smoking-"

"He *hates* smoking."

"And vaping-" Dev popped the lid from his Flat White.

"Completely loathes it."

"And hates BOGOFs-" He took a slurp of his coffee.

"Vehemently."

"Is there anything Freddie Calender *does* like?" Dev asked, licking hot foam from his lips.

Kara flicked ash onto the floor. "You mean *apart* from Freddie Calender? Um...". She puffed out her cheeks in contemplation.

"Ha, yes."

"Jammie Dodgers." Kara lent in toward Dev and whispered conspiratorially. "They're his *secret* vice."

Dev smiled and gazed at Kara snort with laughter at her own joke. He let his eyes linger on her pale and beautiful face, and this time, when she caught him staring, Dev did not look away.

He chipped off the remains of his cigarette and stood up. "The rain seems to be easing up some. If you've finished that, I think we could make a run for it. We shouldn't get too wet."

"Okay." Kara took a final drag and discarded the butt into an encroaching puddle of rainwater. It hissed and fizzled out. "Freddie *hates* it when his coffee is cold."

Freddie Calender slung his foot out of back of the black saloon car and into a puddle of water. "Bollocks!" he swore loudly and pulled his foot back inside, wiping the sides of his pristine white trainers against the tufted car mat. "Fella, you've managed to park on a lake. Can't you find us somewhere drier?"

"Sorry," Dev said and reversed out of the parking bay and manoeuvred it into a empty spot immediately behind. "Is that better?"

Kara cracked open her door and looked down. "Yes, much. Thank you, Dev."

"Yeah, thanks mate," Freddie said, slapping Dev hard on the shoulder as he slid out of the car.

"I've got my phone with me if you need me," Kara mumbled and pulled her bag up onto her lap, rummaging inside. "He's booked for three hours but this shouldn't take much longer than that. You're sure you don't mind waiting?"

"No problem."

"I mean, you don't mind us not paying for you to wait." Kara placed her hand on Dev's arm. "I'm so sorry. I had no idea he was going to suggest that."

Dev smiled and shook his head. "No, that's okay. As Freddie pointed out, it's extremely doubtful I'm gonna get another fare from Marchway back to London. Besides he's promised an autographed photo for my mum. I can't leave before I get that."

"Okay then, see you later." Kara open the car door and got out.

Dev sat back in his seat and watched Kara heft her bag up onto her shoulder, and weave her way through the puddles littering the car park, toward the supermarket. He pulled out his vape stick and switched on the radio. All in all, for his first celebrity fare, he thought it had gone pretty well so far. But Kara? She was definitely the best thing about it.

Freddie saw the expectant delegation of suits and primary coloured uniforms before he stepped through the sliding doors and into the supermarket. He knew they had seen him as soon as he heard a squeal of excitement. There was always a squeal.

"Hello Mr Calender!" Clive called out and strode toward him. "We're so pleased to welcome you to the Marchway Emporium." He grabbed Freddie's hand and pumped it enthusiastically. "Very pleased indeed."

"Yeah, I'm excited to be here." Freddie grinned his trademark grin at the waiting crowd before him and shook the proffered hands. "I can't wait to get cooking."

"Shame about the weather but hopefully it won't put too many people off coming out to see you." Clive placed his hand on the small of Freddie's back and attempted to steer him forward. "This way, we're all set up for you."

Freddie stopped. "Wait. I need to introduce you to my assistant," he said tentatively and swung around, looking for the absent Kara. "There she is. Kara!"

She'd just arrived and was stamping her wet boots on the matting inside the door. Kara looked up and smiled at hearing her name. "Hello. How do you do. Golly, it's extremely wet out there."

Sylvie tottered forward and took Kara's hand. "Yes, it's dreadfully unexpected. I'm Sylvie, the Store Manager's assistant. I can take you to dry off first if you like."

"Kara's my go-to gal, aren't you, Kara?" Freddie wrapped an arm around Kara's shoulders and pulled her in tight. "If anybody needs anything of me, especially whilst I'm cooking, speak to Kara. She's on point. Okay?"

"Ah, well perhaps I should give this to you," Sylvie said to Kara, and loosened a page from her clipboard. "It's all the ingredients specifically requested for today. We just want to make sure there's nothing missing."

Freddie grabbed the paper from Sylvie. "No, I'll check that. I am the chef." He pinched his bottom lip between forefinger and thumb as he scanned the list. "No, that's everything. Thank you."

You arse! Kara thought sourly and plucked the page from Freddie's hand. She'd seen the flush of colour in Sylvie's cheeks and decided a spot of charm might be the best remedy. *It's amazing how skillful I've become at charming people since I started working for you,* she admonished Freddie silently.

She passed the paper back to Sylvie with a toothy smile. "Oh my god, your nails are wonderful, Sylvie!" Kara held Sylvie's hand and studied the finish on her nails. "Did you get those done professionally?"

The flush in Sylvie's cheeks turned to blush. "No, I did them myself. I used transfers. I learnt how to do it on the internet. There are so many videos on YouTube..."

"Well then," Clive said clearing his throat and replaced his hand on the small of Freddie's back, nudging him onward. "Shall we go to the kitchen demonstration area? We've converted part of our Riverside cafe for the day. Temporarily of course, but we think you'll be satisfied with the layout."

"Hey! I thought I might find you out here," Dev called out and ambled over to Kara. He passed her a cardboard carton, a wisp of steam curled out from the hole in its lid. "I thought maybe you could do with one of these."

Kara was stood smoking alone in the bright sunshine, and rocking on her feet. The free hand she had stuffed in her coat pocket took the coffee from him gratefully. "Hey! Aw, thank you! How did you know that the third cigarette of the day is *especially* good with coffee? Wow. You're a really excellent cab driver, Dev."

"Thank you, Kara."

"In fact, I suggest you prepare yourself for a most effusive customer review."

"Consider me already bowled over," Dev said with a wide smile. "So how's it going with Freddie's demonstration?"

"Pretty good, I think. Despite the earlier bad weather, he's drawn quite a crowd." Kara took a long drag on her cigarette, followed up by a short sip from her coffee cup. "Have you been shopping?"

Dev was carrying a bulging plastic bag, with the primary coloured Emporium logo emblazoned on the front. "I have. Fortunately I had some time to kill this morning, so I thought I'd check out inside."

Kara smiled and released a cloud of smoke into the bright blue sky. "Did you buy anything nice?"

"Yes I did," Dev said pulling his vape stick from his pocket. "I got some presents for my mum."

"That's cool."

"Yeah." Dev took a hit from his vape stick. "Say, Kara, have you had a chance to look around the rest of the store?"

Kara looked at Dev and flicked the ash from her cigarette. She squinted in the sunshine. "No, not really. I've been busy with the demonstration. Why?"

"It might be nothing, but the Emporium seems really keen on BOGOFs."

"What do you mean?"

Dev shrugged his shoulders and sighed. "I mean, *really* keen. They have a whole aisle of 'buy one get one free' ingredients from Freddie's demo dishes and it's jammed with customers."

"No!" Kara could feel the blood draining from her already too pale face.

"Yeah, there are even food bank reps behind the tills collecting BOGOF donations." Dev reached into his shopping bag and pulled out a book. "And then there's this." Freddie Calender's twinkling eyes and trademarked dimpled grin shone from the cover. "They've got a big promotion of these inside as well. All 'buy one get one free'. I bought this and got one of his DVDs with it. What a bargain! Mum thinks Freddie's great."

Kara placed her coffee cup on the floor before taking the book from Dev. She stared at it in astonishment. It was Freddie's latest title, 'Time To Cook', but a large, primary coloured sticker had been placed over the last word. "'Freddie Calender's Time To BOG OFF'?"

Dev tried hard but the giggle that he'd held inside him could no longer be contained. "I've only known Freddie a morning, but even *I* know that he is gonna hate *that*!"

Kara roared with laughter and grabbed Dev's arm. "We'd best not tell him then, eh? We don't want to spoil his day."

Sylvie was typing into her computer when Clive returned to the Emporium's Admin Office. "Well, that all went off very well in the end, I think," he said, sitting down at his desk. A steaming cup of tea and a jam doughnut, with a thoughtfully placed napkin, were waiting for him. "Thank you, Sylvie. That's very kind of you."

"No problem, Clive." Sylvie turned away from her computer screen so that she could watch Clive take the first sugary bite from his doughnut. "Have you spoken to Alan this afternoon?" she asked.

Clive shook his head and continued chewing.

"He stopped by earlier, cock-a-hoop about something he's posted up on Twitter."

Clive swallowed and licked sugar and jam from his lips. "Alan's on Twitter?"

"Yes. I don't know much about Twitter but Alan says he's got a number of followers on there. They've been liking and retweeting a photo he took of our Freddie Calendar book promotion. Apparently it's gone viral."

"Really?" Clive wiped his fingers on the napkin, woke up his computer and opened Twitter. "Did Alan happen to mention the name of his Twitter handle?" he asked, reaching for his tea and taking a large gulp.

"Yes. He posts anonymously on…" Sylvie paused, peered down at her notebook and grimaced. "At silver streaky bacon?"

And for the second time that day, Clive Ambrose found himself unexpectedly soaked.

A Coelacanth in the Bathroom

Martyn K. Jones

Finding a four foot long fish occupying the bath was a bit of a surprise. Especially at six fifteen on a Monday morning and particularly before breakfast. "I know it's an old bathtub." Perry muttered to himself, blinking wearily at the large, strange looking fish peering dopily back at him through vaguely green tinted water. At this time of day his sleep fogged mind was still running far too slowly to register any shock. "But this is ridiculous."

Maybe if he left the bathroom and came back it would maybe disappear. Maybe he was still dreaming. He pinched himself and blinked hard, twice. No. The fish with skin like Van Gogh's starry night turned in the confined space of their claw footed cast iron antique with a sluggish sploshing and waved an amiable tail back at him.

Who had filled the bathtub anyway? Wouldn't they have heard their flats notoriously eccentric pipework in the middle of the night? And greenish water? Their venerable plumbing occasionally dispensed liquid with a brown tinge, but never green. Perry sniffed. Was that the taint of old seaweed? Sea water? This far inland?

Grabbing his electric razor, he shuffled out of the plastic tile floored bathroom with its awful bland magnolia decor, and the strange four foot long Coelacanth splashing lazily... Wait a moment. This had to be a prank, right? Sandra's younger brother was a zoology student. No doubt he found this hilarious. How the hell he'd smuggled a live living fossil into Perry and Sandra's one and a half bedroomed flat overlooking the High Street without waking them both up, plumbed new depths. Yeah, fish. Depths. Funn-ee. Not. Hang on a minute, how the hell had he known it was a Coelacanth?

Right. Close eyes, pinch self again to wake up. Turn around. He went back to the bathroom and took a picture with his smartphone, then did an image search. Oh shit. It really is..."Sands?" He called gently into the main bedroom that still looked like a bomb full of sheets and pillowcases had gone off in it. Sandra stirred, one gym toned leg visible above the sheets, the rest of her buried under the remnants of last night's frenetic bed olympics. "Sands?" Perry called again hesitantly.

"What?" She muttered, dark bob cut hair barely visible.

"Your brother, that's what." Perry said grumpily. "He's pranking us. Again."

"If it's from the Insect house, it's your problem." Her muffled voice replied. "Oh God, it's not even half past six!" Pink rimmed opalescent eyes fluttered open.

"He's put a Coelacanth in our bath." Perry said.

"A what?" Sandra swung upright, sheets falling away to reveal her exquisite chest. Perry tried hard not to stare and failed miserably.

"A Coelacanth. A bloody great should-have-been-extinct Dino-bloody fish. I just looked it up." He passed his smartphone to her, the wikipedia page quite visible on its tiny screen.

"Don't be ridiculous!" Sandra swung out of bed and brushed past him, bathroom bound and still naked, smelling wonderfully of pheromones.

"They don't have Coelacanths at Darren's University. Or his placement." She called back. The toilet flushed, ancient sounding clangs and squeaks rattling the pipes. There was an astonished pause as she peered into the bath. "Fuck!" Sandra squealed as she almost bowled him off his feet, running back into the bedroom before diving beneath the sheets. "Right!" She snapped. Perry heard her phone dialling out and walked back into the bathroom where the antique fish lazily stirred the bath water with those strange rounded fins. Behind him he could hear Sandra swearing at her younger brother over the phone. "Well, who else do I know who puts weird animals in their older sisters bathroom! You're the zoologist of the family, you tell me!" There was a pause. "Don't lie to me Darren. Get here now! Bring whoever you got to help you and get your horrible thing out of my bath!" Another pause. "I don't know."

Perry stood over the bath, muzzily looking down at the fish. The fish looked back up as amiably as its species allowed, fins sculling gently like it was maintaining position. Sandra stomped back in. "Darren says he had nothing to do with it." She said flatly.

"Yeah, right." Perry shook his head. He turned to stare back at the fish in their bath. It gazed back with oddly human eyes.

"Pez, my little brother's a world class dick, but he's crap at lying." She leaned her chin on his shoulder, and Perry took a deep breath as he felt her warmth pressing into his back.

"Sands. I've got to go to work." He groaned.

"I need a shower and there's a bloody big fish in my bathtub." Her hands crept around his waist. "I'm not going to work smelling like this. Everyone will talk, and you know what the rumour mill is like at my place."

"Look. It appeared overnight. Maybe if we go to work and come home again it will have vanished. It could even be an hallucination brought on by overwork. We've both been putting in a hell of a lot of hours recently. Maybe we're just seeing things."

"I've got a cure for that." She breathed onto his neck. Her hands crept under the waistband of his sleep shorts. "Mm. Look who's rising to the occasion." She gave that deliciously svelte chuckle he could never resist. "Time for a little neuro-pressure therapy?"

"Sands." Perry protested weakly. "It's Monday morning."

"We're both pulling a sickie." She said sharply, the palms of her hands pulled flat against his belly, her voice a sexy whisper in his ear. "I've already phoned in."

"Now you mention it, I am feeling a bit feverish." Perry shivered at her touch and tried not to grin.

"Only one place for a sick man. Bed."

"Right. Coming." Perry busily texted a sick day alert to his line manager. It saved the bother of having to do any amateur dramatics over the phone.

"Oh you will be, you will." She took his hand and towed him off to the bedroom with a giggle.

Three hours later they were lying in a tangle of sheets and pillows listening to water lapping gently in the bathtub. Perry's head was still fizzing and Sandra was snuggled up against him, a cunning little smile on her sweetly sleeping face. I must pay someone to put an extinct species in my bathtub again, he thought. Once I've got my breath back.

Sandra's phone rang. She squirmed in annoyance, one eye peeking out from under a wrinkled sheet. "It's yours." Perry told her. Her hand crept from under the covers and retrieved the buzzing annoyance.

"Darren, you little shit. What are you doing about this fish you left in our bathtub?" She demanded from under billows of cotton and viscose. Perry lay mute on his side of the bed, listening to the one sided conversation with interest.

"I don't care. It must have been you."

"Little brother, you're a terrible liar."

"Come and get it or I'll tell Mum it was you who got her car keyed last week."

"Not my problem."

"I don't care!"

"Just do it Darren. I mean now!" A moment later, her phone hurtled across the bedroom and disappeared into the open wardrobe, where it dropped into last nights hastily discarded Star Trek costumes with a muffled thump. Sandra stuck a pillow over her head as it began to ring again. And kept on ringing until the auto-answer kicked in.

"Want some tea?" Perry sat up and took the safest line he could under the circumstances.

"Mph."

"Is your brother coming to get rid of that fish?" He swung to his feet, pulling on sleep shorts.

"Mph."

"I'm making tea." He tried a more decisive tone.

"Mph."

"Was that a yes Mph, or a no Mph?"

"Mph."

"Tea it is." Perry paused for a moment, only to hear the same gentle sloshing from the bathroom. Moving into their cramped little kitchen, he filled their battered kettle and lit the gas stove, occasionally leaning back out of the doorway, ears alert, when he thought the sloshing from the bathtub stopped. Just in case that damned animal had conveniently disappeared of its own accord. The kettle whistled, Perry made two mugs of what is to many English a universal panacea, taking one in to Sandra, who was by now sitting, propped up in bed, wearing a green t-shirt and trawling the Internet for clues.

"It says here that sometimes quantum portals randomly open between dimensions and dump things into new locations." Sandra looked up hopefully from her screen. "Objects and even people slip across time and space to end up many miles and years from their home."

"Straight into our bath seems a bit, well, convenient, doesn't it?" Perry hedged, sitting on the bed. "You'd think it would more likely get dumped into some pond, a lake, another ocean, into a gutter on the high street. Even a bird bath. These things happen elsewhere, not some random bathroom in an arbitrary English market town. That's just so, you know, ordinary."

"Yes. That's why I still think it was my stupid little brother and his idiot student friends."

"You didn't give him a key to the flat, did you?" Perry asked.

"No. I'm a qualified accounts technician, not a moron. Did you lock the main door last night?"

"Of course. *And* I put the security lock on, the bolt, alarm and the safety chain. Before you ask, the windows are all locked, too." Perry turned and pulled a threadbare section of curtain aside, looking out of their front window into the pedestrianised High Street. Few pedestrians were in evidence on the rain swept brick paving, hurrying to get across the gap between shelter before getting soaked to the skin. A baseball cap wearing delivery driver standing inside the shelter of his van was arguing with a very damp parking attendant, waving their respectively uniformed arms at each other in a form of uptight street-semaphore. "All of them. And your brother doesn't have a key to those, either." he glanced back at Sandra. "Does he?"

"Go and check the front door." She snapped. "If he came in that way he can't have left the chain or security lock on, can he?"

"Okay." He turned to leave the bedroom.

"For goodness sake put some better clothes on first. I can almost see your bits through those shorts." She scolded.

"All right." Perry pulled on his jeans and the cleanest looking t-shirt he could find before going downstairs to examine the front door. As he thought, the safety chain was in place and the door alarm glowed a steady red, indicating that it was armed and undisturbed. He was just about to check the peephole when a loud knocking startled him. Peering through the lens he saw the fish eye distorted figure of Sandra's younger brother Darren, wearing his long dark hair in a rain slicked ponytail, leather jacket spattered with rain droplets. To Perry his sharp edged features gave Darren the air of a mildly annoyed ferret.

"Hang on a minute." Perry said loudly as he deactivated the door alarm.
"Who is it?" Called Sandra from the bedroom.
"Darren." There was a muffled thump and hurried rustling of clothing from upstairs.
"Where's this bloody fish then?" Demanded a damp Darren from the other side of the door.
"Bathroom." Perry replied loudly, fiddling with the clumsy lock. The security chain rattled off the door and Perry opened up. Darren gave Perry a sharp look as he half pushed past and jogged up the bare wooden stairs, footsteps echoing off bare peeling paintwork. Rounding the corner as Perry closed the door.

There was the sound of the bathroom door opening, an astounded pause and wordless cry of astonishment. A moment later, Darren reappeared back at the top of the stairwell, eyes wide, slack mouthed and waving hands frantically. "It-it's a Coelacanth!" He finally forced the words out of his mouth.

"Like we said." Sandra appeared behind him, now dressed in jeans and open neck shirt, dark hair neatly tied back with a scrunchie.

"W-what's it doing in your bath? I-it's an endangered species. You've got an endangered species in your bath." Darren sputtered.

"We know." Perry said tartly. He locked the door and began making his way back up the stairs.

"But, but...." Darren's voice trailed off. He waved a hand vaguely in the direction of the bathroom.

"I take it you know *nothing* about it-" said Sandra, icily sweet and acid, sipping tea.

"Where would *we* get one?" Perry asked.

"The Comoro Islands." Darren momentarily rescued a scrap of certainty from his pit of confusion. "Off the east coast of Africa."

"Well, you're the zoology student. You should know. All we know is what's on wikipedia."

"H-how did it get into your bath?" Darren fought back a stammer.

"That's something we thought you were going to tell us." Sandra replied.

"But there's none in captivity." Darren said. "You're breaking international law!"

"Us? We didn't put it there." Said Perry mildly.

"Okay little brother, full marks for acting." Sandra sneered at Darren.

"No, I mean it. There's all sorts of rules and regulations about the transport of rare and endangered species. That's a CITES One species! On the red list of most endangered!" Darren sounded like he was really panicking. "You're not supposed to, to...."

"Not supposed to what?" Asked Sandra.

"It shouldn't be there!" Darren panic-glanced back over his shoulder.

"Well, maybe it's a Guppy that got flushed down someone's loo and mutated in the sewers, yeah?" Perry twisted the knife, thoroughly enjoying some petty vengeance for all Darren's previous pranks. Well, you could only take so much student level hilarity. Especially when Darren's antipathy toward him was so frequently obvious. Or mutual.

"Well, who do we call? Fishbusters?" Sandra said maliciously, relishing her younger brother's confusion.

"The chip shop? Tell them the special is off the menu because it's in our bath?" Perry added nastily.

"No, no. Let me think." Darren hurriedly dug around in his rain slicked black jacket and pulled out his phone. "I'm going to call my professor. He might know what to do."

Perry and Sandra exchanged looks. Is he telling the truth? Perry suddenly had a falling sensation in his gut, a realisation that things were about to get even more weird. Despite that he managed "I see you find humour a difficult concept." In reply, Darren looked back at him with a panicky blankness.

A few minutes later a flustered Darren sat in Perry and Sandra's cramped kitchenette, flicking worried glances between his phone and the peeling grout above the sink piled with a weekend's worth of dirty dishes. Anything but go near the antique fish-haunted bathroom.

"Well?" Sandra demanded from the dining space doorway.

"He's in a lecture. I left a message." Darren replied.

"What did you say?"

"Just that I'd got something special. Really important."

"You didn't tell him Coelacanth?" Sandra said, one eyebrow raised. The one gesture she specifically saved for Star Trek parties, where she would play the sexy Vulcan to Perry's Captain Archer. Perry returned a weak smile.

"I don't want him to think I'm crazy. Or worse, taking the piss." Darren puffed out his cheeks, got up and stalked into the bathroom. He came back. "It's still there." He said with a harassed look on his face, plonking himself heavily into a badly painted yellow kitchen chair. Perry and Sandra exchanged knowing looks over his head and left the kitchen to snuggle up on their sofa and veg out watching Netflix.

Just after noon, Darren's phone rang. Darren grabbed at it, fumbled and almost threw it in the crockery congested sink. After a few seconds he regained control of his hands and answered the call. Sandra entered the kitchenette, waiting to hear the worst.

"Hi, Professor Langmann? I've got an oddity you might want to have a look at. It's a rare tropical species that's turned up at a private home." There was a pause while Darren listened. "No, none of those. It's actually quite large." Another pause. "No, larger than that." Pause. "Well not quite as large as that, I'm sending you a picture I took earlier." A few seconds later the phone exploded, demanding specific information in tones that could be heard, even in the TV room. Then the call clicked off, leaving Darren looking pale faced and shell shocked. "He says he'll be right over. He swears a lot. Sorry in advance, Sis."

Dr Bryant Langmann PhD arrived an hour later in a bad mood, observed in astonishment and stayed in the bathroom, thin lipped mouth wide open exposing rarely brushed teeth. "Where did you bloody well steal this from?" he demanded of Perry and Sandra as they watched his incredulity from the bathroom doorway. "This is a sodding red list endangered species!" He ran a hand through badly buzz cut pale grey, almost white, hair.

"That's what I told them Professor." Darren protested. He received a sharp look for his trouble.

"We didn't steal it." Sandra said, her face saying what her mouth wasn't going to. "We were hoping you could tell us where it came from." The emphasis on "you" would have split diamond.

"If we'd stolen it, we'd hardly have made Darren call you." Perry pointed out sharply. His fingers twitched at the pompous little man who had been let in by a highly discomfited Darren. What was it with people over fifty? You'd think they owned the bloody planet. With his wide face and skinny build he reminded Perry of an ageing Otter with a beard, and just as ill natured. "You can take the bloody thing away now if you like. We don't want it." Perry said bluntly.

"I want my bath back." Sandra added sharply. "I don't care where it's going, but that fish is going. Today."

"You'll need a certificate from the Ministry of Agriculture." Professor Langmann said sharply, glancing at the creature again and stroking his face-fungus in what he obviously thought was a thoughtful manner. "That will take a week or so."

"A week!" Sandra and Perry chorused.

"In advance." Darren spoke for the first time since his course tutor had arrived.

"Why does it take a week?" Perry said plaintively. "Can't you just get some tank from the University, fill it up with water, and take the bloody thing away?"

"Interpol will have to be notified." The professor added loftily.

"Interpol!" Perry cried out. "Why do you have to call them?"

"We don't care what you do with it, we just want it out of our flat." Sandra was almost snarling.

"As it's a foreign species, the Border Agency will have to be informed. The revenue and customs too." Professor Langmann ticked the points off on overlong fingers.

"You're kidding." Perry stared open mouthed.

"And the Police of course."

"The Police? Can't we just take it to a zoo? Let them deal with it?" Sandra asked tartly.

"No, sorry."

"I'm not having the Police tramping through our stuff." Sandra said firmly. They might find her more risqué costumes, the ones she and Perry reserved for role play at home.

"I'm trying to think of a specialist veterinarian who will approve the paperwork." Langmann added. "He has to fill in the forms. Which have to be signed and countersigned by the right people before they go to the Animal and Plant health agency for approval. Possibly even DEFRA."

"That does it!" Snapped Perry, turning toward the bathroom. "I'm going to throw the bloody thing out of the window!"

"No!" Perry suddenly found himself firmly pinned in the doorway, an elbow at his throat, halitosis in his face. For a small man, the professor was surprisingly strong. "Over my dead body!" snapped Langmann, grey eyes flaring.

Surprised by this sudden show of aggression, Perry struggled to push the smaller man out of the way, but after a few seconds realised the situation was hopeless and stepped back. Langmann turned away sneeringly, took three quick strides, and slammed the bathroom door behind him. There was the sound of the lock clicking shut. A few moments later there was the muffled sound of a phone conversation. Perry kicked the wall in frustration.

"We're screwed. He's just called the Police." Said Darren. "I'm off. See you." His footsteps rapidly dopplered down the stairs, the keychain rattling loudly as the front door slammed shut behind him.

Perry looked across the hallway at Sandra, whose heart shaped face was frozen into a rictus of panic. "Shit." he said after punching a search into his smartphone. There it was on the screen. Maximum penalty two years imprisonment. "They could put us in prison. Two years. Each."

"But we haven't done anything!" Sandra wailed.

"Sands, you know that and so do I, but will the Police?"

"Erm. No." Sandra rapidly got to the answer she was dreading.

"They'll never believe us." he said. "They'll think we stole it."

"If we get arrested or even taken in for questioning we're going to lose our jobs." She stared back at him, heart in mouth. "You know what HR at my place is like."

There was a sudden heavy knocking from downstairs. "Too late." Perry groaned.

A single slightly embarrassed looking Policewoman in high-viz yellow gave him a blank look when he answered. "Professor Langmann?" she asked.

"He's upstairs. He's locked himself in our bathroom." said Perry tersely, working on the assumption of the least said, the better. Maybe this Police officer would simply arrest Langmann and leave them all in peace.

"My colleague will be along shortly." she said and tramped up the stairs, leaving a trail of water as the rain dripped off her waterproof jacket.

Perry looked up the narrow stairwell. "He's in there." he heard Sandra say tartly. Perry opened the door to another knock, and a younger male Policeman entered, giving Perry a suspicious glance. "In the bathroom, with the fish." Perry said. The second Policeman didn't even crack a smile at the Cluedo-inspired wisecrack. He clumped up the stairs to where the Policewoman was knocking at the bathroom door. Sandra appeared at the top of the crowded landing, she and Perry sharing an exasperated look. He heard the bathroom door open and a muffled conversation punctuated by a single startled guffaw from one of the Police Officers. He overheard the crackling of radios as the Police called their base for instructions. With a sigh he closed the front door and went back upstairs.

Perry wearily trudged up the stairs, resigned to whatever nastiness the world was about to dump on him and Sandra. Professor Langmann was arguing with the Policewoman about moving the fish. "To you it's evidence, to zoology it's a precious resource." He was waving an angry finger in their faces. Never a good idea with the Police. "It has to stay until the correct authorities have been informed."

"What about us?" Sandra chimed in, Perry winced. Please don't Sands, things are bad enough already.

"That's for us to decide." said the Policewoman tartly.

"No it isn't!" Langmann raised his voice. "You will do as I tell you!"

The following silence could be cut with a knife as Langmann realised his error. From his position in the stairwell, Perry saw the younger officer reaching to the back of his belt. There was a glint of handcuffs.

What happened next was a bit of a blur. Sandra shouted something about it wasn't her fault that someone had dumped a stupid dinofish in her bathroom and threatened to pull the plug in the bath. She started to open the bathroom door. In response, Langmann lunged at her and the Police reacted.

A uniform cap bounced down the stairwell, stopping next to Perry's feet on the landing. For a moment he stared at the discarded headgear like it was a rain of breaded cod portions. Then looked up. Langmann was face down and red faced with exertion with the younger officer kneeling on his back. There was a ratcheting sound of handcuffs. Sandra had her hand to her mouth, the Policewoman's truncheon underneath her chin pinning her to the wall. There was more crackling of radios and Perry stood paralysed as two more Hi-viz jacketed officers entered and tramped up the stairs.

Hang on, something was missing. He let the police push him gently aside as a sputtering Langmann was dragged to his feet and firmly guided downstairs. The threat of violence receded. What had stopped? Oh yes, the sloshing sound from the bathroom. Sandra was being walked past him in handcuffs by the woman Police officer, tears streaking her face. As she passed she gave him a look which said; this is all your fault. The Policewoman gave him a sidelong, quirky half smile. With a sense of vague horror he could see one officer in their bedroom examining a costume. Oh God, not that one!

From the top of the stairs he heard the voice of an older officer say. "Where's this fish then? My youngest wanted a picture to show her friends."

"What fish?" said someone else.

"Excuse me sir. Did you call us?" Another officer nudged a stricken Perry.

"No. No. Professor Langmann, the man with the beard did." Perry replied distractedly.

The fish was gone? Had he imagined the whole thing? No-one stopped him as he made his way into the bathroom. He stared. The bath was empty. No fish, no green tinted water, only the vaguest hint of sea-smell still tainting the air.

Another man arrived in the bathroom doorway. Mid thirties, receding hairline, wearing a navy blue rain jacket, jeans and a professionally neutral expression. Obviously a plain-clothes policeman. "Sir?" He said in a pronounced Welsh accent.

"I don't know. I really don't know." was all Perry could manage.

"You need a doctor? A counsellor maybe?"

"No, no, I'm okay."

There was a gravid pause. "Yeah, it's things like these that put a crimp in my day too."

"Does this happen often?" Perry asked.

"No." The plain clothes policeman glanced at the bathtub. A dour civilian pushed past him carrying a long lensed camera and small black carry case. "This it Dave?" The newcomer said to the plainclothes officer.

"So I'm told." Said 'Dave'.

"Another day, another non-crime scene." commented the grey haired civilian. "Could you give me some room here sir?" He said to Perry as he began photographing the bathtub and surrounding area. Perry moved over to the doorway. Dave let him pass.

Perry found Sandra in the bedroom, sourly rubbing at her wrists. "They let me go." She sniffed. He sat down on the bed and put a comforting arm around her. "They arrested that professor bloke though." She added with grim satisfaction.

After ten minutes, Dave appeared in the doorway. "Ah good. Can I have a word?" Sandra and Perry nodded mutely. "Read and sign the copies of the official secrets act I'm about to give you." He said cheerily. "Just a formality really. Everything's back to normal, see." He nodded back at the bathroom and handed over two formal looking documents. "Not that anyone will believe you even if you do say anything."

"Were we hallucinating? The Coelacanth and all?" Sandra asked.

"No. These things happen now and again. What can I say?" Dave replied amiably. "It's a bit strange, but the human mind is pretty good at blanking these things out. Best not to worry about it. Oh, and no talking to the Fortean Times or David Icke if you don't mind. That would definitely deep six your credibility."

"W-who are you?" Perry managed.

"Detective Sergeant Dafydd Llewellyn-Evans. Regional Anomaly Task Force."

"Anomaly?" Chorused Perry and Sandra, who giggled hysterically.

"We investigate weird stuff like your alleged fish in the bath." Dave explained patiently. "Not that we can do anything, just put in reports about student pranks and such." He seemed resigned to a fate investigating non-crimes.

"You cover them up?" Perry said.

"Not as such, no. We don't need to." Dave shrugged, handing over a pen. "Just sign where I put the X's. You could try talking to your local press, but frankly they've only one reporter left who mostly covers council meetings and society weddings. If there hasn't been a murder or a lost kitten, frankly she won't be interested." He took back the signed documents with a tired smile. "Take my advice. Go out and see a movie. Have a nice afternoon out. Forget it even happened. I find that helps."

With that polite rejoinder, Detective Sergeant Dafydd Llewellyn-Evans, sole member of the UK Police Anomaly Task Force (Western Division), left the stunned couple to deal with matters in their own way. As he was closing the door at the bottom of the stairs his phone buzzed with a text message.

Oh hell! A rogue Unicorn, a rampant stallion no less, had turned up again. This time in the Tennis courts at an exclusive private girls' school. Much to the alarm of over-protective staff and thorough amusement of their upper crust pupils. Dave sighed heavily, then pulled up his rain hood and stepped out into the High Street. It was going to be one of those Mondays.

A Moment in Time

Mark Ellott

My thanks to my sister Sharon for the idea that set this story in motion.

Thailand.
Hannah Ramsey made her way gingerly forward in the semi-darkness of the cave, reaching out a hand against the wet walls to steady herself. Cold water dripped from the stalactites to the floor, making it slippery underfoot and uneven with the corresponding stalagmites, rising to meet their brothers in the middle, having formed over millennia. Little drips over time, great edifices had created. The yellow beam from her torch illuminated these crystalline structures in this ethereal world, usually hidden from human eyes. She paused and listened, allowing her ears to adapt to the near silence apart from the almost inaudible dripping of those mineral laden drops, straining to hear any sign of life.

Then she caught it. Echoing softly through the darkness, bouncing on the walls and structures of the caliginous crystalline cathedral, the distant sound of voices: whispers moving through the cave system like ethereal spirits in the night. Children's voices. Lost and afraid.

Hannah reached for her radio. "I can hear something. I'm going further in."

She pocketed the radio and moved on, the torch her only guide, in search of the voices' owners.

Then everything stopped. The drips from the stalactites suspended in the air caught in the beam of her torch as she stood completely still like a statue. Frozen as if time itself had no idea what to do next in the claustrophobic silence.

Twenty years earlier, somewhere in the North Sea.
Jack "Hawkeye" Travis looked down at the grey sea below as he piloted the Sikorsky S-92 helicopter in search of survivors from a capsized yacht. The choppy waves gave way to the down-thrust of the helicopter's rotors that created a shallow circular crater on the water's surface. The wind was brisk, gusting at about thirty knots and he continually massaged the controls to keep the craft steady in the air.

As he scanned the sea he could see the keel of the upturned yacht bobbing among the waves—a bright red ellipse contrasting against the stormy grey sea.

"I make it six in the water," he said over the radio.

"Same here. Should be another somewhere," Frank Landers replied from the back of the craft as he peered out of the open hatch at the same patch of grey sea.

Jack tilted the helicopter and turned to get a better view and scanned the waves for a sign of the missing child that he knew was there somewhere. Jack had earned the moniker Hawkeye for good reason, he was able to spot the tiny speck long before anyone else and in that grey, featureless desert of the ocean. It made the difference between life and death for maritime survivors.

"There! Beyond the boat. A child by the look of it."

"Okay, I see. Drop me down and I'll start to get them out," Frank said.

Jack gently lowered the craft towards the sea, holding it steady as the crew lowered the winch with Frank clasping the harness. As he reached the water, he held out a hand and grasped the child, pulling her close as the winch was hoisted back up.

Then time froze.

Everything stopped.

The sea could have been ice, the waves still and silent in mid-air. The rotors ceased to spin and the helicopter remained suspended like a model aeroplane held to a child's ceiling with fishing line and drawing pins.

Time, it seemed, didn't know what to do next.

Thirty five years previously, Bristol.

Sandra Morgan stepped outside her front door and pulled it shut. She adjusted her woollen beret and turned to lift her bicycle from the garden wall against which it currently leaned. Then she stopped and went back to the door, giving it one final check before going back to the bike. Then, just to make sure, she went back again, opened the door, walked through the flat to the kitchen and checked that the gas hob was switched off, before returning to the front door, pulling it closed then pushing and pulling a few more times to be absolutely certain that it was locked shut.

Satisfied, she put her bag and books into the basket on the handlebars and wheeled the machine out through the gate. Looking up and down the street, she moved the bike into the road and sat astride it, facing down to the traffic light junction at the bottom of the hill. Pushing away from the kerb, she pedalled lightly to get moving and then allowed the machine to freewheel as it picked up speed.

She didn't notice the ginger cat called Zorro sitting on the wall as she passed by. He looked up briefly and resumed his morning toilet, focussing his attention on the important task of licking his paws and wiping his whiskers. The open tin of tuna that he had stolen had gone down well even if it had made him temporarily *cattus non grata*. He decided that the prize had been worth the minor inconvenience of being chased out of the house and held in disgrace. The tuna was now in his stomach, so that was a win as far as he was concerned.

Charlie Sutton was running late. He down shifted and accelerated, ignoring the 30mph speed limit. The loud aftermarket exhaust fitted to his mundane Ford Focus made more noise than speed, but he enjoyed the cacophony even if those he passed on the pavement were less enthusiastic. He turned up the stereo and started tapping the steering wheel in time to the monotonous beat.

Archie Travis shut the front door with one hand and tried to restrain his excitable dog, Toby, with the other.

"Toby, wait!" He scolded, fiddling with the lock. Finally the door was secure and he could make the way to the garden gate. As he shut it behind him, he could see along the road to the traffic lights and Sandra setting off down the hill a hundred yards or so away. His heart skipped a beat and he sighed. One day perhaps he would pluck up the courage to do more than shout a breathless "hi" when they passed. As it was, this morning he didn't even get that opportunity. Toby was one of those gangling dogs of indeterminate ancestry with more legs than seemed decent and a boundless enthusiasm for everything except discipline, so Archie had wasted several minutes calming him down enough to put on the collar and lead. Consequently, the brief morning exchange with his crush had been missed.

"Come on," he said with a dispirited sigh. Toby needed no encouragement and bounded forwards, dragging Archie behind him.

And Death waited. He sat astride his horse atop the hill where he could see everything unfold. He looked across to the right, through the buildings to Charlie's car now making steady progress towards the lights from that direction. *Too fast,* Death thought to himself. Currently Charlie was in luck as they were green in his favour and red against Sandra.

Death looked down from his saddle at the young woman freewheeling down the hill and sighed. He fished about in his cape and pulled out his phone. Tapping the app, stabbing at the screen with a bony digit with irritation, he got the same display as before.

"It still says there is an error message," He muttered to no one in particular. *"Why are these messages so unhelpful?"* He frowned at the phone, which was pretty good going, given that he had neither flesh on his forehead nor eyebrows to frown with, but he managed it nonetheless.

"What is an out of memory error supposed to be anyway? Why don't they tell you in plain English what they mean? Bloody technology!" Death looked back on the old days with some fondness—when he had a room full of hourglasses to work with. Sure, he thought to himself, it might be crude from a technology point of view, but it worked and was reliable—not like

this modern stuff and its vague "out of memory" messages, which could mean anything. It hadn't been the same since the IT guys took over and changed everything for the better—when they weren't fannying about with Grand Theft Auto. Besides, he thought darkly, "better" is a subjective term. "Better" for him was a room full of nice comforting hourglasses in tactile wood and glass that you could touch and look at and worked as they were supposed to, not like this technology stuff that worked in ways mysterious to the mind of supernatural beings, lost in electrons and opaque gadgetry.

He snorted to himself as he watched events unfolding. Something wasn't in tune here and he didn't like it. Then he made a decision.

"No, no, no, this isn't right. Not at all." He snapped his fingers and time stopped. Just like that. Charlie at the wheel of his battered focus, fingers mid tap on the steering wheel, Sandra with her coat and skirt flying in the wind, one hand holding onto her woollen beret as she rolled down to the junction, Zorro, mid lick, Toby straining at the lead as he took Archie for a walk and Archie struggling to keep the dog in check and failing.

Everything stopped. The tableau became a frozen moment in time as time waited for events to happen.

Death turned his horse and rode off, leaving everything as it was.

Death dismounted and looked about him. The red brick structure stood above the bleak, empty landscape and was so tall that it came close to touching the ominous grey clouds that scudded across the dreary sky, oozing desolation for all who entered and dared to face the eternal bureaucracy that resided therein. He sighed as he looped the reins around a post, leaving his horse outside the building as he went inside with a heavy heart, for despite his better instincts, he had no choice.

Upon arriving at reception, he presented himself at a cubicle where a middle-aged woman with brassy hair looked at him with a disinterested stare, her cigarette dangling from the corner of her mouth.

"Yes?"

"I need to speak to someone about this," Death said, waving the phone in front of the glass partition that separated them.

The woman glanced down briefly. "That's an IT issue."

"Well, I need to speak to someone about it."

She shrugged and glanced up at a screen on the wall opposite. The screen had a number on it: 137. She pulled a ticket from a reel and pushed it under the glass screen.

"Well, you will have to wait your turn."

Death picked up the ticket. *"Number two."* He looked about him at the room full of entities all waiting patiently for their number to come up. The screen changed to 136 and a man in full Napoleonic uniform of the Imperial Guard got up and walked across the room to the door.

"French," Death muttered. *"What are the French doing here?"*

"We welcome all sorts here, you know. We do equal opportunities. You need to get with the programme. Have you been on the diversity course?"

Death glared a negative then grunted. *"But the **French**..."*

"Go and sit down and stop making a fuss before someone puts your name down for one."

Death concluded that this was not going well already and he was not going on a diversity course come what may—he had other, more useful, things to be getting on with. He had managed to avoid going so far and intended to keep it that way so decided to drop the matter and wait. He realised looking at the room that this was not going to be a speedy affair and resigned himself to a long wait. He nodded down to the packet of cigarettes lying on the counter in front of the receptionist.

"Er, do you mind?"

She sighed. "Do you ever plan to buy any of your own? You do realise that you have a reputation for bumming ciggies off people?"

"I'm a supernatural being made of ectoplasm that exists in the folds of time and space. I don't have any money to buy cigarettes. Besides, I have been banned from the local tobacconists."

The receptionist raised an eyebrow. "Do tell."

"Apparently I was frightening the clientele."

She laughed and pushed the packet across the counter. "Here, take the packet."

Death thanked her and walked across the room to an empty chair where he sat. He lit a cigarette and watched the plume of smoke as it spiralled into the air, up towards a cobweb that hung from the ceiling.

"Ahem!"

Death started out of his reverie and looked about him, but didn't see the owner of the cough, so returned to idly watching the cobweb.

"Ahem!"

Again, Death looked about him. This time he identified the cougher. A goblin of indistinct age and gender with bright green spiky hair, a lobster coloured face and large pebble glasses. The black eyes seemed to leap out from the glasses and punch Death in the face with suppressed anger.

"Nasty cough, you have there," Death said pleasantly, taking another drag on the cigarette. *"You should try some throat pastilles."*

The lobster face went from pink to puce. Death thought to himself that the colour really didn't match the green hair, but kept the thought to himself. The eyes leapt in and out of the pebble glasses in an attempt to spear him with their intensity.

"A*HEM*!!!!"

Death realised that the goblin creature wasn't looking at him at all. Indeed, he followed the line of the gimlet gaze, realising that it was fixed on an area above his head. He looked upwards, but saw nothing other than the cobweb and he thought it unlikely that the goblin creature was angry about that. Although, he thought idly, perhaps getting angry at cobwebs was a thing these days. He could never keep up with the latest trends.

This time the "AAAHEEEEMMM!!!" was accompanied by a stabbing finger as well as an exaggerated thumping of the chest with the other hand, just to make the point.

Death realised now that it was the wall behind him that was the problem, so he shifted in his chair and turned around to look at the "no smoking" sign above his head. The sign he had failed to notice when he sat down.

"Ah," he said, glancing at the ashtray on the table between them, not missing the incongruity, *"I see. Well, I wouldn't worry about it, no one is alive in this room, so no harm done, what?"*

"I'll report you! You aren't allowed to smoke in here!"

Death nodded to the ashtray filled with stubs and ash. *"So why is this provided?"* he asked pleasantly.

"I'm telling you, you can't…"

Death was growing weary of the exchange. *"Well, now you've told me, so report away,"* he said, taking another drag and leaning back in the chair with no obvious sign that he planned to comply.

The goblin clenched its fists and huffed a bit before deciding that this was not a winning strategy, so muttered loudly to anyone who would listen—which wasn't anyone at all—that Death's cigarette made an offensive smell and took itself over to the other side of the room where it cast sulky glares across at Death, who by this time had forgotten the exchange, having returned his attention to the cobweb, which was far more interesting.

After what seemed an aeon, but was probably closer to an aeon and a half, Death noticed that the lobster-faced goblin had gone and his own number was now showing on the screen.

He stood, pulled his cape about him and hefted his scythe over his shoulder and walked to the door, turned the handle and stepped inside.

The room was empty. By empty, I mean devoid of anything. A complete lack of thing. Not even an atom. Like space but without the stars, planets and space junk. A void. Most would be alarmed by this, but Death was unperturbed. He stood there in the lightless emptiness and waited.

"OH, IT'S YOU." The voice echoed across the ages of time and space.

"Yes."

"WELL, WHAT DO YOU WANT? I DON'T HAVE ALL DAY, YOU KNOW."

"I have a problem. It's an error message on my phone."

There was silence for a moment—or maybe longer. It was difficult to tell. It could have been seconds, years, or decades, but Death became aware of a crossing of arms, a tapping foot impatiently urging him to get to the point and stop fannying about complaining about his mobile phone.

"THIS IS NOT THE IT DEPARTMENT. AND YOU SHOULD NOT BE MESSING ABOUT ON YOUR PHONE WHILE WORKING."

"It's the work phone," Death replied, deadpan. *"It has an out of memory error and keeps sending me to the same point in time. There's something wrong."*

"THAT'S IT? SOMETHING WRONG WITH YOUR PHONE? DO I LOOK LIKE AN IT TECHNICIAN? I DON'T EVEN KNOW HOW TO PLAY GRAND THEFT AUTO."

Death sighed. This wasn't going to plan. He tried again. *"It's sending me to the wrong moment in time."*

The voice went silent for another moment and Death could have sworn there was some shuffling going on.

"I DON'T PAY YOU TO…"

"Actually, you don't pay me—my being a supernatural being consisting of ectoplasm and all that."

"DON'T GET SMART. HAVE YOU TRIED…"

"Switching it off and on again? Yes, of course." Death sighed heavily, which merely served to irritate the voice even more. *"I even did a factory reset, but it keeps doing the same thing—sending me to a specific point in time and space. The **wrong** point in time and space."*

"AND HOW DO YOU KNOW IT IS THE WRONG POINT IN TIME AND SPACE? ARE YOU BETTER THAN THE TECHNOLOGY? OR IS IT JUST A HUNCH?"

*"I just **know**. Because I am aware of all of time."*

The voice sighed. "IF YOU THINK THERE IS A FAULT WITH THE PHONE, THEN TAKE IT TO SUPPORT—ASSUMING THEY AREN'T FANNYING ABOUT WITH GRAND THEFT AUTO. HOWEVER, AS I AM ALSO AWARE OF ALL THINGS ALL OF THE TIME, I AM NOT COGNISANT OF ANY ERROR, SO GO AND DO THE JOB YOU ARE PAID TO DO."

"Actually… That payment thing… Seeing as you mentioned it…"

"ENOUGH! GET BACK TO WORK AND COMPLETE THE JOB YOU WERE SENT TO DO. TAKE THE PHONE TO THE IT DEPARTMENT WHEN YOU ARE NEXT IN THE OFFICE."

There was a flash of light, indicating that the interview was over and Death found himself again at the road in Bristol, sitting astride his horse. *"That went well."*

He fished out the phone and it still showed this time and date along with the error message. *"Bugger!"*

He contemplated matters for a moment or two and then made a decision. He looked across at the cat, Zorro, catching his eye. Zorro nodded, stood up and stretched. He then dropped onto the pavement directly in front of Toby, trying desperately to ignore the face full of bone breath that came his way accompanied by a sou'wester awash with canine drool. He arched his back, bushed out his tail, hissed and swiped the unfortunate dog across the nose, before turning and running down the hill.

Toby couldn't help himself. He sprang into action and tore off after Zorro, legs and ears flapping in the breeze. Taken completely by surprise, Archie was pulled forwards, tripped on a loose paving slab and fell face forwards on the pavement releasing his tenuous grip on the leash. His glasses slid along the pavement after the departing dog. He was aware of a pain in his right knee as it hit the concrete. "Toby! Come back!" he yelled, to no avail.

Zorro hurtled down the hill, passing Sandra just as her bike was picking up speed. Once well clear, he executed a right turn between two parked cars, across the road and up a tree on the far side where he watched the hapless Toby try to follow. The dog's brain was willing, but his hind quarters were slow to react and with feet flailing, he skidded, rolled and finally shot out between the cars directly into Sandra's path.

Sandra yelped in alarm and grabbed the bicycle's brakes, causing the front wheel to lock with the inevitable result. She somersaulted over the handlebars to land flat on her back among the debris of her books that had flown from the basket on the handlebars. She lay there, winded and aware that there was pain in various parts of her body, but mostly her ribs.

Archie, having dragged himself to his feet and replaced his glasses, limped across to where she lay, oblivious to the rip in his trousers or the blood seeping from the wound in his left knee.

"Are you alright? I'm so sorry!"

She sat gingerly and winced as he lifted her. "Ow! I may have cracked a rib."

"Here, let me help you."

Death looked down at the junction and noticed that the traffic lights had changed to green, which meant that Charlie was now approaching a red light. He was travelling too fast to react. His right foot briefly moved over the brake but he realised that he wasn't going to stop, so put it back on the accelerator and pushed hard, sailing across the empty junction against a red light.

Death smiled.

Archie was helping Sandra get herself and her bike back on the pavement and was fussing over her like a mother hen. Zorro was sitting in the tree nonchalantly dangling his tail, teasing Toby who tried to leap up the tree with an enthusiastic bark.

Death pulled his phone out. The error message was gone. *"Another sixty-five years,"* he said to no one in particular. *"That's more like it."*

He looked up at Zorro and exchanged a glance. He lifted a bony finger in salute and the cat nodded.

"Thanks for that," he said. *"She becomes a surgeon, you know. Saves countless lives during her career, but there's something even more important. They have a son,"* he explained as he looked across at the couple busily picking up books from the road. *"Becomes a helicopter pilot with Air Sea Rescue. He too saves lives. But he has a knack of seeing what others miss. One of his rescues involves a little girl. No one else could see her in the sea. If he hadn't been there, she would have died. Which means that the children she will rescue from the caves in Thailand years later would also have died."*

He sat watching the couple who were now in animated conversation. Archie finally got his wish to talk to the woman he had adored from afar. And Death was pleased with himself—being a bit of an old romantic at heart. He wondered briefly if perhaps he was in the wrong job.

"If she had died today, none of those other lives would have happened," he said, returning his glance to Zorro who by this time had become bored with tormenting Toby. He was busy licking his nether regions with a loud slurping noise that bordered on the disgusting. Death grunted. *"Talk to myself why not? Ah, well…"*

He flicked the reins and nudged his horse into motion.

"Come on, we had better get back. I'm in enough trouble as it is."

Kevin's Grand Adventure

Mark Ellott

What follows is mostly true—apart from the bits that aren't.

Marika Spalding had been reflecting on the state of life, the universe and everything while examining the insides of her eyelids when the chiming of her mobile disturbed her reverie. She dropped her feet from the desk, sat up and reached for the phone.

Marika had retired from the police force a few years earlier and, deciding that her detective skills should not go to waste, set up a pet detective agency with her husband Nick, who, like her had worked on the force and shared her love of animals—although he was more a dog person while Marika preferred cats. Their experience and contacts within the police enabled them to track down lost and stolen pets with a high success rate when the police were disinterested in what they tended to refer to as petty crime. Petty to them, Marika had once observed sharply, but not to the owners of the missing pets. Nick frequently found himself attempting to curb Marika's acid tongue but without much success. He worried that good relations with the police might suffer as a result. Marika sometimes appeared to him to have no such concerns.

"Good afternoon, Spalding Pet Detectives, Marika speaking." She reached across the desk for a notepad and pen, scribbling notes as she listened.

"At what time was this? Eleven thirty. And that was yesterday. I see. And there has been no contact at all? Okay, that's fine. Do you have a description of the vehicle? Oh, good, yes, a licence plate will help enormously. A white camper van. Yes, I've got that. And the suspect? Yes, yes, I've got that, thank you. And finally, Mrs Sheldon, the animal? Kevin? That's an unusual name for a cat… Ah, right, I see, yes, I get it. Long haired ginger and white, yellow eyes. Well, I think I have enough to go on for now. I'll be in touch. In the meantime, yes keep phoning around the local veterinary surgeries and animal charities. Oh, and let the chip company know."

She disconnected the phone.

"Nick!"

"Yes," he said, coming into the room. "No need to shout, I do have functioning ears, you know…"

"Yeah, yeah, you're usually in a world of your own, so waking you up from it is necessary. Anyway, we need to pack."

"Anywhere interesting?"

"Devon. A stolen cat."

Nick took the wheel and Marika briefed him as he drove.

"So we have a fourteen year old cat kidnapped by a man in his fifties. Eleven thirty yesterday morning."

"Any special breed?"

"Moggy."

"What circumstances do we have?" Nick asked.

"A neighbour of Mrs Sheldon, Kevin's owner...."

"*Kevin*?" He arched his eyebrows and glanced across at her.

"Yeah, something to do with football, I gather."

"Oh, okay. Go on."

"Well, anyway, this neighbour," she checked her notes, "Patricia Longmuir, noticed someone behaving suspiciously in her front garden, so she went out to confront him. At which point he grabbed the cat who was sunning himself in the garden and said something about taking it to the RSPCA. Mrs Longmuir explained that the cat belonged to a neighbour..."

"Mrs Sheldon."

"Yes, Mrs Sheldon. Anyway, he took the cat to his camper van and made his escape. Mrs Longmuir tried to prevent him from getting away and was nearly run over as he got away. She was lucky not to be injured. All of this was witnessed by her daughter." She checked her notes again. "Helen."

"Is there a police report?"

"Yes. I plan to contact the investigating officer when we arrive. However, I understand from Mrs Sheldon that they are only interested in the cat in the context of the altercation between Mrs Longmuir and the suspect."

Marika lapsed into silence as Nick drove. Marika looked across at her husband and mentally noted that his tousled brown hair was in need of a tidy-up. Indeed, at his age, the flecks of grey would normally look distinguished, but distinguished and Nick weren't so much ships that passed in the night as ships on different oceans on different months of the year on different hemispheres. His attire was similarly casual—faded jeans, tee shirt and threadbare corduroy jacket were his usual garb, contrasting starkly with Marika's immaculate two-piece navy suit and white blouse. She looked in the vanity mirror and adjusted the not quite natural raven hair that fell in curtains around her heart-shaped face.

"Do we have a description of the van?" he asked.

"Better than that—we have a registration number, so we can contact DVLA for the owner's details. It'll take time, though. As always. The police will also be looking for it, but from what I've gathered so far, no one has seen it."

On arrival, they agreed to split their resources. Marika wanted to speak to the investigating officer. "I'll see what I can find out about the vehicle," Nick said as he dropped her off. "Meet up later and compare notes, eh?"

She slammed the door shut and walked up the steps to the small provincial police station. Eventually she was led to an interview room where a blonde woman joined her and closed the door. She held out her hand "DC Samantha Reynolds," she said. "So, Ms Spalding, I believe you are ex-job. What is it that you want to know?"

Marika outlined what she knew so far. "Details of the vehicle's owner would help. Speed things up a bit."

Reynolds shook her head. "Sorry, I can't help with that. All I can say is that we haven't yet located it."

Marika wasn't surprised. However, she pressed on. "How far has your investigation into the missing cat got?"

Reynolds sighed. "I'll be frank with you, Ms Spalding, we are not concerned about the cat. It is not our business to be looking for missing pets—more yours, I presume—we are, however, interested in apprehending this person due to the attempted assault on Mrs Longmuir.

Marika leaned back in her chair and studied the younger woman sitting across the table opposite. "DC Reynolds, I should not have to remind you of the Theft Act of 1968 and that a cat is deemed to be chattel under the terms of the act. So, despite them being regarded as wild animals as far as the Animal Welfare Act 2006 is concerned, the theft of this animal is very much in your jurisdiction."

The frosty look on Reynolds' face told Marika that this interview was now at an end and that she probably hadn't made a friend here. Once more her tongue had got the better of her. She wasn't a DI anymore and there were times when it rankled. Not that she worried overmuch on this occasion as she didn't think that the local plod were going to be much of an asset to her anyway.

She stood to leave. "Well, thank you for your time, DC Reynolds. If I uncover anything that will help with your investigation, I'll be in touch."

She was outside the station when her phone chirruped.

"Nick? What have you found?"

"Big fat zero. I've been to the petrol stations in the area—all two of 'em—and no sign. One had CCTV, but that didn't show up anything either. What about you?"

"Local plod is being local plod."

She heard him snort with barely suppressed laughter. "Did you expect anything else?"

"Nope."

"So, now what?"

"The victim, I think"

"I'll pick you up."

"Okay, how far away are you?"

"About ten minutes."

They drove to the edge of the town where Sandy Sheldon lived with her

43

small son and a menagerie of animals including five cats, a couple of dogs, and several rodents. A slightly worried looking woman with greying dark hair, she greeted her guests and invited them in.

Having been swamped by the attentions of two cocker spaniels that were rather more enthusiastic in their greeting than Marika and Nick were expecting, they sat, whereupon the animals each chose a lap and parked themselves.

"Tea?" Sandy asked.

"Thank you."

As she started towards the kitchen, the doorbell rang and Sandy rushed to the door, just about beating the spaniels, who leapt off their respective laps and lunged towards the door, barking with enthusiasm.

She opened the door and ushered in the two arrivals, a woman in her early forties and a girl of around twelve.

"This is my neighbour, Pat and her daughter, Helen. I thought you would want to speak to them." She then disappeared into the kitchen followed by the dogs and a couple of cats who felt that this was an opportunity not to be passed up.

"So, Helen, I understand you saw everything," Marika started.

"Yes, I was outside in the street when I saw this man. He was in our garden and I thought it a bit odd."

"Can you describe him?"

"He was old. Well, older than thirty, *very* old…"

Marika and Nick exchanged glances. *Well, that's us done for, then.*

"Go on."

"He had a scruffy coat. He had jeans on and a woolly hat."

Marika turned to the girl's mother. "Anything to add to that, Mrs Longmuir?"

"I'd say he was probably in his fifties. About my own height. As Helen said, scruffy. He hadn't shaved in several days—nor washed." She wrinkled her nose at the memory.

"Dark hair? Light hair? Balding? Thick set? Skinny?"

"Oh, yes, dark hair… going a bit grey, I think… and fairly thick set, I'd say."

Marika made notes as she listened. "And the vehicle? It was a camper van, I understand?"

"Yes, we got the number. We gave it to the police."

"So I understand. A white converted Transit, I believe?"

"Yes. Tatty. Rust everywhere."

"We've set up a Facebook page," Helen said as Sandy came in with a tray of tea, followed by the dogs, who seemed disappointed that there was nothing for them.

"And I have informed all of the local vets and animal charities," Sandy said, putting the tray down on one of the few clear spaces. The dogs padded their way over to Nick and made themselves comfortable snuggling up to him on the sofa.

"Okay, let me see the page," Marika said. Helen proffered a tablet with the site open and Marika scrolled down the screen, noting that it had already generated a great deal of attention. Cat kidnapping struck a chord with people. They didn't like it. "Right, put up a post on the page stating that he needs to have his medication."

Sandy frowned. "Apart from his flea treatment, he doesn't need any."

Marika smiled. "You know that. I know that. Our kidnapper doesn't. If we assume that he cares for the animal in any way, he will start to worry. The page tells him that the local vets know the animal is missing. There is a photograph, so disguising him will be difficult. He is microchipped. Taking him to a vet for treatment is now a problem. And we tell him that this is precisely what he needs to do."

She turned to Pat. "Which way did the van go after you tried to stop it?"

Pat took a sip of her tea. "Along the road towards the edge of town. That is, away from the town centre. He nearly ran me over. I've told the police this."

Marika nodded. "Yes, I spoke to DC Reynolds. She is actively investigating the attempted assault. However, she has no interest in the cat, unfortunately. That's going to be our job."

"I wondered if it was an attempted burglary gone wrong," Pat said. "He was prowling about and I disturbed him. He then grabbed Kevin and muttered something about taking him to the RSPCA, but there isn't an office locally for them anyway."

"Could be," Nick replied. "For the moment, I suggest we stick to the cat being kidnapped angle. That said, I could take a drive along in that direction. Gander about, ask if anyone's seen him in case he was dumped once the perp made his getaway."

"Good idea," Marika said.

Marika finished her tea and stood, followed by Nick. "Well, there's not much else we can do today. Nick and I will continue our enquiries tomorrow. In the meantime, publish the posts we suggested on the web along with any more pictures you have of Kevin. Call me if there are any developments."

Sandy showed them to the door. "Do you think we will get him back?"

"We have a good success rate," Marika soothed. "Try not to worry too much."

Nick drove them out of the town to the guest house Marika had booked. They settled in for the night and waited, for waiting was all they could do now. The plan for the following morning was to trace the direction the van had taken and do some door-to-door enquiries. Unless anything else happened in the meantime.

As it was, something else did happen in the meantime.

Marika woke early. Sleeping in a strange bed always affected her ability to sleep. She got up and went outside as the sun lifted itself lazily over the treeline. At this time of the year there was a haze of mist over the fields across from the guesthouse. She hugged a mug of tea to her chest and watched the world wake up to the new day, the sun a red ball casting light upwards onto the mackerel clouds turning them pink sand red, the chill air forming wispy grey fronds that evaporated as the warmth of the sun caught them. Her phone chirruped.

"Is that Mrs Spalding?"

"It is."

"Oh, er, I understand that you are looking for Kevin."

"That's right. Who am I speaking to?"

"Oh, um… I'm a neighbour of the Longmuirs. Well, I know them, they live nearby. Er… It's just that I know where he is… the cat, that is… but…" She trailed off.

Marika prompted her. "And you would like to return him?"

"It's not me who took him, see? It's just that I know who did, but…"

"I understand. Can we meet?"

After a light breakfast, they packed their overnight bags into the boot of the car and drove back into the town. Nick pulled up a few streets along from where Sandy Sheldon lived. As they walked up the drive a middle-aged women came to the door, cigarette in hand. "You must be the pet detectives," she said, looking them up and down with a practiced eye, while waving the cigarette with agitation.

Nick held out a hand. "Nick Spalding. My wife, Marika."

"Tracy. Tracy Briggs."

Marika shook Tracy's hand and they followed her indoors.

Tracy sat on the sofa and gestured to the Spaldings to do likewise.

"Well," she said. "It's a bit complicated."

"Go on," Nick prompted.

"Allan isn't all there. And… Well, he wanted a cat."

"Allan?"

"Allan who took the cat, like."

"Ah, yes. I see," Nick said.

"So he just took one that belonged to someone else," Marika observed flatly.

"It wasn't like that. Not really."

"It was to the owner."

Tracy started shifting uncomfortably and Nick, being the peacemaker, intervened. "Do you know where he is?"

"Yes, but I don't want to get him into any trouble. I've spoken to him, like. Told him the cat is sick and needed to go to the vets."

Marika glanced across at Nick and caught his eye—that social media trick had worked.

"Can you take us to him?" Nick asked.

There was an awkward pause as Tracy struggled with her conscience. "Okay," she said eventually, stubbing the cigarette out in an ashtray. "Just let me do the talking. He doesn't like strangers."

"We'll take you in our car," Nick said.

The van was more rust than metal. Where once it had been gleaming white and chrome, now it was mostly a dull reddish colour from years of iron oxide formation. There were holes in the bodywork and Marika expected that if the owner bothered to get the thing MOTd, it would be a magnificent failure. Their checks online with the DVLA had also revealed that it was uninsured, which explained why its owner was hiding away in the woods at the end of a rutted track. They parked the car some distance from the van and alighted. Marika went to the back and opened the boot. She rummaged around among the debris therein and pulled out a cat carrier.

Tracy gestured the Spaldings to hold back while she went up to the vehicle. She rapped on the door. "Allan, love. You in there?"

"What do you want?" came a muffled voice from within.

"Can we come in, Hun?"

The door opened and Allan appeared. Dirty coal tar darkened his chin and a grubby woollen hat sat on his scalp, exposing wild greying curls bursting out underneath. His shirt and jeans had, once, seen the inside of a washing machine. "Who are they?" He nodded suspiciously towards the Spaldings.

"Friends," Tracy said. "They want to talk to you about the cat." She looked down at Kevin who had come to the door, noting the handsome long ginger and white hair. Kevin looked about for a moment and then went back inside where he promptly vomited whatever Allan had given him for breakfast.

"What have you been feeding him on?"

"Food."

"What type of food? He is under the vet, you know."

"I didn't know that."

"Well, he is. You can't just give him anything, you will make him ill." She looked back and caught Marika's eye and gestured for her to come forward.

"Hi, Allan, isn't it? I'm Marika. Can we come in? We need to talk about Kevin going back home."

Allan stood aside and let them enter. Kevin had settled on one of the sofas that surrounded the sitting area. Marika went over to him and picked him up, whereupon she gave him a quick check over.

"What were you playing at, Allan?" Tracy asked. "You knew the cat belonged to someone."

"I'd seen him about and he's always outside meowing. A mate of mine who live opposite says so, so I thought I'd look after him."

"He has a round," Nick said. "He goes to the neighbours. That's why he meows. To get let in. It's fairly common among cats to have multiple homes like that."

"Anyway, he needs to go back home now," Tracy said. Allan scowled but didn't object. He realised that he was outnumbered and while the others were talking, Marika had slipped Kevin into her cat carrier, much to the animal's annoyance. "Allan," she said. "Were you casing the place?"

Allan shifted awkwardly and avoided her gaze, confirming something that Pat Longmuir had suspected all along.

"I don't want Allan to get into trouble over this," Tracy said.

"Well, as far as Mrs Sheldon is concerned, all she wants is Kevin back safe," Marika replied. "It's up to her if she wants to take it further and Mrs Longmuir regarding the near miss with the van. Not me. The police might want to take it further. We will have to wait and see."

After they left, they drove the short distance back to the Sheldon's house where Kevin was let out of the cat carrier. Having been released, he promptly went through the house and out via the cat flap. "He'll be looking for Helen, no doubt," Sandy observed drily as the flap rattled behind him, a fluffy ginger tail disappearing as it closed.

DC Reynolds looked up from her desk as Marika and Nick came in later that morning. She stood. "Well?"

"Well," Marika responded, "we have found the cat and returned him to his owner."

"So, case closed then."

"Presumably you have your investigation to conclude," Marika said, expecting nothing much, but she thought that she would mention it anyway. "After all, there was a near miss and the vehicle is uninsured and untaxed. Are you planning to follow these matters up? Mrs Sheldon doesn't wish to bother any further now that she has her cat back."

Reynolds sighed. "We do have other things to do, you know, than deal with this kind of petty crime."

Marika looked about her, taking in the insouciance—the desk sergeant absorbed in his newspaper, the telephones noticeable by their silence. "Experiencing a crime wave, are we?"

DC Reynolds opened her mouth to issue a rebuke, but Nick got in first. Grasping his wife by the arm, he smiled at Reynolds. "Thank you for your time, DC Reynolds, we will go now."

"What did you think you were doing in there?" Marika snapped angrily as they walked back to the car.

"We were in danger of outstaying our welcome. That or ending up as house guests."

"If I was still a DI, I'd have…"

"Yeah, but you're not. Let's go home."

As she opened the door of the car, Marika's phone chirruped. She shot a scowl at Nick as she answered it. "Spalding Pet Detectives, Marika speaking. How can I help you? Okay, let me take some details…"

Danish Boy

Daniel Royer

    Mr. Brewster studied the resume in his office. He pressed the intercom button. "Suzie, is she in yet?"
    "Not yet, Mr. Brewster." He could tell that Suzie was chewing gum. He sighed, looked at the resume once more.

Anita Volstead
Internal Auditor at Stockdale Bank
Employment: 1989- 2019
Finance Degree, Harvard University
Valedictorian

    Anita Volstead's resume was impressive—far more so than any of the other applicants. Mr. Brewster was a branch manager at Pickering National Bank. It was no secret that his branch was the least successful of all the locations in the district. In fact, his branch was an outright joke. The rival branch managers would openly mock it at the company barbecues. Mr. Brewster's branch had more embezzlement probes, harassment accusations, and employee drug charges than all the branches in the district combined. Even worse, his branch failed to meet its numbers on an almost monthly basis. Mr. Brewster himself was currently the defendant in a class-action lawsuit. Times were tough for Mr. Brewster and his bank branch. He was wrapping up a grueling hiring process for the branch assistant manager position. The former branch assistant manager was forced to flee the country after that nasty loansharking scandal.
    Mr. Brewster checked his watch. Ms. Volstead was thirty minutes late for her interview. All these resumes and interviews were giving Mr. Brewster a headache. He needed something to eat. What he really craved was a donut. Mrs. Brewster had stopped packing him sweets in his lunchbox because he was gaining weight.
    Mr. Brewster ignored the headache, and studied Ms. Volstead's resume some more. No criminal convictions, no arrests, no reason to believe that she wouldn't be exactly the branch assistant he was looking for. He would follow this up with a few phone calls after the interview of course. Ms. Volstead had graduated first in her class at Harvard University, and had worked at Stockdale Bank since 1989. Thirty years of banking experience would put Ms. Volstead at least in her fifties. Mr. Brewster knew that he was not allowed to ask the age of the applicants directly—questions about race, religion, and sexual orientation were frowned upon as well. The

corporate lawyer had sent him a memo saying so. Mr. Brewster really didn't care about any of that stuff—he just needed his assistant to hit the bank's target numbers, namely by pushing the rewards credit card. Corporate was starting to get impatient. The branch had fallen short of its quota five quarters straight. Corporate was threatening to shut them all down. One more miss, and Mr. Brewster would certainly be fired. If he lost his job, Mrs. Brewster would probably divorce him because he wasn't making money—also because he was fat.

Mr. Brewster glanced at the surveillance monitor. Most of his employees were texting on their cell phones. His loan officer had his feet up on his desk licking a lollipop. Mr. Brewster studied the monitor closer. He saw a teller reach into the register with both hands and stuff cash into his pockets. Mr. Brewster shook his head. He needed his new branch assistant manager to change a few things around this place. He had a feeling Ms. Volstead may be just the person to do it.

Mr. Brewster's intercom buzzed. "Mr. Brewster?" It was his receptionist Suzie. She was still chewing gum.

"Yes?"

"Your next interview is here." He heard her pop a bubble.

"Thank you. Send her in."

The door opened and a young woman entered. She was a short slender brunette who appeared to be in her early twenties. Mr. Brewster glanced down at the resume. *Thirty years of banking experience...*

"Uh... Ms. Volstead...?"

"Yes sir. Please call me Anita." She shook his hand.

"Anita. I'm Mr. Brewster. Please, have a seat." Anita Volstead took a seat in the chair across from him at his desk. Mr. Brewster studied her. She had green eyes. They were smart and assertive. She held his gaze as she sat comfortably and confidently.

"Well, as you know, I am hiring for our branch assistant manager position... I'll be blunt, what I really need is someone who can get us to hit our numbers. Our top priority is our rewards credit card. Corporate's real big on that. It's one of those credit cards with points. I'm sure Stockdale Bank has something like that. We've had a little trouble hitting our quota lately..."

"I can fix that."

Mr. Brewster picked up her resume. He made a show of studying it. "I see you went to Harvard University..."

"Actually, not yet. But I plan to go to Harvard."

"I beg your pardon... Your resume says that you went to Harvard. It says you have a degree in Finance."

"I would love to major in Finance," said Ms. Volstead.

"Then what *is* your educational background?"

"I did a couple semesters at Hacienda Community College. Total honesty, I was expelled for cheating on a couple tests. But I'm fighting that."

Mr. Brewster did not know what to make of this. He crossed Harvard off of the resume. "Okay... Your resume says you've worked at Stockdale Bank for... thirty years..."

"That's actually not quite accurate Mr. Brewster."

Mr. Brewster chuckled. "No, I didn't think it was... How long have you worked there?"

"Technically, I've never worked at Stockdale Bank. I have an account there though."

"But your resume says that you *work* there."

"I can see how that was misleading," she said.

"What *is* your banking experience, Ms. Volstead?"

"I have none. I work part-time at a smoothie shop. Before that, I worked at Sunshine Video." She looked right at him as she said this without shame or nervousness. Mr. Brewster fidgeted with the resume, not knowing what to do. He wondered if this was all some sort of misunderstanding, or if the girl was an outright liar. Ms. Volstead watched him from across the desk with those discerning green eyes.

Finally he said, "And how does your smoothie experience qualify you to run my branch?"

"It doesn't," she said. "But I promise you I can get your branch to hit its numbers."

Mr. Brewster sighed. The Anita Volstead resume had seemed so promising. He dropped the paper in the waste basket. "Why did you write those things, Ms. Volstead?"

"Isn't it obvious? To get an interview with you. Would you have considered a community college dropout who used to work at a bankrupt video store? Of course not. I'm sure your resume basket is filled with Ivy Leaguers with all sorts of financial experience. That looks good on paper, but all the degrees and experience in the world isn't enough to save this branch. Just walking from the parking lot to your office, two of your employees hit on me, and another one tried to sell me weed. And that receptionist you've got out there, the bubblegum queen, she's an idiot all together. There's graffiti all over your building and your lobby smells like mildew. And it's obvious your tellers are stealing from you. I've looked into your branch, Mr. Brewster. I'm guessing it has about three months until it's shut down. Am I right? You don't have the time to flirt with those over-educated white-shirts. You need me. I can get your branch to hit its numbers."

"Why would I even *consider* you?" said Mr. Brewster. "You have no experience. You're deceitful, and you're arrogant. And you're... young."

"And don't forget I was late, sir. I'll tell you now, I have a real problem with tardiness."

"So again, why on Earth would I hire you?"

"Because I'm able to see opportunities where others can't."

"I don't know what that means. And besides, how can I even trust you? Your entire resume's a lie. You're a liar, Ms. Volstead."

"I *am* a liar, Mr. Brewster. I make no bones about it. I'm a liar, a cheat, and an opportunist. I'm also smarter than you, and everyone that works for you. I will do anything it takes to get this place to hit its numbers. And I mean *anything*. When I'm in charge, your branch will reach whatever target goals your corporate office sets. *Guaranteed*. I told you, I'm able to see opportunities where others can't." She sat back in the chair, staring at him. "May I ask," she continued, "what does this position pay?"

Mr. Brewster told her.

"I'm going to require significantly more than that," said Anita Volstead. "I'm afraid that's non-negotiable."

"This is outrageous," said Mr. Brewster. "I want you out of my office."

Just then, the door opened, and a young man came in wheeling a cart. The man was freckled and blonde, and looked to be in his twenties. He wore a name tag that said "Skippy." He wheeled the cart straight up to Mr. Brewster's desk.

"Danish for sale!" said the young man.

"Who are you?" shouted Mr. Brewster. "What is the meaning of this?"

"I'm Skippy! I've got Danish for sale. I've got cherry, cream cheese, and cinnamon! Take your pick!"

"How the hell did you get in here?" Mr. Brewster pressed the intercom button. "Suzie, who is this guy who just walked in my office?"

"He's Skippy," the receptionist said. Her mouth was full. "He's got Danish for sale!"

"But what's he doing in my office?"

"He's got the ones with raisins," she said.

Mr. Brewster hung up. He turned to the Danish boy. "How dare you come into my office. I'm doing an interview here."

"Hey, man," said the Danish boy. "I've got a right to be here. I'm just a poor struggling Danish boy trying to sell some homemade cheer. I'm broke, and I'm about to get evicted from my apartment. I'm just trying to make ends meet. How many Danish would you like to buy?"

"Get the hell out of my office, kid! This is a place of business! I've got no time for—"

Anita Volstead interrupted. "Just a minute, Mr. Brewster." She turned to the Danish boy. "Your name's Skippy, right?"

"Sure is," said Skippy. "I've got Danish for sale!"

"That's great, Skippy. My name is Anita. May I ask, with whom do you do your banking?"

"I don't bank with anyone," said Skippy. "Banks cost too much. I keep my Danish money in a shoe box under my bed."

"Well, Skippy," said Anita. "If you bank with Pickering National, we can open you up a *free* checking account, *and* a savings account that will collect you interest on all that Danish money."

"That sounds pretty sweet," said Skippy.

"I'll tell you something even sweeter," said Anita Volstead. "If you sign up for our rewards credit card, you can get points with all your purchases. Every one of them. With all those extra points, you can buy yourself a fancier cart and even fresher ingredients. You'll have even more customers. And with all that extra money and all that savings, you can even move out of your apartment, and buy yourself a home. Mr. Brewster and I can introduce you to our loan officer, and he can set you up with a very reasonable mortgage. Isn't that right, Mr. Brewster?"

Mr. Brewster stared at Anita Volstead dumbly. "That's right, Ms. Volstead," he managed to say.

Skippy spoke up. "That all sounds like a pretty sweet deal. I want one of those cards with points! I'm going to make lots of Danish money. No more shoe box for me! From now on, I'm going to do all my banking at Pickering National!"

"That's the idea, Skippy," said Anita. "Why don't you meet with me and Mr. Brewster first thing tomorrow morning. We'll set you up with a checking and savings, and our special card with points."

"You've got a deal, miss! Would either of you like to buy a Danish?"

Mr. Brewster was too stunned to speak. Anita spoke up. "I think I *would* like to buy a Danish, Skippy. A cherry Danish for my boss Mr. Brewster here."

Mr. Brewster nodded mechanically. Anita payed the Danish boy. The Danish boy handed Mr. Brewster his cherry Danish.

Skippy said, "You two won't regret this. Not one bit. I'm going to tell all my family about this place. They're in the muffin business. They have lots of muffin money! That's a lot of shoe boxes! I'm also going to tell my girlfriend. She sells turnovers. You'll see! I'm going to make a lot of Danish money! You have a customer for life, I can tell you that!" Skippy wheeled the cart out of the office. He closed the door behind him.

Mr. Brewster sat at his desk. He stared at Anita Volstead. The green eyes stared back. *Who was this girl?*

"You see opportunities where others can't?" he asked.

The green eyes locked. "That's right, Mr. Brewster."

Mr. Brewster averted her gaze. He bit into his cherry Danish. It was stale, but good. Mrs. Brewster didn't let him eat this stuff anymore. He looked up at the girl. "When can you start?"

Anita Volstead stepped out of the bank. She walked to the alley behind the building. Skippy was leaning up against his cart smoking a cigarette. Anita took a drag off the cigarette. She handed it back to him.

"Nice bit about the shoe box," she said.

Skippy smiled. "Did he make an offer?"

"Yes."

"More than the other bank this morning?"

Anita nodded. "Give me one of those Danish," she said. "I'm starving."

Skippy handed her a cream cheese. She bit into it. "These are getting stale," she said. "Get some new ones. I've got an interview with Citibank in an hour."

New Fish

Daniel Royer

The lady walked fast. That was the first thing Roger Barton noticed as he was given the tour of the sprinkler factory. The second thing was that the lady clearly wore a thong beneath her Capri pants.

"Punch in at nine a.m. sharp," she told him as they walked through the lobby. "Punch in a minute late and you're working the rest of the hour for free. You are required to make no fewer than ten sales a day. Fall a sale short and you lose the commission on the previous nine. Lose an existing client and you lose the commission. Failure to sign a new client, there is no commission. Commission is one percent. As for your hourly wage, there is none. You will only be paid in commission."

It was Roger Barton's first day at Snyder Sprinklers United, a fire sprinkler manufacturer claiming to specialize in both home and industrial protection. A quick Web search told Barton that the company was not a particularly reputable one in the industry. In fact, it seemed the only thing in which Snyder Sprinklers United specialized was drawing lawsuits. Barton had a feeling he would fit right in with the place.

The woman giving him the tour was his new boss Madam Snyder, the founder and head partner of the company. She was a pale gangly woman somewhere north of fifty. Her hair was frayed and unruly, a blend of gray and strawberry-blonde that had probably once been a prominent red. Her clothes were tight and revealing. Barton figured she had once been a pretty woman, and was probably operating under the erroneous notion that she still was.

"Hey, new fish," she said to him, "you getting all this?"

"Yes, ma'am."

"Good. Because I'm not going to repeat it. The Go-Away is our industrial model. The Go-Home is our residential. The Go-Green is our environmentally friendly model. Every five units sold saves a whale. Make sure you tell the customers that." Barton was a little unclear of how selling a few sprinklers to someone could possibly save a whale, but there was so much about the sprinkler industry that he did not know. "The Go-Light-Green is our quasi Eco-friendly brand. It takes about a dozen units to save a whale. Maybe more. It's been a while since we've done the math. We don't sell many anyways. Forget the Go-Light-Green, kid. Push the Go-Green model instead. The EPA's been busting my hump lately."

With notepad and pen, Barton tried to write it all down and still keep up with the woman as she walked. She stopped and lit a cigarette. Growing up, Barton's mother and teachers had always told him that smoking was bad.

Barton was also fairly certain that smoking in a public building not operated by Indians was against the law. Barton had smoked once with his friend Chuckles, back when they were teenagers. The cool kids at school dared them. The smoke made Barton queasy, and he threw up. The pretty girls made fun of him. Barton didn't do a whole lot of partying in his youth. He and his friends usually played video games in Chuckles' basement. It was hard to get dates. Most of the girls at his high school thought he was a loser. Most girls liked guys who played football and smoked cigarettes—not guys who played space games and drank soda.

"Madam Snyder, isn't smoking bad?"

"The world is a dangerous place, new fish. You've got to be tough. I hire men, not little girls. This place is for grownups. If you want to work here, you got to act like a man. Not a little girl with a pink dress and pigtails. Besides, the way I see it, a fire sprinkler factory is just about the safest place to light up anyway." Barton knew she had a point there. He also knew he would have to butch up if he wanted to work for this woman. The lady continued smoking and talking as Barton watched the contours of her thong shift with her stride.

Roger Barton was thirty-five years old. His father had been a master salesman many years before. The old man's status in the local sales community was legendary. There wasn't a person who had met Barton Senior that hadn't heard the story of him selling sand to that guy in the Mojave Dessert. Or the stereo to that deaf lady. Or when Barton Senior had had a few cocktails in him, the video camera to that Amish guy. Growing up, young Barton had heard all of his father's war-stories, usually while sitting on the floor cross-legged at the tip of the man's loafers as he drank his dinner from several highball glasses. The kid would gaze up at Barton Senior with an open-mouthed awe that only a small boy looking at his dad can have.

In the late 1980's Barton Senior focused his sales endeavors on sports equipment. Things were good until the Major League Baseball strike of '94. That was the year the Barton family lost their house. It was also the year that Barton Senior put a gun in his mouth and messed up the wallpaper. Roger Barton was eleven years old then. He cried a lot at school after that. The boys at school teased him. They told him he cried like a girl.

Young Barton admired his late father's success, though he never thought of himself as a salesman growing up. He was never sure he had the guts. In truth, he lived in fear of never being able to live up to the salesman family totem that his father had set. The death of Barton Senior had only made the man's status grow among other salesmen to the point of legendary. It was a lot of pressure for young Barton.

After high school he enrolled in a community college. He took classes in the day. At night he played video games and drank soda. He had crushes.

He got rejections. After dropping out of college, he found himself still living with his mother as he wandered around without focus or prospects. He dabbled in many different trades and got fired just as often. The ice cream parlor said he was no good, and the sunglass hut said he wasn't up to snuff. His most recent venture into party deejaying proved disastrous when he was fired and blackballed from the industry after playing AC/DC's "Highway to Hell" at a funeral gig. In the daytime, Barton sat in his mother's living room eating cereal. She told him to get a job. At night he played video games with Chuckles and their buddies.

And then there was the redhead—the sweet redhead that worked at the cookie shop in the mall. She had freckles and dimples. Barton had bought a lot of chocolate chunks from her over the past few months. He had been trying to woo her—flowers, love notes, *a cappella* serenades at the cookie counter. No dice. The redhead refused to go on a date with him. The redhead said she only dated salesmen with lots of money. She only dated closers. She called Barton a loser. She said he wasn't man enough to date her. Barton vowed to get a job, to be a salesman just like his old man. Roger Barton called an old sales buddy of his dad's. The sales buddy knew of a place. It was run by some old lady he used to have the hots for. He referred young Barton to Snyder Sprinklers United.

Madam Snyder guided Barton through the corridors of the factory. She led him into the sprinkler laboratory. The lab had all the clichés of a bad 1950's science fiction movie. There were Bunsen burners, Tesla coils, test tubes, and unlabeled beakers filled to their brim with bubbling liquids. Flashes of light lit up the lab from the arc rays of the welders. The sound of crunching metal pierced the room as the machinists cut pipe. Engineers scurried around the lab shouting at each other. Snaking around the floor were exposed wires circuiting through puddles of water and what appeared to be some sort of smoking acid.

"Here's where *all* the magic happens," Madam Snyder said with the wave of her hand, as if she was Merlin showing him the backstage of Camelot. Madam Snyder directed Barton's attention to one of the welders. "This is our top man, Stu Milwaukee," she said to Barton. Milwaukee was welding without a mask. He squinted into the arc ray. Milwaukee pulled out a pack of cigarettes. He shook one loose. He lit it up with his his torch.

"Milwaukee, this is... what's your name again, new fish?"

"Barton."

"This is our new salesman," she said to Milwaukee. Milwaukee shook Barton's hand. The welder's hands were rough and callused. His face was red and his eyes were blood-shot. Barton never took metal shop in high school—labor-induced calluses interfered with his gaming thumbs—but he knew people that did. He knew that those people usually wore masks while welding. The masks were for protection. This was Barton's chance to look smart.

"Good to meet you, sir," said Barton. "But shouldn't you be welding with a mask?"

"Masks are for sissies, new fish," said Milwaukee. "I'm a man. I have muscles. I don't need protection. Masks are for little old ladies wearing Mother Goose shoes." Stu Milwaukee grunted, and went back to his work, squinting into the arc ray.

Madam Snyder led Barton out of the laboratory.

"Stu Milwaukee is right, you know," said Madam Snyder. "I have *men* working for me. Sweaty, sturdy, rugged *men*. Men who don't give a damn about getting a boo-boo, only about getting the job done. I thought we went over this already. I hire men who have grit, not damsels walking around with a parasol. Which are you, new fish?"

"I'm a man."

"Good. Now, I was trying to tell you that Milwaukee is responsible for the Go-Green model. Milwaukee's a man. He's got the stuff. Joe Gouda says those sprinklers are selling like candy bars. Gouda's got the stuff too—he's our top salesman. Milwaukee and Gouda are definitely guys you'll want to take notes from."

Madam Snyder led Barton to the second floor where the salesmen hung out. The offices on the floor were cramped and cluttered. They walked into a small conference room. The salesmen were huddled at a table. They were checking out a girly magazine.

"Boys, this is our new salesman, Barton."

"Pleased to meet you, Barton," said one of the salesman. "I'm Joe Gouda. If you got any questions, just ask me. These sprinklers may seem tough to sell at first, but they're not. Not if you're tough enough. Not if you're a man. It takes a real salesman to push this stuff. We move our product pretty hard here. I'm talking about cold-calling on the street. I'm talking about knocking on some guy's door and not leaving until he's got a sprinkler in his hand. We're *salesman*. We're not a bunch of Brownie Scouts with boxes of chocolate chunk in front of the grocery store." He held up the girly magazine. It was a cheesecake centerfold. "Check out the legs on this one."

If Barton wanted to fit in, he needed to turn up the testosterone—and fast. He whistled, and said, "Sweet!"

"You like the ladies, new fish?" asked Madam Snyder.

"Sure do," said Barton. "The ladies are my favorite. Also cigarettes." Joe Gouda nodded, and went back to his girly magazine. The other salesmen joined him.

Madam Snyder led Barton to his new office. To call it an office would be using the term loosely. During the glory-days of his father's sales success when the Barton family lived in a mansion, Barton's mother had a bigger shoe closet. The office was a nothing more than a bunker with a desk and a chair. There was also a window that overlooked the parking lot below. Barton looked outside. There appeared to be a man urinating between two parked cars. When finished, the man zipped up, and walked into the building.

"Welcome to your new digs," said Madam Snyder like a proud bellboy showing off a suite at the Ritz. Barton took a seat in the chair. He felt a spring dig into his rear. The chair wobbled and squeaked. He noticed there was not a telephone on his desk.

"Madam Snyder, how do I make calls?"

"What do you mean?"

"To sell the sprinklers I'll need to make calls."

"Then kid, I'd suggest you get a telephone." She lit another cigarette. In hindsight, Barton really should not have been surprised that the illustrious Snyder Sprinklers United, which didn't provide masks to its welders, was too ill-equipped to provide its salesmen with wild extravagances such as telephones and functioning chairs. The absence of the telephone posed a problem though, as Barton did not own one. A few months back, his mom canceled his service and took away his phone. She said he had to grow up and pay for his own telephone.

With that aside, another question posed itself. Customers. "Okay, but *who* do I call? Who am I selling our sprinklers to?"

"To *people*," she said smartly, as if Barton might have thought he was selling sprinklers to animals and robots.

"Do we have a list of possible clients or anything? Do we have any leads?"

"*Leads?*" scoffed Madam Snyder. "Kid, this isn't a Mamet play. There are no leads." She tossed her cigarette to the floor, stubbing it out with her heel. She was getting bored.

"Okay, but how—"

"Just make sure you make ten sales today or you get no commission." She lit another cigarette. "If you have any other questions you can ask Joe Gouda," she said, walking out of the office. Barton watched the thong sway through the doorway and into the hallway. He rubbed his temples.

Barton had to admit that he was a bit apprehensive of a job where his wages were unknown. In fact, it seemed that not only were his wages unknown, but it was actually possible he would not be paid at all—assuming he fell short of ten sales a day. And without a telephone, how could he *not* fall short of ten sales a day? Or even *one* sale a day?

Barton thought of the redhead at the cookie shop. He had hoped that this job would impress her. He had hoped to make lots of money. But if not money, then at the very least, this job offered him a place to hang out without his crazy mom shouting her head off. Barton put his feet up on the desk. He stared at his shoes. The right one had a pretty big hole on the toe.

Joe Gouda and a few other salesmen hung their head in his doorway.

"Hey new fish," said Gouda. "We're going out for shots and porterhouses. Wanna join us?" Barton looked at his watch. It was 9:30. Barton usually had cereal and soda at this hour.

"Isn't it a little early for that stuff?" he asked.

"I thought you were a man, new fish. I thought you liked the ladies. We are salesmen here. We drink. We drink and we eat porterhouses. We also make sales. Now, are you a man who takes shots in the morning, or are you a skinny teenage girl who likes chamomile tea?"

"I'm a man."

"Good. Now, the boys and I are going to be over at Scully's getting hammered and hitting on waitresses for the next few hours. Afterwards we're going to make some cold-calls like *real* salesmen. After *that*, we're going down to the mall. There's this sweet redhead at the cookie shop. The word is, she only dates closers. I'll be asking that redhead on a date. And friend, she'll be *accepting* that date because I've got what it takes. If you decide you got what it takes later on, maybe you can join us." Gouda and the boys walked out of the office.

Barton knew he screwed up again. Joe Gouda was going to steal his girl. Barton needed to fix this. He could fix this by proving he was a man. He could prove he was a man by making a sale. To make a sale, he needed to access a telephone. He had remembered seeing a payphone in the lobby during his orientation.

He went downstairs and found the payphone. Wedged beside it was an old tattered phone book. He opened the first page. Adele Aaron. He needed to start somewhere. He dialed Mrs. Aaron's number, but was informed by the operator that he needed to insert a quarter before his call could be patched through. Roger Barton didn't have a quarter, just some lint. He called collect, and dialed Adele Aaron's phone number after the prompt. The operator informed Barton that Mrs. Aaron did not accept the collect call. Barton crossed Adele Aaron's name off the list in the phone book and moved on to Adrian Aaron. Adrian Aaron did not accept his collect call either. Barton crossed his name off too. He repeated the process and moved down through the Aarons. Finally, Cedric Aaron accepted his collect call.

"Yes, who's this?" the man asked.

"Good day to you sir," Barton blurted out. "This is Roger Barton from Snyder Sprinklers United… Uh, I've got some Go-Green Sprinklers for you…" Pause. Barton thought that his pitch would be enough, that the customer would tell Barton how many sprinklers he would buy and afterwards mail Barton the money. Instead the customer didn't say anything. Maybe Mr. Aaron had a hearing problem. "Uh, Mr. Aaron, I have some Go-Green Sprinklers for you!" Barton repeated.

"I heard what you said, son," said Cedric Aaron sharply. "What the blazes is a Go-Green Sprinkler?" The hell if Barton knew. He did remember Madam Snyder saying something about them saving whales though.

"Oh, they're a new red hot sprinkler that'll protect your home *and* save whales..."

"I don't have any whales that need saving right now, son," the man said. "I'll let you know when I do. And I'll tell you one *more* thing, young fellow. I only buy products from *men*. Strong, determined, salt-of-the-Earth *men*. Men who take a bite out of life of life. Men who, when they see a challenge, they light a cigarette and laugh at it. Men who got what it takes. I do *not* buy from little boys—little boys with knee-socks and juice-mustaches. I do *not* buy from—" Roger Barton hung up on him. He crossed Cedric Aaron off the list, and moved on down to Celeste Aaron.

An hour had passed and Gertrude Aaron was the only other customer to accept his collect call. He didn't get a sale though, only some curse words. Barton was discouraged. His head hurt and his mouth was dry. He looked around for a drinking fountain. Instead he found a cigarette vending machine outside the men's restroom. The restroom was boarded up. If he couldn't butch-up by making a sale, perhaps he could smoke a cigarette. That would go some way in restoring his reputation as a man.

The machine charged four dollars, but Barton didn't have four dollars. He punched a hole through the glass and swiped a pack of Montana Strikes. On his way out the lobby he grabbed the phone book and an old newspaper, wrapping his bleeding hand with the Classifieds. He hopped on an elevator and rode up to the sales floor.

He got back to the sales floor, realizing he didn't have a match to light a cigarette. He stopped by Madam Snyder's office to see if he could bum one off of her. He stepped into her office and found her passed out at her desk. A bottle of Jimmy Goodtimes sat by her outstretched hand. The bottle was half full. Barton took her pulse. It was there. He grabbed the bottle and took a hit. He coughed. He wasn't used to the hard stuff. Sometimes he would swipe wine coolers out of his mom's refrigerator and bring them over to Chuckles' basement when they played video games. This stuff was much stronger. He took another swig and put the bottle in his pants. He found a pack of matches on the desk. Next to the matches was a cell phone—Madam Snyder's cell phone. Madam Snyder began to snore. Barton lifted the unconscious woman's hand and pressed her right thumb to the cell phone's screen. The phone unlocked. Roger Barton grabbed the matches and got out of there.

He got back to his office and took the Jimmy Goodtimes out of his pants. He took another hit and lit a cigarette. The cigarette made him cough. He smoked anyway—like a man. He plopped down in his desk chair. He took another drink. The booze warmed him. He got out Madam Snyder's cell phone. He called his friend Chuckles to see if he wanted to buy some sprinklers.

"You mean sprinklers for my lawn?" asked Chuckles.

"No," said Barton. "For your house. In case it catches on fire or something. Remember when you burned that Pop Tart?"

"Um, yeah."

"Well these babies will make sure that never happens again."

"You mean they'll keep my Pop Tarts from burning?"

"No man. They'll put out the fire when your Pop Tarts *do* burn."

"Well that can of Mountain Dew I used last time seemed to work just fine."

"Come on, man, I need to make a sale."

"Well, maybe I can get *one* sprinkler. How much does it cost?"

"I don't know."

Pause. "Well me and Scooter are gonna be playing video games in my mom's basement tonight if you want to join us." Click.

Barton called Scooter and the rest of his buddies. No one was employed, and no one was in the market for an expensive sprinkler system. This day was turning out to be a real bummer. Barton thought of the redhead at the mall. She would think he was a loser. He thought of his old man. He would be disappointed in him. Barton was starting to get discouraged. He took another pull of Jimmy Goodtimes, and lit a cigarette. Suddenly the cell phone rang.

He answered. "Hello?"

"Is Madam Snyder there?" It was a male voice.

Barton thought of Madam Snyder sprawled out at her desk asleep. "Um, she's here, but she can't, like, talk right now."

"Tell her we have her husband and her kid. Tell her it's ten thousand this time, or they're dead meat. Tell her in the alley behind the Dairy Queen by midnight. And tell her no cops." Click. Barton jotted down the message on his notepad.

He took another drink and lit a cigarette. By now he was pretty drunk. He got out the phone book and called up Gloria Aaron. He thought of his old man and the cookie girl. If he wanted to make a sale, he decided he would have to be bolder.

"Hello?" answered Gloria Aaron.

"Do you want to buy a sprinkler?" Barton blurted.

"Who is this?" she asked.

"This is Roger Barton. Do you want to buy a sprinkler?"

"Um... no." Barton hung up. He called Gunther Aaron.

"Do you want to buy a sprinkler?"

"Huh? Who is this?"

"This is Barton. Do you wanna buy a sprinkler or not?"

"No."

"Why not?"

"Who *is* this?" repeated Mr. Aaron. Barton hung up.

He finished up the Aarons around noon. It ended up that many of the Aarons were related to each other, and some were even of the same household. Either way Roger Barton still hadn't made a sale. He was getting discouraged again. Sleepy and discouraged.

He was finishing up the bottle of Jimmy Goodtimes when Madam Snyder stepped into his office. She had sleep creases on her face. Her cell phone rested on his desk. She glanced at the phone and also at the empty bottle of Jimmy Goodtimes. She didn't seem to be making the connection that they used to belong to her.

"You're still here?" she asked.

"Uh yeah," Barton said, wondering how many salesmen had literally walked out on their first day. He picked up his notepad. "Oh, um, some guy called. He says he has your husband and kid."

Madam Snyder nodded as if the information were the most natural in the world. "I'm not too worried about it."

"It sounded pretty serious."

"It's just my husband trying to get attention. He gets jealous of the studs that work for me. He slings scoops at the Dairy Queen with a bunch of other losers. He can be a real girly-girl sometimes. He'll come home tonight when he gets bored."

She leaned in close to Barton. He could see down her blouse. "Has Joe Gouda said anything to you?" She was whispering.

"He said something about shots and porterhouses."

"Anything else?"

"No."

"Good," she said. "Because he can't be trusted. And I think he and Stu Milwaukee are in cahoots." Madam Snyder had just named every employee that Barton had met. She dropped a red folder on his desk. "You're new here, so you haven't been tainted yet. That means I can trust you. I'm giving you the Marshall Henderson file."

Barton held the file, studying it. "What do I do with this?"

"Just take care of it, will you. And don't let Joe Gouda get his Commie hands on it." And with that, she walked out of the office as if all questions had been answered. Barton watched the thong sway out the door. He put the red folder in the desk drawer and lit a cigarette. He continued with his phone book calls.

After Adriana Abigail hung up on him, the cell phone rang. Barton answered.

"This is Marshall Henderson," the voice said. "I need to speak to Madam Snyder."

"Snyder isn't here."

"Then get me Joe Gouda."

"Gouda can't be trusted," said Barton.

"Who's this?" asked Marshall Henderson.

"This is Barton. I have your file. Gouda can't be trusted, and neither can Milwaukee maybe."

"Hot damn," said Marshall Henderson. "Gouda was working on my Go-Light-Greens. Do you think he knows too much?"

"It's being taken care of," said Barton, making it up as he went along. "But I have your file now, so everything's safe."

"You're a real pal, Barton. You've just saved my bacon."

"No sweat," said Barton. "And may I suggest you install our Go-Greens instead. They save more whales than the Go-Light-Greens."

"Is that so?" said Marshall Henderson. "Gouda was saying the Go-Light-Green was top dog."

"Gouda can't be trusted," Barton repeated. "And maybe he tampered with them too. I think you should buy some Go-Greens right away."

"Thank goodness I still have a friend left in this town. Ship me over a batch. Madam Snyder has my accounting information."

"Yes sir," said Barton. "They're on their way."

"And if you ever get tired of working for that old gasbag, you should consider working for *me*. Something tells me you've got the damn horse-sense to be Henderson material. Something tells me you got the stuff. I need *men* working for me, not baby girls who need their diapers changed. My guys will be in touch with you soon." Marshall Henderson hung up.

It was young Barton's first sale. He lit a victory cigarette. He thought of his dad and the redhead. He dialed the number to the cookie store at the mall.

"Hello?" It was the redhead.

"I'm a salesman now!"

"Who is this?"

"It's Roger Barton."

"Oh, the chocolate chunk guy... I told you before, I only date *men*. Men with jobs who make sales. Men who make the big bucks. I don't date teeny-boppers who tweet about their celebrity crushes."

"But I *am* a man! I sold a batch of sprinklers to Marshall Henderson. Want to go out on a date tonight?"

"I'm already going on a date tonight with another stud. Some big-cheese, calls himself Joe Gouda."

"I know Gouda," said Barton. "He ain't no man. I heard he takes bubble baths and goes to flower shows. I heard he doesn't make sales. You should dump his sorry keister and date me instead."

"Sure thing, stud. I'm glad to hear you've toughened up. I'm glad to hear you've swapped your baby bonnet for a cowboy hat. My shift ends at six tonight. Take me dancing. Don't be late." She hung up.

Barton was ecstatic. He wished he could somehow share the moment with his father. But this was no time to be sentimental. He picked up the phone book and continued with the sales.

He spent the rest of the afternoon calling without any luck. It was four o'clock when he called Alan Adams.

"Mr. Adams, this is Roger Barton. Do you want to buy some sprinklers?"

"I sure do, young man. My factory almost burned down last night. We had a small explosion, and my workers got spooked. You hear me? Spooked! Like sheep. Like a herd of baby sheep crying for their mamma. My workers are a bunch of baby sheep who can't handle a little fire. Do you hear what I'm saying, son? They're afraid of matches and they don't want to get burned. They say they need protection. *I* say they need to get weaned from their baby bottles. *I* say they're a bunch of Little Bo-Peeps. Anyway, some lawyer called this morning. *He* says I need to get some sprinklers, or I'm toast. Do you have any of those Go-Light-Greens?"

"The Go-Light-Greens are for suckers, Mr. Adams. The Go-Greens are where it's at. I just installed a batch at Marshall Henderson's and he's loving them."

"Is that a fact, huh?" said Alan Adams. "That Marshall Henderson's some kind of man. A real cowboy. Do you hear what I'm saying? I'm saying he's not afraid of a little fire. I'm saying he's got gumption. Sign me up for several hundred of those Go-Greens. Something tells me—" Suddenly the line went dead. Barton looked up. Madam Snyder was sitting on his desk, her index finger on the phone's power button.

"Do you think he likes me?" she asked.

"Madam Snyder I was about to make a sale. I was about to—"

"Do you think he likes me?" she repeated.

"Who?"

"Joe Gouda," she said, as if that should have been obvious.

"I thought Gouda couldn't be trusted."

"Where'd you get that idea, new fish? Gouda's our top man. You should be at the steakhouse with him... And *sometimes* I see him looking at me."

"Madam Snyder, I'm not sure about this Joe Gouda. First he was our top salesman, then he couldn't be trusted, and now maybe he likes you..."

"Welcome to Snyder Sprinklers United, kid."

"I have no idea what that means, Madam Snyder. Anyway I need to makes some sales calls now if you don't mind."

Madam Snyder stared at him. "You ain't getting girly on me, are you new fish?"

67

"No ma'am."

Suddenly the cell phone rang. Barton answered.

"Is this Barton?" said the voice on the other end. It was Marshall Henderson.

"Yes sir," said Barton. "How are those Go-Greens working out for you?"

"Working out for me?" exclaimed Marshall Henderson. "The damned things damn near burned my office down. The Coast Guard says they've got a dead whale because of them. Joe Gouda's over here cleaning up your mess. He's putting in some Go-Light-Greens to sop up your damage. Afterwards, Gouda and I are going on a double-date. He's got something sweet lined up with a redhead at the mall. He says she's got a friend for me. They only date *closers*. I thought you were a *closer*, Barton. I thought you were a man. I guess I was wrong. You're just a little girl with a pink bow selling lemonade in front of your mamma's house. You're lucky I don't sue your ass!"

"But Mr. Henderson, I thought... I mean I think..." Roger Barton didn't know what he thought anymore—only that he would never get a date with the redhead, or measure up to his father.

"You can think all you want, Barton, but you'll never be Henderson material. And you'll never be a man. Have fun working for that Snyder slut for the rest of your life. Or until the EPA shuts her down. Which should be soon!" Click. Barton lit a cigarette. Madam Snyder picked up the Marshall Henderson file.

"I'll be taking this now," she said. "I don't know how you got it anyway."

Suddenly there was an explosion downstairs. The building shook and the furniture rattled. The office window shattered. Barton nearly fell out of his chair. Madam Snyder braced herself at the desk. The fire alarm sounded off and Barton heard screaming. He looked through the broken window outside. He saw smoke pouring from the factory floor below. Workers scampered out of the building and ran straight to their cars. The office sprinklers above sputtered and hissed. He and Madam Snyder were getting wet.

Madam Snyder pulled a flask from inside her blouse and took a long pull. She handed it to Barton.

"Take a drink, new fish." Barton took a good long drink. The fire alarm turned off, but the sprinklers were still running. The parking lot outside was becoming vacant. Barton offered the flask back to Madam Snyder. She declined. "Keep it for now, kid. I'm leaving."

"Where are you going?"

"Home, kid. I'm going home." She sighed. "The whole damn planet's getting soft on us, new fish. It's getting *real* girly. We've got health food, light beer, and seat-belts. We've got paint without lead and Chinese food without MSG. Hell, we've got presidents who can barely throw a damned baseball. There's fewer men out there like Joe Gouda and Stu Milwaukee and Marshall Henderson. There's fewer men like you. I'll be damned, but *I've* got more grit in me than some of the sissies we've got sashaying around these days. Things are looking real shaky. This world's one big tinderbox, you know. And I think it's about to blow. Lucky for us we have the longest hose... Either way, who gives a damn?" She turned, heading for the door. Barton watched her thong push out of his office. Then it was gone.

Barton settled back in his chair. The office was starting to flood. His big toe was getting wet. He put his feet up on the desk. He tried to light a cigarette. His matches were wet. So were the cigarettes. He chucked them all out the window. He killed off the flask instead and picked up the cell phone. He called back Alan Adams.

He had ten more sales to make that day.

The Janitor

Jeani Rector

Craig parked in the empty lot and got out of the car, his windshield reflecting the glare of the brightly lit school sign. He was tired. Somehow his Monday night shift had come too soon.

He studied the school as he walked toward it. High school kids had to be the messiest people on the planet. He knew if he had paid attention and worked harder during his own high school days, he'd have a better job than this by now. But he hadn't so this was the result.

"Make the best of things," his mother always said. "Being a janitor is an honest living." Yeah, and all good dogs go to heaven.

Craig took the large yellow cleaning can out of the closet, and began to lug it towards the first classroom. It was about the size of an urban garbage can, made of hard plastic, and it was on wheels. It contained all the supplies he needed to do his job.

He cleaned the brightly lit classrooms first. They were the easiest; the teachers always watched the students and made sure they didn't disrupt the rooms too badly. He moved on to the gymnasium, another fairly easy clean.

After he did all he could in the gym, he knew it was time for the rest of his job. He stepped out into the night air, locked the gym door behind him, and started walking across the grassy quad towards the bathrooms, still lugging his cleaning supplies behind him.

He hated cleaning the bathrooms the most. They were in their own small building, boys on one side and girls on the other. Who knew what he would find there; sometimes things he didn't even want to look at, much less touch, so he always left the bathrooms for last.

Everything was locked at night, even the bathrooms. He started fumbling with his key ring as he walked, not seeming to find the right key, when suddenly he understood why he was having so much trouble. He couldn't see the keys very clearly.

Craig hesitated and glanced around. Why was it so dark? He looked ahead and noticed all the poles containing fluorescent lights that surrounded the freshman bathrooms were black. None of the lights were working.

Everything seemed quiet—too quiet. The sense of stillness was overpowering. There was simply no sound, no motion, as if all the night creatures were silently hiding; watching and waiting. No crickets chirped; no owls screeched.

The intense stillness was finally broken, and movement began again, as though the world was releasing the breath it held. A slight wind picked up. A creaking noise sounded as two twisted limbs of an old, gnarled tree rubbed together in the soft breeze. The seed heads of ornamental grasses fluttered with a sighing sound. Clipped boxwood shrubs rustled as branches shuddered in the wind.

Craig felt spooked. He wished he had a flashlight, more for cold comfort than for the visuals it would give him. Everything seemed threatening in the dark; everyday things seemed to take a sinister undertone. It was more of a mood than a lack of sight.

He wanted to turn around and go home but knew he couldn't. He needed this job, as lousy as it was. He couldn't afford to lose it.

You're not a little kid, afraid of your own shadow, he told himself. *Buck up and be a man.*

So he started walking towards the bathrooms once again, resolving to clean them and then move on. It was what he did five nights a week. This night would be no different. So what if none of the lights were working?

When he reached the overhang of the building, it seemed even darker under there. The roof shaded what little light the moon delivered. The bathroom building was brick, and felt cold to his touch as he leaned against it, fumbling with his keys. God, why couldn't he find the right key?

Finally he felt it, the small one with the knob on the tip. Next he had to feel the door to find the keyhole. As his fingertips glided over the metal doorjamb, he noticed how cold it was, colder than the brick. Maybe he had never noticed the temperature before since he could normally see it and didn't have to feel it.

The key connected with the lock, and Craig pushed the door open. He reached to the wall for the light switch. He found it and flipped it up.

Nothing happened. The bathroom remained dark.

No way was he going into that pitch black bathroom. He would have to call the school office in the morning and explain the situation, that he didn't feel safe because none of the lights were working. They couldn't fire him for that, could they?

Craig began to turn around when he dropped his key-ring. He cursed as he heard it bouncing into the bathroom, jangling as it tumbled and rolled the keys end over end.

Oh my God, I can't go in there!

But his car keys were on that ring. Unless he retrieved them, he had to spend the night in these dark school grounds. Which fate was worse?

He needed the keys. He knelt on the cement floor of the bathroom, feeling the coldness of the stone on his knees all the way through his pants. He held the door open with his foot as he leaned over and began feeling around the cement floor, his fingers doing what his eyes could not, searching for the key ring.

He realized that the keys must have fallen further into the room than he initially thought. He crawled forward, and his foot slipped from the door and it slammed shut with a *bang*. Craig could not suppress a small scream before he realized that the door only locked from the outside. From the inside, it could be opened. He was not locked in.

He noticed he was panting. Trying to slow his breathing, he gathered his wits about him and once again began feeling over the cement floor for the key ring.

I can do this. I am not afraid of the dark.

His fingers groped the cement and he felt something on the floor that gave a little at his touch. Craig hesitated, then touched the thing again. It felt wet and...did he feel it move?

A sour scent of musty brine assaulted his nostrils. Craig jerked his fingers back and decided to get the hell out of the bathroom, keys or no keys. He tried to rise to his feet but his legs were like rubber beneath him. He staggered; his body rocked with fear, and made an attempt at reaching the door.

He heard the thing slam against him more than he felt the blow, and understood that whatever was with him in this bathroom was big. He could hear someone sobbing and realized it was he who was doing the crying.

Please God, get me out of here! Please God please God...

The creature dragged him down to the floor with its weight. He tried to push it off, but he couldn't seem to grasp it. Its surface was slimy and his hands slipped off.

He tried again to shove the wet, cold bulk with all his might and finally made contact. His hands seemed to sink into rubbery flesh that enveloped his fingers and didn't slow the assault. Stench of rotted seaweed and polluted ocean filled his nose and his panic rose to desperation.

He pulled back his arm and landed a punch on what he hoped was the face area. The thing grunted and then made a growling sound.

Craig tried to shove his forearm backwards, because he knew that a sharp elbow could be an effective weapon, but he was disoriented in the dark and didn't know where to aim. He was aware of intense, searing pain. It felt like the creature was attacking him for an eternity, although what was left of his rational thoughts assured him it had only been for a few seconds.

He managed to roll out from the creature's grasp. He hoped with all his might that he was rolling in the right direction, towards the door. He honestly didn't know.

And suddenly he felt the door, and he cried out loud with relief and renewed hope. He shoved the door open and the cool outside air slapped his face. He staggered to his feet and began to run across the grassy quad; a loping, lopsided gait because his left leg wasn't functioning properly.

He felt an adrenaline surge as he realized he was going to make it. He was going to escape whatever beast had been in the bathroom. He was going to survive!

And then behind him, he heard the bathroom door open again as the thing came out.

Under the House

Jeani Rector

Her father was yelling again.

Ten year old Kayla cringed, even though this time the screams were directed at her mother, and not at her. Kayla wished for the courage to rush in and save her mother. But she didn't, and despised herself for being the coward that she was.

Instead Kayla began to slink away, out of the house. Because her father's wrath was directed elsewhere, she figured that she would not be noticed as she made her getaway. If she could disappear, perhaps she could avoid her father's fury, which always ended in brutal beatings.

Once outside, Kayla noticed a hole in the clapboards that criss-crossed underneath the back porch. *Well, this is new,* she thought. The hole hadn't been there yesterday.

Could she hide in there? Doubtfully Kayla peered under the stairs. It seemed pretty dark under there.

And then suddenly Kayla heard her father's voice coming closer. No time to decide! She went through the hole in the clapboards and scooted under the house to hide.

The temperature was cooler down here. It smelled funny too…musty, moldy, like mushrooms. Kayla waited for her eyes to adjust to the darkness before she continued further into the underbelly of the house.

Since daylight was streaming in through the hole, she could see a few feet in front of her. The house was held up by wooden supports, surrounded by a brick foundation. The ground was earthen and dark. She saw some garbage, and she wondered, *How did that stuff get here, underneath the house?* There were a few opened cans and some rotting, discarded paper.

It was amazing how much she could hear down here. She could hear her mother and father talking very loudly, and walking about up above her in the house. In fact, this new hiding place would not only be a safety zone, but one in which she could probably eavesdrop as well.

Kayla was thinking that once she was under here, it did not seem as frightening as it had looked from the outside. Perhaps this would indeed make a great hiding place for when…well, for when she had to hide.

And then things upstairs quieted down. Kayla realized that everything had become okay once again. Now there was no more need to hide, because up in the house, all the yelling had suddenly stopped. That gave Kayla the "all clear."

She scrambled back through the hole in the clapboards and stood in the open sunlight. It would be safe to go back into the house now, and check on her mother.

And when her father sobered up, life would become smoother, and her mother would smile once again. The seas of life would remain calm.

Until the next storm.

Groggily she was aware of a noise. It was dark, and when Kayla became fully awake, she realized that she was in her bed. She burrowed deeper into her blankets, and put her hands over her ears because she didn't want to hear the screams coming from the next room.

Despite covering her ears, Kayla heard her mother's voice. "Leave her alone!"

"I'll get that brat up out of bed!" yelled her father. "I'll teach her!"

She heard her mother scream, but Kayla knew that nothing could stop him. So it was to be Kayla this time who became the victim of his wrath, not her mother. Kayla knew her father would burst into her bedroom at any second. She had to get away!

And now she knew where she could go. She knew a place to hide.

Aren't you afraid of the dark? Kayla's inner voice whispered. *It will be dark under the house because it's night time now.*

But anything was better than sticking around here. She made her choice before she gave herself time to think about it. Her father was coming for her!

Kayla threw off the covers and jumped out of bed, landing nimbly on her feet. Rushing to the window, she lifted the sash. Thank god she lived in a one-story house.

Just as she was scrambling out the window, she could hear the door to her bedroom burst open behind her. As Kayla dropped to the outside ground, she could hear her father's voice become a roar of anger as he realized she was escaping. There would be hell to pay now.

Wearing only a cotton nightdress and underpants, Kayla felt the cool grass, slick with dew, under her bare feet. She couldn't take the time to be careful; *Please god, don't let me slip.* She didn't look behind; she couldn't risk any mistakes.

She ran for her life, turning the corner of the house to head for the backyard where she knew the hole in the clapboards waited for her. She leaned into the run, her knees pumping, her breath wheezing, her lungs beginning to hurt. If only she could get under the house in time!

And then she reached the hole under the porch. She took a deep breath and scooted inside. She tumbled across the hardpan dirt and rolled twice until she came to a stop. She tried to be quiet, tried to hold her breath, but her lungs were bursting and she had to breathe hard.

She could hear her father giving chase. Had he seen where she went? She ducked her head under her arm as she heard him run past the hole in the clapboards.

He hadn't seen! Could she dare to relax?

Kayla took her head out from underneath her arm. Better to not risk feeling smug; she had better make sure her father wouldn't find her. She had better go deeper underneath the house.

But it's dark, her inner voice whispered. *You never had a chance to explore here yet. You don't know what's down here.*

Again, Kayla felt faced with the idea that she had no choice. After all, which was she more afraid of? The unknown couldn't be as bad as the known. And her father's drunken rages were very well known to her.

So she scrambled deeper under the house into the bowels of the crawlspace.

The darkness enveloped her; it surrounded her in an almost surreal eclipse of light. Her sense of smell sharpened to compensate for her lack of sight. She could smell moldy, rich earth.

Too short a space to stand, Kayla felt her way over the ground as she crawled on her hands and knees. She could feel small pebbles, and then she felt one of the discarded cans that she had noticed the last time she had been down here. She tossed the can aside, careful not to cut herself on the rusted metal.

Finally she figured she had crawled far enough to not be seen if her father wised up and peered through the hole in the clapboards.

She curled up into a ball and waited, listening intently for sounds coming from the house above her. She could hear the front door open and close. Her father must have made the entire round of the house, and when he didn't find her, he must have gone back inside. What was her mother doing? Kayla could hear nothing upstairs except the sounds made by her father.

Why was her mother so quiet? Even more odd, why wasn't her father yelling? It would be more normal for Kayla to hear him shouting abuses than to hear this silence.

There came a scraping noise that seemed to move across the floorboards. Kayla strained to listen, but she couldn't make sense of the sounds.

And then she heard the back door swing open.

Oh no! Was her father coming back outside to look for her once again?

Cringing in fright, Kayla scrambled sideways like a crab to travel deeper underneath the house. She couldn't see in the darkness, so she started with surprise when she hit a brick wall. She was cornered against the foundation that held up the house. There was nowhere else to go. So she crouched; waiting, fearing. She tried to make herself as small as humanly possible.

An ax! She could hear her father chopping at the clapboards. How had he known she was down here?

Kayla heard the boards being pulled away. He must have put down the ax because now she could hear that he was using his hands. She could see the light entering from the hole he was making. Even though it was night outside, it was still lighter out there than it was underneath the house.

And then something blocked the hole, but only for a moment. Light shined in again. And then her father blocked the hole. He was coming inside! He was pushing something in front of him.

Kayla braced herself. He had found her. Now he would grab her and drag her outside. And then he would take her into the house and beat her within an inch of her life. So she hadn't escaped after all; there was never any escape.

But just as she resigned herself to her fate, her father reversed direction and backed out of the hole. Kayla was stunned. What did that mean?

And then she realized that the hole in the clapboards was being blocked again. Except this time, her father was nailing the boards back into place.

He was closing the hole!

She was being buried alive!

Fear froze her; she remained immobile. She waited for her father to finish nailing the clapboards back into place. Under the house, it became dark as a tomb; as dark as death.

Still Kayla could not bring herself to move. She waited. And then she heard the back door slam, and she understood that her father had gone back inside the house.

Finally Kayla decided to take action. She thought she would crawl to the place where the hole was covered and test her father's handiwork.

Maybe he hadn't taken too much care with the patch job he had done to cover the hole. Maybe he hadn't nailed the boards down very securely.

Maybe Kayla could push the boards back out if she leaned hard on them, and if so, then she could set herself free.

Where she would go once she got out, she didn't know. But she would deal with that later. Now, she just needed to get out from under the house.

She began to creep back over the hardpan earth. She felt her way along, because it was too dark to see. She desperately hoped she remembered the direction of the way out. She had mental images of herself crawling through the bowels of the house for an eternity, hopelessly lost.

But then she could tell she was headed in the right direction, because the dirt began to feel warmer under her fingers. It would make sense that the sunlight had warmed the area closest to the back porch earlier in the day. It had not totally cooled down yet, even though Kayla figured it was probably around midnight now.

She moved forward an inch, touched the ground in front of her, and then moved forward another inch. It was a slow progress, but it was the only way.

And then her fingers felt an obstacle in her path. It seemed to be blocking her way. It must have been the thing that her father had pushed ahead of him when he had entered the crawlspace.

She desperately wished she could see.

Instead, her fingers nervously probed the object in front of her. It felt smooth and clammy; soft and moist. And warm. Repulsed, she quickly withdrew her fingers.

A horrible thought was dawning on her. She suddenly understood.

She had always been such a coward. She had never run for help, had never gone to a neighbor or a teacher. Her father always threatened her to not tell anyone, ever, about the abuse.

But why hadn't her mother done anything? Who was the adult and who was the child?

After Kayla crawled over her mother's prone body, she reached the clapboards. She pushed and pried at the repair job her father had done until a nail holding one of the boards popped free. Kayla knew the boards would come off to make another hole. And then Kayla could escape to a neighbor's house.

She didn't have to worry about what her father would do to her mother anymore if she told.

Pandora's Lost Luggage

H. K. Hillman

"The delegation has arrived, Mr. Blackthorn."

Erasmus Blackthorn tapped the intercom on his desk. "Send them up, Melissa."

He placed his hands on his huge and largely empty desk and swung his chair a little. They had come to dissuade him, but they were too late. His people were already on site and already digging. Erasmus indulged himself a smile, which he knew he would have to lose soon. These people would expect serious conversation and if he was to get what he wanted out of this meeting, he would have to keep it serious.

"Do we have the permits yet?" Charlie West's face was full of concern, but then it always was.

"They are coming. Mr. Blackthorn has cleared this with the authorities. Don't worry, Charlie, we aren't going to get into any trouble." Terry Rarity sighed. Charlie was a worrier. Maybe Terry shouldn't have brought him on this dig but Charlie was a good archaeologist and particularly skilled at noticing the tiny details so many others overlooked. The downside was Charlie's insistence on proper protocol. If he ever found out there were no permits, that the whole thing was a catalogue of Blackthorn's calling in favours, coupled with payoffs and bribes, he'd have a fit.

"You know I'm not comfortable unless it's all above board." Charlie stared at his shoe as he twisted it in the dirt.

"I know. It's fine, Charlie, really. We're just following up on earlier work. The hole we're digging into was first dug in 2001. This isn't some speculative dig, we already know we're onto something."

Charlie sniffed. "Do we know why they stopped work back then?"

"Well," Terry said. "You know the current situation in this country, right? The government had a lot more to worry about than some guys in a hole in the ground and really, they still do. They can't spare time nor money on archaeology. We have Mr. Blackthorn's funding so the country isn't having to pay out, and they get tax revenue and permit fees and they do need the money. That's the only way we've been able to revive this dig."

Charlie shrugged. "I don't understand why nobody did it this way before. It's a fascinating find and it just got ditched for so many years."

Ah, Charlie, you're still at the stage where you think science is pure and scientists don't engage in sneaky, underhand practices to keep the money flowing. "It's about funding. Basically, about keeping funding going by not reaching the end point." Terry held up his hands. "It's the science version of politics, Charlie. Stay one step away from the final discovery for as long as possible, and the money keeps coming. It's the game that has corrupted real science in every field." Terry smiled. "We don't play that game and neither does Mr. Blackthorn. We want to see the end point. We want to see the last secret opened within our lifetime."

Charlie closed one eye in a lopsided smile. "I want that too."

"Gentlemen, welcome. Please, have a seat." Erasmus indicated the three chairs placed in front of his wide desk. "Can I offer anyone a drink?"

The three men exchanged glances and all shook their heads.

"No thank you, Mr. Blackthorn. The matter at hand is urgent, at least to us."

Erasmus recognised Professor Christopher Rooke and extended his hand. "I'm quite certain it is of the utmost importance to you, Professor Rooke."

The Professor ignored Erasmus' proffered handshake and raised his eyebrows. "You know me?"

"Of course." Erasmus let his hand fall to his side. "I do not enter into projects, nor business arrangements, not even meetings, without knowing who I am dealing with." He nodded to the other two men. "Professor Williamson. Doctor Prosser. I haven't studied all your work in detail, of course, that would require rather more time than I have available, but I think I have the general idea." He relaxed into his chair. "Please, gentlemen, be seated, and tell me your concerns."

The three men sat. Professor Rooke placed his arms on the desk, fingers interlocked. "We are here because of the projects you have applied for. The permits you have applied for, I mean. You're clearly in a position to fund the projects yourself."

"Quite so. I have engaged the services of one of your colleagues, a Doctor Rarity, and we are seeking permission for digs in a number of locations."

"Rarity!" Prosser sneered. "He's a treasure hunter, not an archaeologist."

Erasmus smiled. "I am a businessman, not a scientist. I am not interested in discovery for its own sake. I am, as you correctly deduce, in it largely for the profit."

Rooke waved Prosser to silence. "Mr. Blackthorn, what you will find is not treasure. There is no gold in the chambers you propose investigating."

Erasmus smiled wider. "I know, but not all treasure is gold."

Terry looked over the drawing Charlie had made. "So all these stone vials contain pressurised carbon dioxide?"

"Yes," Charlie indicated the lines of vials embedded in the walls and revealed by their ground penetrating radar. "Try to break through by force and we'll release enough of it to asphyxiate ourselves down there. It's heavier than air, and two or three of those would be enough to fill the dig."

"I wonder how they did that?" Terry mused. "We have to get a few of them out intact, for later study."

"Won't be easy." Charlie sniffed. "Those things are embedded in the stones and then there's the vibration down there. Subsonic, makes you feel like crap. We still don't know where that comes from. We have to cycle the diggers because they can't work in there for more than an hour. They certainly can't hold on long enough to extract one of those vials."

"We'll get back to the vials later." Terry scanned the hand drawn diagram. "There must be a way into the thing. I bet the vibrations come from something inside, and if we can find it and stop it, it'll be much easier. I can't see a way in."

"There might be one." Charlie pointed to a mark on the ground scan. "It's in the north face. We're digging down the east face."

Terry squinted at the printout. "Where?"

"It's faint, but it's there. A rectangular patch about halfway down the side of the structure." Charlie took a red pen and circled the spot.

Terry took a deep breath. He had been right to bring Charlie along. Nobody else would have spotted that. "So, can we get to it?"

Charlie shrugged. "The easy way would be to dig another shaft. The quick way would be to tunnel sideways, around the thing, but that has more risk of a tunnel collapse."

"We won't be able to dig another shaft. We're lucky to have access at all, the government here isn't going to like us digging holes wherever we please." Terry tapped his pen against his chin. *The truth is, digging another shaft will get us noticed and we aren't supposed to be here.* "We have to try the tunnel. Just make sure it's well shored up."

"It's not too far around and we're already past the point where we're deep enough. I'll get the ground staff to make a start. Can we get enough wood?"

"No problem. Mr. Blackthorn gave us a generous budget," Terry said. "Just tell me what you need." *And I'll bribe the right people to get it.*

Williamson tapped his fist against his mouth and cleared his throat before speaking. "Mr. Blackthorn, we are all aware of your fascination with the occult. It is likely you expect to find some artefact in the chambers you are interested in. I can assure you, there is nothing of interest in any of them. Nothing that you, nor anyone else, can make use of."

Erasmus raised his eyebrows. "You've opened them?"

All three shifted in their seats. Rooke spoke. "No. We have not opened them because there is no need. We already know what they contain and they have to remain sealed."

Erasmus could raise his eyebrows no further. "Really? So what do they contain?"

Charlie led the way down the steep stairway cut into the sloping shaft. "It's no more than ten or twenty years old. The wood still has local builders' stamps on it."

"You mean someone beat us to it? Damnation." Terry clenched his fists.

"Here we are." Charlie stopped at a hole lined with new wood. "We cut through a few feet of earth and the tunnel was already there. Looks like someone blocked it off but they didn't do a very good job." Ahead, the new wood changed to slightly older, darker wood lining the walls and roof of the tunnel. "I've sent the diggers home for the day. We don't need them now and finding this spooked them a bit." He grinned. "It spooked me a bit too, until I realised it was very recent."

"Maybe they didn't get as far as that entrance you found. Maybe they didn't open it." Terry bit into his lip. If they had lost out, future funding from the Blackthorn group would not be guaranteed.

"Maybe." Charlie handed a flashlight to Terry and turned his own on, then started along the tunnel. "Nobody has been down this passage yet. It might not go all the way."

"We can't tell you." Prosser folded his arms. "You just have to trust us."

Erasmus smiled his broadest smile. "I won't have to worry about trust. One of those chambers will be open soon. Doctor Rarity is digging into it as we speak."

The effect was electric. Erasmus relaxed in his chair and wished he had brought popcorn. All three men shouted at once, all three pulled out cellphones and scrolled through screens of something or other. Contacts,

Erasmus guessed, but who should they call first? Which of the many unexplored chambers, around the planet, was Doctor Rarity about to open?

Professor Rooke was first to grasp the dilemma. He quieted the others then turned to Erasmus, his phone gripped in his hand.

"Which one? Where are you digging?"

Erasmus steepled his fingers. "I can't tell you that. You just have to trust me." He could have laughed at the expression on Rooke's face, but he managed – barely – to contain himself. This was the moment he had planned for all along and now it was here he had to stay in control. This was no time to collapse in helpless laughter. He could do that when his game was over.

Prosser banged his fist on the desk. "You don't know what's in there! You have no idea what you'll release."

"We'll know soon enough." Erasmus looked from one to the other. He had them in a corner, and the looks on their faces told him they knew it.

"The vibrations don't seem so bad in here." Terry ran his hand over his stomach. "I always feel as if I'm about to shit myself in the main shaft, but all I feel in here is a little bit queasy."

"I think the vibrations come from the top of the pyramid and travel down the structure." Charlie placed his hand on one of the side walls, then the other. "Yes, you can feel it on the side that's next to the pyramid. Maybe the wooden walls attenuate it, or perhaps it's all the earth that's still piled against this side."

"Interesting." Terry tested the walls and nodded. "We'll have to have a look at the top of this thing. Might be something we can sell to the military."

"Well, this is where the tunnel turns a corner so we're about halfway." Charlie shone his flashlight along the tunnel. "This might get to the entrance after all."

"I hope not." Terry gritted his teeth. "I hope they gave up just before they reached it, and left it to us to finish the job."

"That would be nice, but it's a long shot. Nobody goes to this much trouble just to give up at the last minute." Charlie started walking again.

Williamson closed his eyes and drew a long, slow breath. He opened them and faced Erasmus. "What will it take to stop your dig? Money?"

This time, Erasmus did laugh. "Money? I have more than I will ever need, thanks. No, you can't buy me off. Try again."

"What is it you want?" Prosser's face showed defeat.

"It's simple." Erasmus tilted his head. "I want to know what's in those chambers. That's why I'm funding Doctor Rarity's expedition. Really, there is nothing complicated about it, gentlemen. I just want to know."

For several long minutes, they sat in silence. Finally, Rooke spoke.

"If we tell you, will you stop the dig?"

Erasmus kept his face impassive. "If you can convince me you're telling the truth, and that it's important to keep the chambers sealed, yes."

"We can't." Prosser put his hand on Rooke's arm. "This is too big to get out."

Rooke's laugh came out as a snort. "If he opens that chamber, it all gets out. And we have no idea how to put it back."

"He's right." Williamson faced Erasmus. "We have to rely on your absolute discretion. Not one word of this can leave this room."

"Of course." Erasmus allowed himself a small smile. "I am a businessman, gentlemen. Keeping secrets is part of the job."

"How much time do we have?" Rooke stared at the desk. "How long before he opens the chamber?"

"He will call me when he finds a way in. I want to be there when it opens. So we have a little time yet." Erasmus put his elbows on the desk. "Begin at the beginning, Professor Rooke."

"What the hell?" Charlie almost dropped his flashlight.

Terry battled the rising nausea in his insides. The vibrations had increased, massively and suddenly and the thing on the floor really wasn't helping. He was sure his gut was going to violently empty at both ends, any second now.

"Charlie..." Terry retched. "Charlie, let's get the hell out. We have to tell Mr. Blackthorn about this."

"We should tell everyone." Charlie stood immobile, his face in a shocked rictus.

"Charlie. Move. Now. Or I'm going without you." Terry started down the tunnel. "Blackthorn is paying us. We tell him first." He was relieved when he heard Charlie's footsteps following, then terrified when his mind wondered if that was really Charlie following. After what they had seen... dare he look back?

Terry picked up the pace and tried not to break into a panicked run.

Professor Rooke tapped his finger on the desk a few times before he spoke. "You are no doubt aware of the, ah, conspiracy theories concerning ancient structures? The pyramids in Egypt, the Göbekli Tepe find, Gunung Padang in Indonesia, the Aztec and Inca ruins, even Stonehenge in England and so on? We have gone to great lengths to keep the things under them secret, even to the extent of announcing the Stonehenge chamber find on April 1st so everyone would think it was a joke."

"The theories that they could not be constructed by modern technology, so must have been of alien origin?" Erasmus smirked. "Surely you aren't going to give me a flying saucer story?"

"No." Rooke's face remained serious. "There was no alien involvement. Those structures were built by, and most were deliberately destroyed or buried by, humans. At a time long before our current ancestors were cavemen."

"I have heard the ideas put around that those structures are so old, they must have been built while we were still making flint tools. It is a difficult idea to put credence in." Erasmus raised his hand. "My apologies for the interruptions, Professor."

"Not at all." Rooke's smile was tight and short lived. "This tale is going to get a lot stranger before the end." He closed his eyes for a moment. "It was almost Utopia. One world, one language, one government with very few laws and most people did what they liked. The Tower of Babel story was almost real. No God did that, humanity broke itself apart deliberately. To save itself, or so they believed. The tinfoil hatters are partly right, but the loss of that advanced civilisation was not the result of a cataclysm. Not a global flood, not an asteroid, nothing like that." He opened his eyes to look directly at Erasmus. "They destroyed it all themselves. All their records, all their achievements, all their technologies. They, in fact, tried to delete themselves from history and returned to the primitive life. They weren't 'contemporary with cavemen' They became those cavemen. Deliberately."

Erasmus shook his head. "Why?"

"They became morose." Williams winced at Rooke's glare. "Sorry. A bad joke."

Rooke sighed. "Bad, but essentially correct." He leaned forward on Erasmus' desk. "They came to believe their technology was bad, that it was destroying the planet, that they were heading for a global catastrophe of their own making. It wasn't true but they believed it and 'morose' is the reason. Or rather, Moros."

Erasmus sat back in his chair, rummaging in his brain for his memories of that name. "Moros was part of Greek mythology. He brought mortals to their doom. I'd have to look up the details, I don't remember this particular character very well."

"You won't need to. Moros was a real entity. As were most of those in the various pantheons of gods. Memories of the old times, passed down and corrupted. Did you ever notice how every single religion has one 'chief' god and then a lot of lesser gods, or angels, or demons, with specific jobs? They are all memories of the same thing. The things the ancients woke, or activated, or perhaps even created, with their technology."

"You don't know?" Erasmus raised one eyebrow.

"There are only fragments left. They did a very good job of erasing themselves. We have a good picture but it's incomplete."

"I understand. So this Moros was human?" Erasmus folded his arms and leaned forward, fascinated.

"No. We have not been able to determine exactly what he, and others, were. They might have been in human form but they were not human. They certainly didn't like humans very much." Rooke snorted. "They spent their time convincing humanity it was doomed, on any level they could get a grip on. They were the ones telling people they were causing their own destruction and they were so convincing, so believable, that humans trying to avoid their own destruction actually caused it."

"So Moros led them to self-destruction, as the legends say." Erasmus sniffed. "However, I don't see how this leads to what is in the chambers. Is it the knowledge they tried to delete? If so, that would be worth a great deal."

Rooke shook his head. "We have some of their technology but we dare not release it, nor use it. Something in their work called up, or let loose, or created Moros and his gang of doomsayers and we don't know what it was. We do know they deliberately tried to destroy or hide absolutely all of it but we don't know which parts are dangerous."

"Well, surely this Moros is long dead by now so you can't call him up again," Erasmus said.

Prosser spluttered. "Aren't you listening? Moros might have been created by their technology so if we try to use it, we might create another one. And this time we don't know how to lock it away."

"I was getting to that." Rooke said. "It's worse than Doctor Prosser suggests. Moros, and his underlings, once created or released or whatever happened, turned out to be immortal."

Prosser piped up. "Also unkillable. The damn thing is indestructible and that's why we don't want to accidentally make another."

Erasmus whistled. "You're telling me this Moros is locked in one of those chambers, right?"

"Exactly right." Rooke leaned further forward. "His gang, his brood, whatever you want to call them, are in the other chambers. Someone worked out how to snare them but we haven't found any record of how they did it. They erased everything and put humans back to the stone age to start again."

"If they had the threat contained, why didn't they just go back to the way things were? Rebuild their civilisation?"

"When the lie gets big enough it cannot be contained. Even when the originator is out of circulation. These were people, just like us, with the same failings. They continued to believe they had to shut everything down." Williamson shrugged. "We don't know for sure, of course, but our best guess is that Moros was contained too late. Those who contained him realised that they had to hide all evidence of what they had done and hope no future generations ever found the chambers."

Rooke smiled. "Curiosity doesn't just kill cats, Mr. Blackthorn. Your expedition could well kill everyone. If those things get out, we don't know how to put them back." He sat back in his chair. "That is why those chambers must never be opened. Or at least, not until we know how to contain the things within them."

Erasmus considered this. "I agree," he said. "An overt demon would commit atrocities, and humanity would react at once. A subtle demon like Moros does not destroy. He incites people to destroy themselves. He could build his plan over decades without being noticed. Sowing division and hate and paranoia until humanity collapses under its own fear. I will of course keep your secret and stop the dig as soon as Doctor Rarity calls me."

"Thank you, Mr. Blackthorn." Williams wore a look of relief, as did the others. "Will you now tell us where he is digging?"

"In the one place I didn't apply for permits. The least known place of all the places so far discovered." Erasmus grinned. "In Croatia, Sevastopol. The buried pyramid discovered by Vitaly Goh in 2001."

"Oh my God. We were just in time." Prosser put his face in his hands.

Rooke shut his eyes, tight. "It's the least known place because it's the one we tried to keep most secret. It's where Moros is contained and if he gets out he can release all the others."

Williamson scoffed. "He'd never get in. The pyramid has a subsonic generator to deter humans and is loaded with asphyxiants. Try to break through and you'll die."

"Fortunately, Doctor Goh documented these things before the military took over the area." Erasmus steepled his fingers. "I sent Doctor Rarity in with full knowledge of those traps. And I'm afraid keeping things secret is very difficult in this digital age. YouTube, in particular, is becoming quite a resource."

Rooke nodded. "The military have been in control of the area since. They were instructed to leave it alone." He looked at Erasmus. "I suppose they have become lax, and open to bribery, since they started?"

Erasmus laughed. "Quite so. An army guarding a hole in the ground for almost two decades does become easily distracted. It wasn't what they signed up for."

"It's no laughing matter." Prosser scowled. "This conversation might just have saved us all from going back to another stone age, although this time Moros might have finished us. We might also have saved your life, Mr. Blackthorn. Moros has been in the box for tens of thousands of years. He will need sustenance. He'll suck all the life out of the first person he hits when the door is open."

"Damn this phone. Why is it taking so long?" Terry glared at the screen, at the low bars of the reception indicator. "If we had WiFi here we could have contacted him that way."

"Military wouldn't allow it in case we tapped into their systems." Charlie sat with his hands in his lap, staring at the floor. "Do you think they know?"

"Of course they know. That corpse was in military uniform. The same uniform they wear on the base." Terry's phone beeped. "At last. Hello? I have to speak with Mr. Erasmus Blackthorn. It's urgent."

"That corpse looked mummified. Like it was a thousand years old." Charlie lowered his head. "How can that be?"

"Quiet, Charlie." Terry waved his hand.

The woman's voice on the phone said: "Mr. Blackthorn is in a meeting. Can you call back?"

"No. No, this is very important. Tell him it's Doctor Rarity. He knows who I am and he'll understand why it's important I speak to him at once."

There was a pause. "I'll get a message to him but I don't think he'll be pleased. He doesn't like being interrupted in meetings. Please hold."

Appalling, tinny music drifted from the phone. "Jesus H. Christ!" Terry forced his grip to relax in case he accidentally crushed the phone in his fingers.

The woman's voice returned, sounding rather less pompous than before. "Mr. Blackthorn will take your call. I'm putting you through, Doctor Rarity."

Terry braced himself. This was likely to be the worst phone call of his life.

Erasmus opened a drawer in his desk and took out an ashtray, lighter, and a box of cigars. "I think this meeting is a success, don't you, gentlemen?" He offered the cigars around. All three declined.

"Isn't it illegal to smoke in your place of work?" Prosser scowled at him.

"Probably." Erasmus lifted a cigar and clipped the ends. "Some of us just don't care."

"Perhaps we should have let you die when that chamber opened. It would be one less smoker on the planet." Prosser's face twisted in a sneer.

"Oh, I had no intention of opening it. No need, really." He lit his cigar. "You see, gentlemen, I wanted you here at this precise moment for a reason. Have you been watching the news? Have you followed the insanity of the world lately? It had a sudden onset, didn't it?"

"What are you talking about?" Rooke narrowed his eyes.

"Well, sure, there has always been a low-level insanity in society. That's normal. The last decade or so though, it has ramped up enormously. Didn't you notice?" Erasmus took a puff and blew a blue cloud into the air. "After your description of the end of that advanced civilisation, did you really not notice?"

Williamson blinked. "Notice what?"

A light blinked on the phone. Cigar clamped in his teeth, Erasmus checked the message on its LCD screen. 'Dr. Rarity calling. Do I put him through?' Erasmus picked up the phone. "Yes, Melissa, put him on. He is relevant to this meeting." He put the phone on 'speaker' and replaced the handset then answered Williamson. "Noticed what I'm about to tell you you should have noticed. If only you scientists had put windows in those ivory towers."

"What?" Rooke leaned forward. "Do you have information we should know?"

"A great deal." Erasmus grinned. "And some you'll never know. This information though, is something you would never have accepted had I not set up this proof."

"We are scientists." Prosser's sneer intensified. "We deal in facts and reality, not the pipe dreams of some money-oriented business-suited smoker."

"Shut up, Prosser." Rooke glared at him. "There's something going on here and we have to listen."

He's getting the idea, Erasmus thought. The phone beeped to signal a call coming through.

"Hello? Mr. Blackthorn?" Terry's voice crackled through the bad connection. "It's Terry Rarity."

Blackthorn took a puff of his cigar and relaxed in his chair. "Yes, Doctor Rarity. You are speaking to me, Professor Rooke, Professor Williamson and Doctor Prosser. You may speak freely."

"Prosser? That arse?"

Erasmus feigned a coughing fit but noticed the little smirk on Rooke's face. "Yes, and as I said, we can all hear you."

"Never mind. Look, we found the entrance and it's open. There's nothing in there."

Erasmus took a slow drag on his cigar. "I told you not to open it until I was there." His voice stayed calm. The other three did not.

"You opened it? You bloody idiot!" Prosser shouted.

"I didn't open it. It was already open." Terry yelled from the speaker. "Listen. There's a corpse, looks mummified but is in modern military uniform. There's a tunnel that Charlie reckons is no more than ten to twenty years old. Someone beat us to it. Calm the hell down, I'm still trying to get this into perspective in my head."

"Would anyone like a whisky?" Erasmus opened another drawer and lifted out a decanter and some glasses.

"You don't seem to be at all surprised." Rooke shook his head. "You knew about this?"

"No, I didn't know for sure, but I suspected." Erasmus poured himself a whisky then set the decanter on the desk. "Help yourselves, gentlemen." He tapped ash from his cigar. "This is exactly what I have been expecting."

"Expecting?" Terry shouted from the speaker. "You sent me on a wild goose chase?"

"What the hell do you mean, you expected it?" Rooke narrowed his eyes.

Erasmus held up his hands. "Gentlemen, please, calm down. We can discuss this in a civil fashion."

"You don't seem to think there is any urgency." Prosser's face had turned bright red. "Didn't you listen?"

Erasmus sighed. "Doctor Rarity has already told us that the chamber has been open for over a decade. The results you fear are already under way."

"What results? What's going on?" Terry sounded baffled.

"Doctor Rarity, thank you for your work on this. I will of course continue to fund the expedition, although you might want to let the military know they have a body down there."

"But the chamber—"

"Is empty, yes." Blackthorn steepled his fingers. "There is still the matter of the subsonic generator. Find that, and it's likely to be worth a fortune."

"Well…" Terry muttered.

"Take a few days off. Give your staff a break too. You'll need to let the military collect the corpse anyway."

There was a pause. "Okay." Terry sounded calmer. "Thanks, Mr. Blackthorn."

"Keep me updated. Goodbye for now, Doctor Rarity." Blackthorn switched off the phone. He faced the others. "Well, gentlemen, we can talk now. I suspect this matter is not something we should be letting Doctor Rarity know about yet, given his delight in publicity."

"Absolutely." Williams nodded.

"That publicity hound would have it on every front page." Prosser sneered.

Rooke leaned forward. "Why are we here, Mr. Blackthorn? You seem to already know everything."

"Not at all," Erasmus said. "I knew the chambers existed, of course. Every late-night geek rummaging on YouTube knows about them. However, I had no idea what was in them. I congratulate you on keeping that part very quiet, by the way. I really didn't know about Moros and his gang of dark whisperers. In fact, I doubt I would ever have thought of that name. He was a very minor character in the mythology we are taught nowadays. No, all I had was a feeling that the buried pyramid in Croatia was likely to have been breached. The little I had heard of the place made it, logically, almost inevitable. I didn't know what was in there but I had a feeling something was released."

"Just feelings? That's a thin reason to pay for an archaeological expedition." Prosser blinked. "You must have had more?"

Erasmus nodded. "I have noticed a massive increase in what I would term 'general lunacy' all over the world. It started in the early 2000s. So I began searching for a link, something big, something that happened around that time. Vitaly Goh's discovery was the biggest anomalous event of the time and it was being kept rather quiet, I thought."

"But he didn't open the chamber. He didn't get very far at all." Rooke shrugged. "Once we realised what he had found, we persuaded the government of the time to declare it a military base and close it. That put a stop to his and all other digs. Until now."

"Not quite." Erasmus pursed his lips. "You didn't think it through, you know. That pyramid contains a subsonic generator that has operated with no apparent power source for tens of thousands of years. Clearly, this is something of interest to a weapons technologist and most definitely of interest to the military." He paused for breath. "Gentlemen, you put a military base on top of a potentially useful weapon and told them to leave it alone. Of course they didn't leave it alone."

"Oh, shit." Rooke put his face in his hands.

"My guess is that they opened it within a year of you closing it down. Which means Moros was released in 2002 or 2003. Which fits with when the world really started cracking up." Erasmus took a sip of his whisky and stubbed out his cigar.

"Doesn't make sense," Williamson said. "If they got as far as opening it and lost a man in the process, why didn't they carry on looking for that generator?"

"As with all of this, we can only guess at most of it." Erasmus refilled his glass. "Maybe Moros caused them to forget what was down there.

Maybe they were scared – soldiers are human too, remember. Maybe they decided to close the dig until they could find another way in. Maybe… maybe they thought they'd let some actual archaeologists do the job and pick up the device when they found it." He waved his hand. "Any guess is as good as any other at this point."

"And none of them matter." Prosser glowered. "Moros is out, and has been for almost two decades. He's had plenty of time to release all the others. Who knows what they might have been doing?"

Erasmus snorted. "Really? After all you've just told me? You don't know what they've been up to?" He held up his hand and unfolded one finger at a time. "The planet is doomed unless we give up all our technology. People are splitting into smaller and smaller factions and fighting over differences that really don't matter. People are outraged if someone utters one word out of place." He closed his hand and banged the desk. "And so much more. How could you not have noticed, when you were the ones with the answer to why it was happening?"

Rooke still had his hands over his face. He lowered them to reveal new lines in his skin. "We thought the chambers were intact. We didn't know."

"Ha!" Erasmus bared his teeth. "And if you had known where Doctor Rarity was digging, you would have blocked it and we still wouldn't know." He sighed. "Well there's no point getting angry about it. Pandora's box is open."

Williamson laughed, a hollow sound. "Box? This is Pandora's entire luggage set for a year-long round-the-world cruise. We were supposed to be the baggage handlers and we've lost the lot."

Erasmus stood and leaned on his desk. "Gentlemen, I will need access to every bit of that ancient technology you have deciphered. Every fragment, no matter how apparently inconsequential. If we are to put this thing back in its box, we need every clue available, and it is not going to be easy. Whatever trick those ancient people used to get Moros and his horde contained will not work again. We have to know what that trick was, and how they made those containment chambers." He stared at the three stunned faces before him. "What do we do first?"

Rooke eyed the decanter. "I think I'd like to accept that drink now."

A Little Knowledge...

H.K. Hillman

First published in 2011 as a stand-alone eBook

The six-foot pole stood upright in the middle of the field. At its top, a white plastic bag flapped and fluttered in the wind, like a fish on a line.

"That the best you can do, Dimmy?" Javier laughed aloud and pointed at the bag.

"Don't call me that." Jimmy's face hung in a sulk. "It's not nice to laugh at me. I do the best I can."

"Those crows are gonna laugh, long and hard. Most people scare them away. You lay on entertainment."

"I do the best I can."

"You do just fine." Javier patted his brother's broad shoulder. "You just have no imagination."

"You're so clever, you make the scarecrow. You don't do nothing." Jimmy walked back towards the house, his head low between his shoulders.

Javier stared at his brother's retreating back. What Jimmy said was true. Since the death of their parents, Jimmy had done all the work around the farm, while Javier had concentrated on his studies. Javier made it to college. Jimmy, the older brother, had barely made it past fourth grade.

We make a fine pair, Javier thought as he leaned on the fence and watched Jimmy's makeshift scarecrow rustling over the newly-planted field. *Jimmy's all muscle and no brain, and I'm all brain, and no muscle.* Jimmy supported Javier through college. Jimmy grew their food, ran the farm, made their money. Jimmy ploughed. Jimmy planted. Jimmy harvested. Javier studied. He pushed himself from the fence and ran after his brother.

Jimmy pitched hay in the barn, lifting bales onto a cart to take to the cows. They had no horse. When the cart was full, Jimmy would pull it himself. Jimmy glared at Javier.

"What now? You come to make fun of me again?"

"No, Jimmy." Javier shifted his feet. "I came to say sorry. I know you don't think as fast as me, but I also know you work hard to look after me."

"Hard, yes. It's what I know. I do it the best I can, and all you do is make fun. It's not nice, Jave."

"I know. I don't mean it. It's just the way my mind works. You know, I take your name, change one letter, and Jimmy becomes Dimmy. I don't mean any harm."

Jimmy narrowed his eyes. "Is that what imagination does?"

"Yes." Javier smiled. "Imagination lets you think of new things."

"Don't like it." Jimmy hefted another bale onto the cart. "Sounds like all it does is make people sad."

"No, it's not like that. Sure, sometimes my jokes are cruel, but I don't mean them to be." Javier leaned against the cart. "Look, you must have some imagination. You're my brother."

"You got the brains. I got the muscle. That's what Dad always said." Jimmy moved to the front of the cart and lifted the heavy wooden yoke. "I farm. You learn. That's how Mom said it should be."

"Not forever, Jimmy. Once I graduate, I'll earn loads of money. Then I can look after you."

"Don't need looking after. I can look after myself." Jimmy heaved. The cart rolled forward. "I look after you, don't I?"

"Right. You do a great job." Javier walked alongside Jimmy. "But we'll get older. You could do with help around the farm. Hell, Jimmy, we can't even afford a horse to pull this cart."

"College costs money." Jimmy grunted under the weight of the cart. Sweat beaded on his forehead.

"I learn a lot of stuff there." Javier struggled for the simple words. College had increased his vocabulary well beyond Jimmy's ability to follow. "I could teach you some of it. I taught you to read, didn't I?"

"You did, Jave. Not much use for it round here though." Jimmy stopped and lowered the yoke to the ground. He wiped the sleeve of his overalls across his face. "This college learning. Anything about farming in there?"

"No." Javier chuckled. "I'm learning to be a historian. Ancient traditions, languages and cultures. Nothing about farming, at least nothing you could use."

"Well, I know a language." Jimmy lifted the yoke again. "Don't need more than one. I just need to know how to farm."

"Yeah, but Jimmy, just think how much better you'd be with some imagination. You'd work out a way to move this cart, I bet. And you'd make a real good scarecrow."

Jimmy stared down at Javier. "Imagination does that? It can do good things?"

"Sure it can. You just need to work out how to use it."

"Right. You can tell me." Jimmy hefted the yoke and pulled. "First I gotta feed the cows."

Javier watched until the cart obscured his view of his brother, then went back to the house. It was time he repaid Jimmy for all his effort.

Javier grinned at the look on Jimmy's face. They stood in the main hall of the library, a building Javier knew Jimmy had only ever seen from the outside.

"Someone wrote all these books?" Jimmy spoke in an awed whisper.

"Not one person, Jimmy. Lots of people. Some wrote a dozen, some wrote just one. It took a long, long time to make them all."

"I'll bet. How many have you read?"

"Oh, I've read some. There's lots here I've never even opened. You could spend your life in here and never finish." Javier smiled at his brother's astonishment. This was all part of their agreement. Javier would learn about the way Jimmy ran the farm. Jimmy, in turn, would see first-hand what Javier was doing with the money Jimmy earned.

"Wow." Jimmy's gaze roamed along the shelves. "You say we can take some home? For a little while, anyway?"

"Yes, we can borrow a few at a time. We have to bring them back though, so other people can read them."

"That's only fair." Jimmy nodded his agreement.

Javier took Jimmy's arm. "Come and look at this." He led Jimmy through an archway, along a corridor and into his favorite part of the library. Jimmy had no hope of understanding the books Javier wanted to show him. Later, Javier would take him to the westerns, the thrillers, the formulaic stories Jimmy would enjoy. First, he wanted to show his brother the old books.

Javier pushed open a door and stood back to let Jimmy enter.

"Look at these, Jimmy. These books are centuries old." Javier inhaled the dry, papery scent of the room.

Jimmy wrinkled his nose. "They smell like old people."

Javier grinned. "Dead people, Jimmy. The folk who wrote these books are all long since turned to dust. Their words live forever though, on these pages." He stepped into the room and spread his arms wide. Jimmy ducked under the low door frame and followed.

"There aren't so many as in the big room. Didn't they write so much in the old days?"

"Well, maybe, maybe not. Lots of old books went missing, you know. These are just the ones that are left." Javier ran his finger along the worn leather spines on the shelf. "They didn't have any printing press back then. If you wanted a copy, you had to write it out yourself."

"Really?" Jimmy lifted a slim book from the shelf and opened it. "You're right. This is all in real writing. Not like the ones we get at the gas station. It's heavy, too."

"We have to be careful with these." Javier held his breath as his brother turned the pages. "There aren't any others. You can't just buy a new one if the book is damaged."

Jimmy narrowed his eyes. "I'm not stupid, Jave. I won't hurt it. I'm just looking, that's all."

Javier pursed his lips. He had made a promise not to treat Jimmy as if he was an idiot. Jimmy knew how to handle books. Javier had shown him. Cradle the spine in your hand. Never bend it backwards. Don't open it further than it wants to go and never, ever fold down the corners of the pages. He turned his back for a moment, an expression of trust his brother must surely understand. Javier pretended interest in the shelved books until he could take no more.

When he turned around, Jimmy's hands were empty. Javier forced himself to hold down the relieved sigh he wanted to release. Despite his love for his brother, Javier decided it was safer to take Jimmy out of this room. *Sure, Jimmy wouldn't deliberately damage anything, but his hands are made for plough and spade, not paper and bindings,* Javier thought. He led Jimmy back into the main room of the library, to the paperback popular-novel section, and left him with the instruction to choose two books. Javier then went to busy himself with his favorite historical texts.

After supper, Javier grimaced at Jimmy's constant murmur. He couldn't concentrate; Jimmy had not yet developed his reading skills to the point where he could read in silence. Every word on the page formed on Jimmy's lips, sometimes accompanied by the wrinkling of his face as he struggled with a long or unfamiliar word. Eventually, Javier gave up and carried his books upstairs to his room.

The old bed creaked and sagged under Javier's weight. Jimmy had allowed him to use their parent's old bed, the one with the sprung mattress. Jimmy always insisted he preferred the harder bunks anyway, although Javier had caught him, more than once, stretching and rubbing at his back in the morning. He reached for one of his books, stacked on his bedside cabinet, and rolled over to cradle it on his pillow. He shifted position until the single bare bulb illuminated the pages sufficiently for him to read.

It was late when the creaking stairs announced Jimmy's arrival upstairs. Javier checked the old alarm clock beside his bed. Ten-fifteen. Much too late for Jimmy, who used no clocks, marked no time other than sunrise and sunset.

Jimmy's heavy tread padded past Javier's door. It was clear Jimmy did his best to walk quietly, but the tired floorboards groaned under his weight, reporting every step he took.

"Must have been a good book," Javier muttered to himself. He doubted Jimmy had finished, not at the speed he usually read, but he must have been engrossed in his story. Javier closed his own book, switched off the light and rolled himself in his blankets. The library had been a new experience for Jimmy. Tomorrow, Javier had to repay his brother by taking an interest in the farm. Jimmy was to wake him early, so Javier needed to sleep. The brothers had always held completely different definitions of 'early'.

Sunlight bored through the holes in Javier's worn curtains and lanced into his eyes. He blinked awake and stared at his clock. Nine-thirty. Far too early to be up and about.

Early. Javier sat upright in bed. Jimmy was supposed to wake him, and nine-thirty was equivalent to 'nearly lunchtime' in Jimmy's definition of a day. He scrambled from his bed, washed and dressed in a hurry and ran downstairs. The scents and sounds of frying reached for him before he made it to the kitchen.

"Hey, Jave. You want some eggs?" Jimmy stood at the stove, poking at the frying pan with a wooden spatula.

"Late breakfast, Jimmy?" Javier smirked. "I thought you were getting up early today. Too much late-night reading, eh?"

"I was up with the sun. I always am. Had breakfast ages ago." Jimmy flipped the eggs onto a plate and cracked two more into the pan. He passed the plate to Javier.

"So what's this?" Javier accepted the eggs. He might question Jimmy's timing, but he wasn't about to turn away breakfast. Javier lifted his fork.

"Snack," Jimmy said. "Work's all done for the day."

Javier's fork stopped, halfway to his mouth. "What?"

"All done. Didn't need to wake you. I thought you could help out later, but there's no need."

"Come on, Jimmy. You work all day, every day. I've never seen you do otherwise."

"Times change." Jimmy flipped his eggs onto another plate, switched off the stove and joined Javier at the table. "I have time to read more now. I have to practice."

Javier lowered his fork. "Hey, look, Jimmy. I know that library's a great place, but you can't just let the farm fall apart. I'll help you with your reading, if you want, but the farm's our only income at the moment."

Jimmy spoke through a mouthful of egg. "Farm's fine. Better than ever. Got some help."

"Help? We can't afford help."

"Don't cost nothing. I just had to agree to something, that's all." Jimmy finished his eggs and eyed the two cooling on Javier's plate. "Don't you want those?"

Javier pushed the plate to Jimmy, who switched it with his own and continued eating.

"Jimmy, what are you talking about?" Javier's stomach rumbled at the sight of Jimmy's voracious appetite, although the confusion in Javier's mind occluded his hunger.

"Show you. In a minute." Jimmy wiped yolk from his chin. "I did what you said. Used my imagination. And that book from the library."

Javier shook his head. Jimmy had selected *The Wizard of Oz*, and some Sam Spade novel Javier couldn't remember the title of. Where in those books did he learn his new super-efficient farming methods? Had the characters come to life and opted for a pastoral existence? The image of the Tin Man ploughing the fields flitted through Javier's mind. He laughed, despite his worries. The scarecrow would certainly come in handy.

"It was in the wizard book. That gave me the idea. The other book showed me how." Jimmy picked up the plates and placed them in the sink. "In the wizard book, things come to life. A scarecrow, a man made out of pots and pans, things like that. I thought well, if I can't make a scarecrow, why not just magic one up?" Jimmy ran hot water into the sink. "Then I thought, why stop there? Why not magic up some farm workers? If they're not real, they don't need to eat so they won't cost nothing." He washed the plates and set them to dry.

"Jimmy, magic isn't real. It's just—"

"Imagination. I know. But you told me imagination could do good things, so I tried. It worked. The book showed me how."

"I don't get it." Javier rose from his seat. "You learned magic from a Sam Spade book?"

"Haven't read that one yet." Jimmy wiped his hands on a towel. "Just some of the wizard book, and some of the other one."

"Whoa." Javier raised his hands. "What other one?"

Jimmy trapped his upper lip between his teeth and stared at the floor.

"I know that look." Javier walked around the table to face his brother. "That's your guilty look. What have you done?"

"I only borrowed. We can take it back next time we go. You said it was okay to borrow from there. You said that's what it was for."

"Jimmy." Javier assumed his father's authoritative voice. "Show me this book."

Jimmy's face reddened. "You're just going to shout."

"I won't shout." Javier lowered his voice. If Jimmy had taken a book from the library without checking it out, it was probably Javier's own fault anyway. *I should have explained things more clearly*, he thought.

Jimmy opened a drawer below the table and took out a heavy, leather-bound book. Javier's eyes widened.

"That's one of the rare books." Javier took the volume from Jimmy's hands. "We're not supposed to take it out of the library. Jimmy, this is serious. We could be in big trouble."

"We'll take it back. It's only borrowed." Jimmy bit at his lip again. "I'm sorry, Jave. I didn't know."

Javier patted his brother's shoulder. "It's all right. We'll sneak it back in the same way you sneaked it out. Inside those baggy overalls, I'll bet." Javier hefted the book in his hands. "We'd better go today. If we're quick, it might not be missed."

"Can't we keep it for a while? Just till next week?" Jimmy reached for the book.

"No, Jimmy, we can't. What if the library calls the police?" Javier turned the book over and read the title.

'An account of the Witchcraft used by Peter Sykes, Farmer.'

Javier stared at the title for a while. Jimmy's hand rested on the book, and pulled. It left Javier's unresisting fingers.

"It's a farming book, Jave. Farming with magic. It works." Jimmy hugged the book to his chest.

"No." Javier whispered the word. "Magic isn't real. It can't work."

"Yeah? Come and look at this." Jimmy strode from the kitchen and into the yard. Javier followed in silence, a silence that was echoed by the animals on their small farm.

The chickens formed an orderly series of queues at their feeding trough. In the low field, the few cows munched at grass, standing alongside each other and maintaining this line as they moved along the field. Where Jimmy had planted wheat, a scarecrow stood guard. Not a plastic bag on a stick, but a dummy with arms outstretched and a tattered old hat on its head. Javier realized he had stopped breathing and drew a long, shuddering breath.

"You did all this today? In the few hours since the sun came up? How did you train the animals to do that?" Javier's mind struggled to accept the images his eyes saw.

"No, I did it last night. It's not perfect, not yet. I read slow. I do the best I can." Jimmy pressed the book into his chest. "I just need it for a few days more."

"It has to go back." Javier blinked. Something his brother said came back to him. "Jimmy, you said you had to agree to something. What was it?"

Jimmy giggled. "That's the best part. See, I remembered what you told me about the church. How all that stuff was made up, long ago, to keep people in line. So they'd do what they were told."

"Jimmy, just tell me." The morning air turned cold. Javier shivered.

"Well, the book said I have to give up my immortal soul. So I promised. I read the words and I promised."

Javier closed his eyes.

"It's all right, Jave. There's no such thing as a soul. You told me. So I didn't really give up mine, 'cause I don't have one to give. All this stuff comes for free."

Javier opened his eyes and stared at his brother. *I only told you that to get out of going to church on Sundays!*

He had never admitted it, but Javier did believe in the existence of the soul. He just didn't believe in getting up early on a Sunday. Besides, watching Jimmy gawp at the preacher's sermons, believing every word, had been too much of a temptation. He had exploited Jimmy's credulity once more, and set him on this course.

"Jimmy—" Javier's voice caught in his throat. The cart rolled out of the barn. Its yoke had been removed, and it was piled high with bales. In the chicken coop, a small, grey, leathery creature strolled from the hen house with a basket of eggs. The cart rolled onto the track leading to the cows. High on the bales, three more of the creatures sat. Jimmy hugged his book and grinned.

"Jimmy, what in Hell's name are those?"

"See? I told you I had help. I read about them in this book. I imagined them, I read the words and they came out of the pages. They work hard. They're good."

Javier's bowels churned, and not with hunger. "They're demons."

"No, no." Jimmy opened the book and ruffled through its pages. "Imps. They're called imps."

Javier's legs gave up the struggle to support him. He fell to his knees.

"Jave? You all right? You haven't eaten, that's the trouble. I'll fry up some more eggs." Jimmy grinned at his diminutive farm workers once more. Before turning back into the house, he waved towards the scarecrow in the field.

The scarecrow waved back.

Claiming Number Eight

H. K. Hillman

First published in The Horror Zine, January 2011

As the sole occupant of Oort Explorer Twelve, four years out from Earth and now at the edge of the solar system itself, I really had not expected to meet anyone. The helmeted figure at my window came as a considerable surprise. I was, in that moment, grateful for the urinary tube they had grafted into me before I was installed in this ship.

Wait. I'm getting ahead of myself. You don't yet know who I am, why I'm here or what I'm doing.

I am Tiberius Dominic Blackthorn, and I am sane. It sounds a strange boast but since I'm the only Oort Explorer in this section who's managed to avoid flying gibbering into a planetoid or firing all boosters and vanishing into space, it is a proud boast indeed. My sanity has been intact throughout the flight – although the ghastly face I glimpsed when that space-suited man tapped my window did make me wonder if my time, too, might be short. Is that how it was for the others before they cracked? We had limited ship-to-ship communication but there was never any way to tell who was going loopy, or when they would flake out altogether. It just happened. One by one.

It's better not to think about that.

The man outside is real, I'm sure. A line from his suit has tangled around some part of the external apparatus and he's drifting along with me now. Once in a while he floats past a window or a camera. If I'm lucky he has his back to me when it happens.

He is real. I am still sane. Of this I am sure with ninety-nine, okay, ninety-five per cent confidence.

I've set the computer to the task of estimating where he came from, and reassigned four close-range and two long-range detectors to look for his ship. I can't spare more. I have to watch out for the rocks.

Ah yes, I wanted to tell you what I'm doing. The Oort Cloud is a messy place. Composed of bits of ice and rock, all flying around with no sense of order or direction, it surrounds our entire solar system and constitutes what I suppose you might call a hazard to future shipping. My job, and that of any Oort Explorer who manages to keep his head on straight, is to map it.

That's not strictly true. The computer maps it. All I do is adjust, scan data and send samples. If artificial intelligence had ever worked as it should I wouldn't even be here. I'm the 'human element'—and if you could see me you'd laugh at that claim—here to cope with the unexpected. I use my intuition to decide where to aim the sensors for best effect. I fiddle with the programs when something goes out of alignment. I control the sampling arm. I select chunks of rock and ice for the boffins on Earth. Those go back in little pods. Sometimes I use the sampling arm to bat rocks around, just to watch the computer remap their trajectories.

I don't think the computer was at all surprised to find the astronaut out there. In fact—let me check—yes, it's mapped him, and it continues to map him as he floats around. Stupid machine doesn't realise he's stuck to the ship.

There he is again, floating past my window. I can't quite make out his face but it looks like someone—but it can't be him. If it is him then I've definitely lost it. I'll be aiming for the nearest big rock soon enough. It can't be him. He's dead, six years in Earth's soil. Soil I'll never walk on again.

No, I can't think that way. I'm alive and it's better than the alternative. Besides, even if I did somehow go back, I no longer have legs. These ships have stringent weight restrictions. You don't take along anything you won't need. Torso and head are essential, as is one arm. The rest is just excess baggage.

The man floating outside is entire. I must admit to a twinge of jealousy, yet I am alive and he is not. That must mean I have the better deal. It must. I have to believe that. Concentrate on life, be grateful for it. It keeps me sane. I think.

Sometimes, over the past four years, I've wished I had taken the injection. Those thoughts came often the first year, less so the second, less again the third. Now I've grown accustomed to my condition and marvelled at my adaptability. It seems people really can get used to anything.

I killed seven people. There, I've said it. No use denying it now anyway, I was convicted and condemned for it. Then saved, if that's the right word. Oh, it is. I've seen Neptune close up. How many could say that?

I hope my sanity, and this ship's systems, last a long while yet. I'd really like to see what's out there in interstellar space. Like Yuri Gagarin, the first man to leave Earth's atmosphere. T.D. Blackthorn, the first man to leave the solar system. The big difference is that Gagarin came back.

Maybe I'll still be travelling when the first of the interstellar ships passes by. That would be something to see. I could congratulate myself on making it possible with the maps and trajectories I've sent back from my little vessel. I doubt they'd even stop to say hello. Nobody likes a serial killer.

Well, not quite nobody. The space geeks came to see me on Death Row. All I had to look forward to was a little prick from the Oblivion Needle. Instead I met a little prick from the Space Agency.

You fit the profile, he said. I know, I said, they're going to baste me in death-juice for it next week.

No, he said. He meant I was a loner. Someone who preferred to be away from people. He had a proposal. I signed up, quick as a flash, when I found out it could get me out of that place. After a couple of months on Death Row, I'd have signed a contract with the Devil himself. I wish he had visited. He might have had a better deal.

Now here's Death looking me in the eye. That couldn't be Tom Santini, my fifth victim, who taps my window with his stiff gloved fingers and grins his desiccated, frozen grin through the thick glass. Taunting me with his limbs and teeth. It couldn't be him. Yet the face is so like him, the same death-mask. There are letters on his helmet, written in red. Not a word, just a mess of letters in blood red. The thought of blood makes me lick my gums. It's been a long time since I cut those numbers into my victims' foreheads. The letters might mean something to the computer so in they go. C-C-C-P.

Where was I? Oh yes, the space agency guy. Well, as soon as I signed the form I was handcuffed and ankle-chained and taken away in a van. They trained me in a mock-up cockpit which had more space than this one. I still had all my limbs then. Once they were satisfied I could do the job, off I went to surgery. Chop-chop, stitch and heal, counselling and more training. I had no choice by then. Take the ship, or take the needle. I had been through too much to turn back.

Four years. It's been good, in a way. Sure, I don't have space to move much, which is a little ironic when you consider that just outside my window is more space than anyone could ever need. Still, nobody bothered me until the astronaut turned up so I had four years of peace. The ship feeds me some tasteless mush, takes away my crap and does something with it. I never asked what because I have a feeling I don't really want to know. I even have TV, of a sort. Nothing but reruns but then that's all there ever was anyway. Once in a while someone from Earth asks how I'm doing. Once in a while I get around to answering. I know they don't care about me. It's the ship they're worried about. They've lost too many and these little babies aren't cheap.

The computer's found something. A conspiracy-theory archive from its memory. I shouldn't be surprised, since even phones had gigabytes of memory when I left Earth. This damn thing probably has a record of everything that was known when I set out, and might even have been updated on the way. Computer memory is far more important than body parts when it comes to weight limits.

A story, a rumour, a tale of Italian brothers named Judica-Cordiglia who listened in on early Russian space shots. A theory about a cosmonaut, pre-Gagarin, whose ship went up and up but never came down. You know, I'd never given it a second's thought before. Yuri Gagarin's space trip was a perfect success. It never occurred to me to wonder how they managed to get it right first time. It seems they didn't.

For the first time in a very long time, I feel a sense of companionship. Outside my ship is proof of a story that Earth regards as legend. The cosmonaut before Gagarin. The failed mission nobody spoke of. The man who just floated away. A myth, a story, a tale for dark nights and firesides and tinfoil-hats and geeks with computers who have too much time on their hands. Yet here he is grinning into my ship. Seems I caught up with him. On the same one-way trip, but still alive, I'm facing another who had little choice in the matter.

So it's not Tom after all, and I'm still sane. I can continue through the Oort cloud and see what's on the other side. What to do with this corpse though? I'd rather not have him peering in at me. Kindred spirit or no, he's hardly engaging company. I can cut him loose with the sampling arm and send him on his way.

Oh, wait. I have an idea, but first I have to confess to something. Are you listening, Space Agency geeks? The reason the cockpit camera broke, three weeks out, is that I broke it. I didn't want you watching me. I've made some adjustments to the system in front of me over the last four years. These transmissions, coded so only you guys can hear them? Well, I finally found out how to disable that coding system. This transmission is going out broadband, all frequencies, uncoded, just like all the others I've sent over the last three months. Anyone can hear me. By now, everyone knows your 'automated' probes are manned by partially-dissected convicts. I'm not another conspiracy theory you can deny. I'm real and I'm about to prove it. Suck on that, space boys.

You geeks must have worked out I'd broken the encoder. I've been thinking about that. You'll be spreading the word that it's all a hoax. You'll pretend it's some kid in his bedroom making up my transmissions and bouncing them off satellites. Oh, I know you haven't told the people of Earth how these ships work, and whose mangled bodies are stuck in them. I also know you can't stop me transmitting. Even if you fire a missile, I'm so far away it'll take years to reach me and I am a very small target in a big pile of rocks.

I've been wondering how to prove I'm real. I could maybe use the cutter to write on a rock sample, but the Space Agency gets them first anyway. The dead Russian here changes everything. This corpse, and this message, are linked. If the corpse comes home then the message is proven. His conspiracy theory and mine can both be proven.

This is going to embarrass Russia and cause all kinds of diplomatic incidents. Maybe even war. Yes, I might still be responsible for deaths on Earth from millions of miles away. So let's start this game.

I've caught him with the grabber part of the arm. If I can just move the cutter over his helmet, I can burn a mark there. Done. Now I have to trap his suit-line in one of the sample pods and cut him free from the ship. No problem.

It's a big thrill to press that fire button and watch him towed away. Hey, Earth. Your prodigal is coming home. I have no idea how long he'll be but he's on his way. Watch the skies. If you want to hush this up, space-geeks, if you want me to sound like just some Earthly fraud, you'd better get scrabbling for that evidence. Lots of countries have space programs now. Who will find him first?

You'll know him when you find him, and you'll know I sent him. I burned an '8' into his helmet. Okay, I didn't kill this one but I'm claiming him as number eight anyway. He's proof of that old story and he's proof I'm out here too.

It's going to be years before Russki gets home but he's my reason for staying alive now. I want to hear what happens when he gets there.

The anticipation will help keep me sane.

Tears

Justin Sanebridge

It was a Saturday night in the autumn of 1980, and outside the wind was busy piling huge mounds of dead leaves against the businesses that lined the street. As usual, we were hanging out at our favourite haunt, the Tromsø, a pub right in the heart of Antwerp's red light district. As befitted its location, it was hemmed in by whorehouses on all sides: row upon row of windowed prostitution, behind which sat scantily-clad girls advertising their wares. Although the whores made brief visits between clients, the pub's exclusively male regulars came for no other purpose than to quietly and assiduously drink. It was like a desert island for castaways who'd temporarily lost interest in their cocks.

The Tromsø was managed by Nelly, an Antwerp native with a butt that drooped like a pair of saddlebags and a set of massive, sagging tits. Her assets reminded me of a photograph of African tribal women I'd once seen in an old copy of National Geographic Magazine. She was cursed with long, ruler-straight brown hair, which hung limp and lifeless around her hips and did nothing to add to her allure. Her sole saving grace was her unusual height, which helped disguise her considerable bulk. In all other respects, she was about as glamorous as an unmade bed.

Knut, her Norwegian husband, had washed up on the shores of Antwerp a long time ago. He'd married Dominque and bought the Tromsø soon after, naming it after his home town. This was his sole contribution to the business so far as I could tell, because he delegated all the real work to his unlovely wife. I'd sometimes tease him about his life of leisure: "Knut, you command the sea," I'd say. The joke – a reference to the ancient legend of King Knut – was lost on him, but he smiled nonetheless, assuming it to be a compliment.

Unlike his namesake, Knut made no effort to control the tidal wave of alcohol that ruled his life. His day began at sunset, when he rolled out of bed and attacked his daily quota: thirty or forty whiskies spread over the course of the night, plus about twenty beers to offset the thirst. Whenever the conversation turned to food, Knut always looked as if the customers were talking about something dirty. I guessed that he never ate any more. For the most part, he seemed content to sit in silence and stare at something we couldn't see. He probably missed the fjords or his former life in the Norwegian fishing fleet, but he was too far gone to ever leave his pub.

Anyway, as I was saying, it was a Saturday night and I was sitting with Serge as we nursed our drinks and awaited the arrival of Fat Bert, who was even later than usual. We'd despatched Lazaros to the phone box outside to find out where the hell he'd got to, and Serge's patience was almost exhausted by the time a sudden rush of wind and dead leaves signalled his return.

"Fat Bert can't come, he has a blockage," declared Lazaros, a Greek who had learned his Flemish* in the underworld of Antwerp.

Flemish is the form of Dutch spoken in Belgium. Some Flemish words are not understood by the Dutch, or have a different meaning in Dutch.

"A blockage? What's wrong with him? He can't shit?" asked Serge. He was a Walloon* who had learned Dutch in Amsterdam.

Walloons are French-speaking Belgians.

"No, Serge," I replied with a wry smile. "Blockage is the Flemish word for lower back pain. It sounds like Fat Bert has a nerve blockage, a trapped nerve. I imagine he can shit just fine."

Serge was an impressively well-built guy whose massive frame disguised a terminal case of cancer of the soul. Despite his size and physique, I suspected that he could be felled with a single blow, like a Dutch Elm tree ravaged by beetles and fungus. He went to great lengths to disguise his condition with trendy three piece suits and talk of a life free from the usual money worries, but his careworn face told a different story. One glance at his deeply furrowed brow told me that he was tired of life, even if he didn't want to admit it.

"Godverdomme*," spat Serge. His French 'R' rolled like the pebbles on the banks of the River Meuse when a barge passes by. "If Fat Bert doesn't come, I can't get any coke."

Meaning 'Goddamn it' in Dutch.

I should explain that Serge had moved to the city during the summer and was relatively new to Antwerp. His source of income was an inheritance bequeathed to him by a dead aunt, plus private disability insurance payments awarded him after an unspecified 'accident' at work. He bore no obvious signs of physical impairment, so I concluded that his 'disability' was psychological in nature, if not entirely fictitious. His wife had divorced him shortly before his aunt's death, and if you believed Serge then this was the best thing that had ever happened to him. He now had his aunt's money all to himself, and seemed intent on snorting most of it up his nose.

"Bert needs to be very, very careful," I said. "The police are looking for a reason to arrest him again. They're pissed off that he was acquitted of drug dealing. It wasn't easy, but I managed to get him off the hook on a procedural error."

"Long live our lawyer!" yelled Lazaros and smacked the top of the bar to get Nelly's attention. "Nelly, give Johan here another whisky, a real one, a Johnny!"

Nelly poured a whisky for me, then turned to her husband and said something in Norwegian. Knut replied with what sounded like a curse and descended from his bar stool with difficulty. He disappeared behind the door next to the bar and returned a moment later with something in his hand.

"From Fat Bert," he said as he slipped the package across the bar to Serge. "You pay now."

Serge paid up and retired to the toilet, from where he emerged a few minutes later looking very pleased with himself and the whole world. He immediately bought a fresh round of drinks for us all.

"It's thanks to you that Bert isn't in prison right now," he said as he slapped my back.

"Long live our lawyer!" yelled Lazaros again as he saluted me with his glass of whisky, showering most of it over the bar.

Lazaros resembled a field mouse – skittish, speedy, and never at rest – but had the moral principles of a gutter rat. He was a long time resident of Antwerp and a frequent participant in the illicit trade that was conducted down in the docks area of the port.

Fuelled by a heady mixture of whisky, beer, and cocaine, Serge suddenly broke into an impromptu recital of a poem by Verlaine, waving his arms about for dramatic effect. His poem of choice was admirably suited to the atmosphere of an autumnal evening in the Tromsø. "Les sanglots longs de l'automne," he began, slurring the words slightly.

Nobody paid any attention to him. Knut was propping up the bar in a drunken stupor.

Lazaros emerged from the toilet a matter of seconds later. Serge must have been sloppy with his coke, because Lazaros looked very happy and his nose was speckled with a white residue. With his gutter rat mentality, he'd probably snorted it straight from the toilet lid.

"Poupehan," said Serge out of the blue. He pronounced the word reverently, the way a Muslim says 'Allah'. "Poupehan, that's a small village in the Belgian Ardennes region. I was born there and my auntie Amélie too. It's the most beautiful village in the world. Fresh air, beautiful forests and meadows, the banks of the Semois river, tasty trout, it's wonderful over there. I had a happy childhood there with my auntie Amélie. I was an orphan, you see..."

His voice faltered and a tear rolled down his cheek. "What am I doing here in this stinking pub? I should go back to Poupehan, in the fresh open air, because fresh air is the most beautiful thing on earth."

Serge didn't get a chance to continue his lyrical reflections on Poupehan, because Lazaros interrupted him with a speech in favour of the Greek islands. Specifically, the island of Skopelos where he came from. Of course, Skopelos was the most beautiful island on earth and the air there was even fresher than it was in Poupehan. Lazaros' soliloquy aroused Knut, who raised his head and yelled in a kind of Dutch: "The fjords, most beautiful, much better."

Serge wiped the tears from his eyes, but his sadness had changed the atmosphere in the pub. Is sadness contagious when several men in a pub are in the grip of alcohol? I was perplexed when Lazaros, the hardened criminal, ordered another whisky with tears in his eyes.

"Something wrong with you?" I asked.

"It's my son," he said. The tears were flowing now. He looked miserable. "Yesterday he visited me. I'm divorced. He lives with my ex-wife, but once a week he comes to my house. He's six years old, a beautiful child. I sometimes wonder how an ugly man like me managed to produce such a beautiful boy. I love him more than anything else in the world."

He gulped down the whisky and ordered another one.

"I had a visitor, I was in another room talking business with him and when the man left, I went into the kitchen. My boy was sitting at the table. He had found my great-grandmother's jewellery box. It's been in our family for ages. He was scratching it with a knife. I got so angry that I slapped his cheek. And then I looked at the box. He had scratched *I love you Dad* on the lid of the box."

I paid my bill and left the pub. I had seen enough tears that night.

The Mother of God

Justin Sanebridge

God's mother called him to one side.
"What's that thing you're playing with, son?"
"One of my balls, mom. I call this ball Earth."
"Ah! A blue ball. Beautiful. Did you experiment with it?"
"A little bit, Mom. I threw a meteor at it, and life began over there."
"Life is not a game, son. Do you have everything under control?"
"Yes, yes, Mom."
"But can you keep the atmosphere stable?"
"Yes, Mom, of course. And I created living things. I experimented with oxygen, carbon, hydrogen, nitrogen, calcium, and phosphorus. At first they were very primitive beings. I had done something wrong. Those hominids died out. I even had a race of dwarfs, the hominids of the Indonesian island of Flores, but these morons became extinct, not my fault, they were too stupid."
"But right now, what beings are there now? Do they have consciousness?"
"Yes, Mom, and they are able to communicate with each other."
"How are they doing?"
"Not bad. I let them discover the feeling of love."
"And hormones?"
"Hmm ... they have those too."
"It won't work, son. If you give them testosterone, then they will become competitive. You know what happened to your big brother ..."
"Mom, I gave them the capacity to love one another."
"All this is not good, boy. Testosterone and love cause a lot of suffering. Listen, God, I asked your older brother to have a look at your planet. He told me that he was not a welcome guest there. According to these arrogant beings your brother doesn't exist at all!"
"Well, it's too confusing for them ... one world and so many gods, so they believed in the story that there is one God who sends someone to spell it all out. And what could I do? They began to see Me in everything and all. My sisters and brothers threw them into confusion, Mom. That's why I told one group that I sent a peasant with a long beard chained to a cross, and I said to another group that I sent a peasant who would be on his knees 5 times a day to pray."
"And is that better? Previously, everyone could have their own god, now they are fighting for the fact that only their god is real."
"But Mom, they are all under Me."

"They will destroy each other, son!"

"I gave them morality and the ability to think."

"But they are not stupid, son. They simply say that they are good and others are bad. They will continue to confuse each other. And then there are too many of them! They can't stop breeding. And they pump everything out of the soil in order to live as comfortably as possible. How will you solve that problem?"

"I don't know. If everything goes bad, I'll start somewhere else all over again. I still have a lot of balls."

"No, you are not starting anywhere else anymore. I won't give you any more balls to play with until you prove that you can get this one right."

Grudgingly God went back to his own place. "What if I moved the moon from its place with my fingertip and let it rotate very close to the earth?" he mused. "Or I could suck up the remaining oil through a straw. Or have more wind here and there?"

He lit a cigarette. Yes, he had given mankind this secret weapon. Every god knew that nicotine has a positive effect on brain activity, and that it slows down the manifestation of dementia.

God smokes seven packs of cigarettes a day.

He shrugged. Why bother again with the Earth or any other ball, blue or not blue? His Mom wanted her own fireworks. She had already hinted at making the Andromeda galaxy collide with the Milky Way.

Exchange Students

Cade F.O.N Apollyon

The days have lost their darkness. Like all of the seasons, Spring brings many of its own wonders. Some we like, some we don't. Some we notice, others...not so much. One of the wonders that Spring brings, at least in this part of the world, is the erasure of the embedded darkness in the days.

Many seem not to notice, but it is there. A hazy, embedded darkness in each and every Winter day, that keeps Sol's heat at bay so that Winter can do her work. Spring carries a key to releasing the grip of this Winter darkness. It usually happens over the span of a single day in late Winter, each year, and for those who are looking, it is very easy to see.

Today's date is the 22nd of March in the year 2019 CE, and by my own accounting, the darkness first started to be released a week or so ago. You can tell, because the shade of the sky is...different. Brighter at a certain time of the day than it was at or around the same time on the previous day. That embedded darkness will not return until Fall and Winter return. And, there will be several more increases in the light over the coming months. The brightness will reach its peaks in the months of July and August; the months in which here, the temperature will usually rise to oppressive levels. Day after day of a sweltering and inescapable heat. No embedded darkness to shield us.

Why am I writing about all of this darkness and light business, you might ask? Perhaps you are one who enjoys seeing wonders, and never knew that such a thing even existed. This phenomenon of a change in the sky's opacity and luminescence is not something that you can actually sit, wait and watch to happen. You just need to be mindful of it. If you watch the sky enough, you can train yourself to notice variations in the shades and colors of the skies.

Today, I am sitting out back, banging away on the laptop, and thinking about the sky I am currently seeing. Thinking about the skies I've seen. Comparing those skies in my mind to what I am actually seeing in real time. All the while, taking some notes.

It occurs to me to suggest that this darkness phenomenon is akin to seeing the sky go dark, then turn light again during a solar eclipse. Winter brings an embedded darkness to our days, ands Spring bri...woah!

Apologies for the interruption, but something just flew in front of the Sun; a plane I'm guessing. There was that rapid change in the Sun's brightness that lasted for but a fraction of a second. I suppose my heart is beating so fast and my mind racing because I am, ironically, writing on just this very topic.

Um...it just happened again. That blip of a rapid change in the Sun's brightness, and it happened in less than a minute after the previous. I know a bit about aviation, so I know enough to know that aircraft are spaced further apart than that. A bird perhaps? Circling vultures or some large bird of prey? They are quite common here. Busy airways in this area, so there are many possibilities at this point.

There is a high, thin layer of cloud today, but the Sun is still very bright, and plenty of blue sky. I only mention this because that blip just happened for a third time, then almost immediately a fourth. I see no planes, I hear no planes, I see no birds. Of course I am stopping my typing occasionally to observe, and I know that I am somewhat straying off topic, but this whatever it turns out to be is interesting to me. I have observed this phenomenon many times before, but *never* with this frequency. Not even close.

It is still happening, and I've now lost count of how many times it has happened. I cannot look directly at the sun, but I certainly cannot see anything on the perimeter of the Sun's disk that might be causing this. The frequency is too often. Something very odd happening here. Almost like someone waving their hand rapidly in front of the light bulb on a lamp. But in this case, I cannot actually see what is causing the Sun to be blotted temporarily.

My heart is beating out of my chest as I write this. The frequency and duration have both dramatically increased, and I suddenly feel I'm at some weird daytime Rave. I've experienced some weird shit in my life, but this is completely fucking new.

WHAT IN THE ACTUAL FUCK!!!
OMG!!!
I CANNOT BELIEVE WHAT I AM SEEING!!!
Gotta stop writing.
Be right back...I hope.

I just had...the weirdest fucking conversation...that I have ever had in my entire life.

Um...give me a second to get my bearings so that I can accurately relate the completely fucked up shit that just happened to me. My heart is pumping hard in my chest again, but it's only because I'm trying to figure out what in the fuck to do at this point. How to try and grasp the meaning of what happened and how to relate it. Perhaps even if I should. If so, to whom?

OK...I've already dismissed the urge to contact MUFON and file a report. Police? Not a fucking chance. The military? Yeah right. A friend? Fuck no...I have no friends, not for something like this. Local government? NASA? Ghostbusters? Who in the fuck do you call? What do you do?

This is something, that in all my years of watching Bigfoot, UFO and other weird documentaries, I have never considered before now. Now what? You wanted the experience, you got it, now what?

The fucker is now gone, but as you may have guessed, yes, I just saw a goddamn UFO. I've seen plenty of UFOs in my lifetime, but there are only a very few of my own personal sightings that I cannot explain. ***This*** fucker, just landed in my back yard, no bullshit. I seem to be able to explain this one just fine...or maybe not. Digress.

I'm sitting outside in one these fucked up sun-chaser outdoor recliners, typing all that bullshit above about the sky changing, then all that weird crap started happening. I stopped writing when I finally saw what was dancing all wiggly in front of the sun and causing that rapid "micro-shade" or whatever it might be called. Just when I thought I was going to have a seizure from all that flashing, this purple and green...ship...came into full view. It descended down from right above me, and plopped itself down in this tiny-assed backyard of mine.

Weird, because the fucker looked HUGE in the sky, but the closer it got to the ground, the smaller it got. No idea how it fitted in this tiny yard. Made no sense whatsoever, and I don't want to speculate about the shrinking and growing possibilities at this particular junction. None of this shit makes any sense. Least of all...that totally bizarre and completely fucked up exchange between...us. I have no idea what that was. But yes...us.

I am sitting here, hands shaking, trying to get my head wrapped around all this crap, what to tell and how. But holy SHIT...all I can think about is that conversation I just had. Yes, an "alien" got out of their spaceship, and they fucking talked to me.

You know what? Fuck this noise. I'm gonna play transcriptionist here, and try my best to make an accurate record of the conversation while it is still fresh in my mind.

My mind...my fucking mind.

Jesus H. Christ...where in the fuck is my fucking mind right now?

Alien: Where is your mating orifice!?
Me: ???

NOTE: I said nothing of course. But if ever in my life there was cartoon bubble containing question marks floating over my head, it was precisely at this exact moment in time.

Alien: Do you speak?

Me: Yes, I speak.

Alien: Then you likely also have the capacity to hear. *Where is your mating orifice!?*

Me: Um...I don't have a mating orifice...that I am aware of.

Alien: *All beings having mating orifices! Where is yours!?*

Me: At work?

Alien: At work. Ah, so it is already currently active in a utilization sequence?

Me: No, not that I'm aware of. It better not be anyway.

Alien: Is your culture one that speaks only in riddles?

Me: Not...always, no.

Alien: *Then explain how your mating orifice can be in an active utilization sequence when you do not know where it is located!*

Me: I was thinking of my girlfriend.

Alien: You think of others while your mating orifice is in use?

Me: No, I don't think of...wait. *I,* do not have a mating orifice. I think my girlfriend does though.

NOTE: It was at this point in which I realized, that my childish desire to please had suddenly taken a turn. Am I, completely by accident, about to inadvertently pimp out my girlfriend to an alien?

Alien: I have traveled the length and breadth of the great void and seen it's many wonders, and I tell *you,* that I have never encountered a being that does not have a mating orifice! *Where is yours!?*

Me: And I'm telling *you,* that I'm pretty sure to an accuracy of almost 100%, that *I* do not have a mating orifice. I was simply thinking that I may know where one is.

Alien: Where is it? And why it is there and not here!?

Me: My girlfriend. Your unusual request initially made me think of my girlfriend. She's at work.

Alien: This girlfriend has a mating orifice?

Me: Maybe. Before I came to my senses, it had occurred to me to perhaps call her.

Alien: Her?

Me: Yes, her. I'd thought to call her.

Alien: Call?

Me: My girlfriend.

Alien: Girlfriend?

Me: On the phone.

Alien: Phone?

Me: At her job.

Alien: Job?

Me: My girlfriend, she's at work, I'd have to call her, on the phone, at her job, to verify the mating orifice...status.

Alien: *WHY ARE THERE SO MANY INTERMEDIARIES BETWEEN YOU AND YOUR MATING ORIFICE!!!*

Me: Now that I think of it, that's a *damn* good question.

Alien: If this query is in fact good, *why have you not obtained an answer to it!?*

Me: That's an even better question.

Alien: Where do you currently stand in your quest to obtain these answers!?

Me: Your questions keep getting better and better. Keep this line of questioning up, and you could probably rule this planet in the span of a week if you wanted.

Alien: I have no desire to rule your planet! *I seek a mating orifice!!*

Me: If anything, that's one point we both seem to be clear on.

Alien: You are trying to deceive me with your riddles in order to hide your mating orifice?! *Immediately remove your veils for verification!!*

Me: !!!

NOTE: *Now, I admit that I'd been sitting outside in the sun, nothing on but a t-shirt and jogging shorts, not wearing any underwear, and it occurred to me that it would be real fucking simple to answer a whole lot of questions and possibly solve a lot mysteries if I were to simply pull my shorts down posthaste and forthwith. But there was no fucking way that I was going to drop-trou just because some alien shows up, looking to get laid, all whilst experiencing some gender confusion in this particular quadrant of the galaxy, then demands that I present my junk for their inspection. And so, at the speed of light I might add, that's exactly what I did.*

Alien: Ah, I see. Not very well, but I do see. You are Pleggbah. Equipped with doingy doinger...like Muuk!

Me: If there is a God, I pray to them now, that *you* are Muuk?

Alien: I am Muuk...The Pleaser.

Me: Pleased...er sorry, to meet you...Muuk...The Pleaser. I'm not sorry to meet you, was just going to say "pleased to meet you" and kinda got tripped up.

Alien: A simple "greetings" would have sufficed in this exchange.

Me: Noted protocol for future reference. My name is Phillip. You may call me Phil if you like.

Alien: Phillip called Phil, you are in fact *not* equipped with doingy doinger like Muuk.

Me: I'm continuing to make mental notes of the pertinent details whilst dealing with the flood of data. Some contextual clues are beginning to form some pictures for me though.

Alien: While making notes, do not again use subversion to covertly ask Muuk about the existence of God.

Me: Noted...no religion, and I'm guessing no politics either?

Alien: *Guess all you care to!* Met God once or twice. Unpleasant type. No sense of humor.

Me: That revelation would not surprise me in the least were it not for the bullshit that is currently going down right here and now.

Alien: Going down like veils that previously concealed Phillip Phil's doingy doinger?

Me: Among other things.

Alien: *Save your existential riddles for your institutions of higher learning!*

Me: Will do. And, for the sake of clarity, a "doingy doinger", I'm guessing, is in fact this thing right here between my legs that I'm about to go to jail for unleashing in public even though I'm in my own back yard?

Alien: Correct. Muuk has many doingy doingers.

Me: Ironically, I sense a monologue in my very near future. With no pun intended there.

Alien: Many mating orifices exist in the void. Many dimensions to cover, many needs, much work, and there is only one Muuk. One Muuk has many doingy doingers for many occasions.

Me: You have many of *these* things? And before you respond, I'm going to take what you tell me as gospel truth at your word. I don't require visual confirmation of *any* kind whatsoever, even though I admit that a video camera would come in *really* fucking handy at this precise moment for all kinds of reasons.

Alien: Muuk, known as The Pleaser, evolved many a doingy doinger over many cycles of time to please many a mating orifice through the ages.

Me: I could see where that might come in handy for the right... Pleggbah? I think it was?

Alien: Being with doingy doinger is Pleggbah. Muuk is Pleggbah. Phil...is...*slightly* above the curve according to initial rough estimates.

Me: I'm going to sleep the sleep of angels tonight in that knowledge.

Alien: Muuk has utilized my ship's surveillance units during conversational exchange to take the dimensions of your doingy doinger. Will craft duplicate. May come in handy for Muuk.

Me: My dimensions sometimes come in handy for me.

Alien: Muuk may encounter being that desires displeasure or dissatisfaction.

Me: Thanks for that exclamation point on the matter.

Alien: My pleasure. *Hararar rarah!* That was humor since pleasure will be Muuk's.

Me: You laugh at your own jokes. I have that problem too.

Alien: Laugh at own jokes is only problem Muuk have. Phil have Muuk at numerical disadvantage in the category of problems to have.

Me: That sleep of angels coming tonight will be haunted by nightmares of demons shitting on every second of it.

Alien: Displeasure is need like any other.

Me: I'll spend the rest of my days knowing an exact replica dick of mine is causing displeasure and dissatisfaction all over the Universe.

Alien: Everywhere but here.

Me: What?!

Alien: Everywhere but here...Phil.

Me: Uh...I...

Alien: Utilization. Proper utilization of available supplies or components. Old universal parable... *"It is not the dimensions of the craft, but the vectors of the matter."*

Me: We sorta have that same saying here... *"It's not the size of the ship, but the motion of the ocean"*.

Alien: You say tomato, I say vincherapine.

Me: I guess I can relate to that...somewhat...eventually perhaps. Maybe after some heavy cycles of Thorazine and Quaalude therapy.

Alien: You will recover without medication cycles. Take your time.

Me: Another note to make in what is now likely to be my psychiatric journal.

Alien: I must go, and now.

Me: So soon?

Alien: No mating orifices to be found here.

Me: Well, there actually *are* some to be found here. You just need take your time. Maybe heed some of your own advice?

Alien: Noted. Farewell Phillip called Phil.

Me: See you around Muuk.

Alien: It is assured you will see me again.

Me: Great. I mean, yeah. Great.

Alien: Muuk serious. Will return.

Me: Seriously?

Alien: Yes. Someday, Muuk The Pleaser will return to Phillip. But not *for* Philip. As in...

Me: I think I get the gist Muuk.

Alien: Going now. Be back later.

Me: In that case, I'll see you when I see you. Travel well Muuk...be safe.

Alien: Will try. Earth orbit treacherous. Much junk. Many debris.

Approach and departure risky.

Me: We're actually working on that, believe it or not.

Alien: Stay on it. Outlook currently grim. Now, Muuk go get lost in void. Find orifices to please.

Me: Later Muuk. Good luck with the ladies.

Alien: And Phil, retract your garment to it's original configuration and/or placement.

Me: Thanks.

And so, that's it. I just had an honest to God, UFO + extra-terrestrial close encounter of the *you-gotta-be-shitting-me* kind. In my own yard. In the broad daylight.

I was left standing there in my backyard, mouth agape, shorts down. Wondering what chance there was that a video of this event was going to somehow materialize and wind up on the Internet, and if so, what I would think about that. I just had the most bizarre exchange of my life in a "what the fuck" moment of epic proportions, involving an alien being of some kind who I guess was looking to get laid.

I pulled my shorts up, watched this weird looking spacecraft lift-off into space from my backyard, and started to contemplate the weird fucker named Muuk who was piloting it. A space cowboy with a bunch of penises. Then I sat down, grabbed the laptop, and I've been at it ever since.

Thinking about it now, my penis has multiple dimensions...sorta. Something like multiple penises, except in a single package. It get's bigger, it gets smaller, lots of dimensions between here and there. Interesting. Digress.

I do wonder if he and his fabled many doingy doingers will actually be back. Not that I care about the bouncy bits. Hell, they may not even exist. I didn't see a doingy doinger, let alone many. Maybe he was some interstellar perv pulling some intergalactic prank for some channel on the Milky Way's version of YouTube? Fuck. I feel like a complete dunce all of sudden.

At least I didn't get the "industry standard" type probing.

Just gave an alien the full Monty in the Spring sunshine.

Full frontal nudity.

Or thereabouts, in my case.

She's In The Shower

Cade F.O.N Apollyon

Before I go, I thought I might pass along a few thoughts that I've had about timelines and those who travel them. My name is Arton Arin. I am a 43 tri-season old resident of Bollinger in the Southern Midlands of Eggland, and I've been told that I am preparing to pass of a diseize called Cancera Molingua.

Before you become too distressed at my predicament, know that I actually feel quite well as of this writing, and I would prefer that you hear the tale I have to tell before making too many judgments about how you should feel about me and my current Medicull outlook. I simply thought it best to relay to you a bit about who I am, when and where I come from, and maybe a bit about why I am writing this story.

To be completely forthright, I am bored. My diseize is very rare, but highly contagious. Therefore, I spend most of my days in total isolation, pacing the length and breadth of my isolated hopspittle tangle, thinking about days gone by. If there is a bright side, it is that after the first two weeks of infection, which I am told is usually spent in a comatoe, the remainder of whatever time is left is spent mostly symptom-free. Or so I am told. However, I am also told that I will once again, sometime in the near future, slip into a comatoe from which I will not wake. Typical.

One might think that someone in my current state may perhaps spend most of their time lamenting a future that will never come. Sorrows, woes, and oh no's. All those glorious dreams of future endeavors, forever lost because of some new form of Cancera that has chosen to spring up in myself and a few other unfortunates. All of us scattered here and there, in and around a world that I do not know very well at all. But I find myself thinking about such things only when contemplating the thoughts of others and how they might view me. And what I mean to say there, with impunity to you who are reading this, is that I do not think about the future nor why I shall not be in it, unless I think about those who are actually there. Someone such as you.

You are there already...reading this...written by someone who *might* have been there, but is, alas, not. Cancera Molingua decided we should be apart. Or perhaps, decided it better that we meet in a different fashion. Were I not preparing to pass, I would not be writing this. Were I not already passed, you would not be reading it. It is a pleasure to make your acquaintance, whoever you are. But let us get back to my boredom and why I've decided to explore a bit further the topic of those who travel timelines differently than others.

As stated previously, I am quite bored. My waking hours are spent in the past. Spent recalling tales told to me in my youth by parents and grandparents, relatives and friends; a cross section of everything from absolute truth, to complete and total flabber. Some of the more strange and interesting tales were those told to me by my grandfather. My grandfather confided in me later that these tales were actually told to him by his grandfather, although my grandfather sometimes painted himself in the main role to make the storytelling more relatable. "*After all*," he explained, "*these are strange tales of a time where both morta and godda alike intermingled with the firmament of the cosmos!*" Grandfather liked to recall in a mighty voice. They were sometimes indeed difficult tales to understand. Difficult tales to follow.

Of course, in my grandfather's grandfather's time, the names were different as the language was different. These were the times before "The Great Buyout" when the last of the free lands were deeded. Before "The Final Four Closure" when all ownership tytulle changed hands, which intern caused "The Sudden Shift" of morta peepwholes moving to and from all corvers of the planets. Before "The Age Of The Tri-Season" where the cold and hot seasons came with some regularity, and our primary planet did not linger for unspecified times in rethrograde nor anterograde orbits. Before "The Great Shaming Of All Nations" when all language was changed, and all memory of what came before was changed forever.

I am only telling you this, because I just realized that some of my words may not mean the same to you as they do to me, as I have no idea who you are, nor when and where you will be reading this. Pity that I have no idea which words you may understand, and which words you may not. I suppose it just an unfortunate side-defect of time's progression, and I suppose I'll just have to do the best that I can.

My grandfather told tales of times and places before The Shifts. Of course, the peepwhole then too were different, but they are gone, whereas I am told that many of these places that he spoke of still exist in some forms in fashion. Old places with new names and new destinies in new times. Many places that I should have loved to see had I reached the required traveling age of 45 tri-seasons. Alas, I am told that I shall not.

I suppose in looking back now, the interesting thing to me is that the tales my grandfather told me seem now to have been an up-building. A gathering of wanders and their wonders. Strange events I once thought fiction, leading from a time of knowing, to a time of non-knowing. Only through my illness have I had the time to reflect on these tales and what they could potentially mean. By that, I mean that I can avoid reflecting on a future that never is, mine, by reflecting instead on a future that perhaps never was. Perhaps because of these events, a future without me in it, was somehow avoided? Perhaps I am here only because of The Shifts?

I have begun to believe that perhaps there is truth in these stories my grandfather told me. Perhaps there is a certain deliberate vibration of sorts through time, and *only* through time and *only* with our attention can we begin to understand the wisdom in this. Perhaps this vibration crafts the never *was*, the is *not*, and the *never will be*, into something...more tolerable? More palatable? A deliberate and direct intervention on the part of some unseen will who guides us to where we actually need be, as opposed to where we want or think we need be?

I apologize to you if I am straying off point. And I realize that I have not yet told to you any of my grandfather's tales. But as I write this, I cannot help but feel some degree of sorrow for a certain place from one of grandfather's stories I shall never see. A place that I have dreamed of seeing since I first heard the story of "The Lady In The Shower Ring", and it all took place in a land of dry, in a small town ship that no longer exists, called Text Sass.

We in my time are allowed to know anything, but we are not allowed to know it until a certain age is attained. There is no reason given for this as no one is said to know how this process came to be nor why. But the general consenseus is that it is to maintain a balance of want and need within society in times of limited resources. The less we know, the less we want, and the less we want, the more that our needs will be both true and inline with their actual necessity. This reasoning makes sense to me as it does most others that I have spoken with on the subject. But until I became sick and eventually became to be housed at the hopspittle with my own private tangle, I had no real knowledge of what "a shower ring" really was, nor that they actually existed.

L'water is plentiful in my time. As far as I am aware, even those who live in lands of dry never attain a thirst that cannot be squenched. We are allowed to totally immerse ourselves in L'water for cleaning twice every season within the tri-season, and both M'water and N'waters can be used for cleaning and swashing. You cannot consume these waters because of a tiny unseen organism called Blass Ticks that are too numerous for our internals, but these waters are more than adequate for daily cleanings. The Blass Ticks are even said to be good for swashing and cleansing the hepadermis. However, in my grandfather's stories that his grandfather told him, he spoke of times before The Shifts when morta peepwholes had unlimited access to L'waters, and would sprinkle their bodies with it daily in an area of their residences called The Shower Ring.

My tangle here at the hopspittle has a shower ring. It is a tangle like where I now spend my days but much smaller; two long sides, two shorter sides. A small tangle, within a larger tangle, that is specifically for swashing and cleansing. Due to its shape, I admit I am confused as to why it is called "a shower ring". Perhaps someday I will ask one of the Fizzicans who checks on me each weakly.

I can swash and cleanse as much as I like, but you do not totally immerse in the shower ring. In fact, you do not immerse at all. A'waters, which are a yellowish, orange/brown Medicull water with something called "munkee blod" in it, sprays from a pipe on the wall, and all I need do is stand in the shower ring to swash. The water droplets that fall from the pipe in the shower ring remind me of the stories of "The Time Of Many Reigns". Before The Shifts, reigns fell from the skies without intervention from peepwholes. No one knows why, but reigns of L'water fell without prompting, at many and all times during the four seasons that were said to have existed prior to the times of the tri-season. To preserve the purity of processes, we are disallowed from standing in the reigns when those who reign over all pour their L'water freely from the skies. But this shower ring is what I imagine that must be like.

So many things seem to have conspired to land me in my own tangle with my own shower ring. And I am told that I will know that the time is close when I feel my toes start to become numb. What a strange concept to ponder...the feeling, of numbness. I fear I've gone too long on myself already, so pondering here the concept of what it is to feel nothing or how nothing feels, I shall save for perhaps another time.

I shall now tale you the tell I was told by my grandfather. The story of The Lady In The Shower Ring. The story of the lady with tool eggs, and four harms. The story, of She Vah and my grandfather's grandfather in the shower ring.

My grandfather was not a holy man, neither was he good. But nor was he unholy, neither was he evil.

There was no good...there was no bad...only the conflict of the two was in him.

Empty, some might say. As empty as a nothing which had no end.

Yet all and any was at his beckoning and at his whim.

For the two mighty Ones held sway over him...The One, and The Other One.

The Other One was to The One, as The One was to The Other One.

Two Ones, which is, and are, the same One, from different times, who *sought out my grandfather, in the same time, **at** the same time.*

The time before The Times Of The Shifts.

Both of The Ones were sometimes hidden from him, and both sometimes seen, and brought with them their manys and alls to test him.

To both teach him and to remove his teachings...and learn my grandfather did.

To taunt him, confuse him, cause fear in him...and fear and become confused my grandfather did.

To break him...and break my grandfather they did...many times.

The Ones and their goddas versus the lone morta.

How and why you may wonder? Why did the goddas show up? Why did they show up in Text Sass? Why did they choose my grandfather? What could he as a morta possibly have to offer the goddas, and what purpose could he possibly serve?

My grandfather said he never knew why they chose him, except to say "well that fuckin' figures."

Breaking after breaking my grandfather withstood.

Each and every time, the Ones wagered whether this be his last...but my grandfather found his feet again each time. More resilient and more determined after every breaking. Determined to know...why him...why now.

My grandfather had nothing. That is not to say he had "nothing", for he had many things in his life that he loved dear. But in the time of those times, and in the eyes of those in and of those times, he was considered to be a man who had nothing. Alone, in a tangle, without possession, old and broken, separated from those he loved, and he knew not why.

And it was at this time, that The Ones and their goddas arrived.

Arrived in all manners. Arrived in all forms imaginable, and in many forms unfathomable. Via any and every channel available them, they arrived. Sight, sound, smell, song, memory, knowing, and more. With all tools in the hands of the masters that created and crafted them, they arrived. Completely unannounced, they arrived.

My grandfather said of their arrival..."Pretty god damn unwelcome to be honest."

I asked of my grandfather why he did not ask of them "why?"

He smiled at me and said, "It honestly made perfect sense at the time, and I also know now that they arrived just in time. I just...didn't expect it, and certainly not in the way and ways that it happened. I had no idea what to do, nor how to do it. Cornered, I was."

Emptiness, *my grandfather told me,* **is a portal into the realm of the absurd. And to begin to understand the absurd and its absurdities, is to gain insight into the concept of love. Insight into the concept of love, provides us with a glimpse into the concept of hate. From there, the**

knowing of all knowing cascades in, out, and through, any and every emotion you can think of. Before long, you find yourself falling through nothing, into nothing, surrounded by everything, and somehow, you see all.

To fall forever is a completely absurd notion, my grandfather told me. *Why would anything, ever need to exist, or ever even be contemplated as potentially needing to exist, which would cause one to fall forever. The answer that I arrived at from time to time, after much deliberation, was love. Neither One wanted me, but neither One could bring themselves to destroy me. This is the best I could arrive at, after countless years and tears of contemplation...was hope. I fall forever in hope. They allow me to fall forever, in their hoping. Hoping that I may someday, when needed, be what it is I need be. They about their business, and me about mine. Time for all of us, to arrive at the time we all need be at, when we need be there, as we need be. Ready, for whatever we need be ready for.*

May as well busy myself having some fun doing something, while I fall forever doing nothing...
...heh, heh, heh.

I was his grandson, and you are mine, and let me assure you that humility was always on my grandfather's mind. How to remain hidden. How to be wise. To temper a blade of his own fury that cuts without cutting, and vanquish any foe while the blade remains sheathed. Yet to stand, not bowed nor cowered, yet still in all humility, before the goddas and speak as one might speak...to a friend.
Knowing these are not my friends, but neither are they my enemies.
In fact, they don't even know who I am.
My grandfather broke into singing a strange rhyming tune that was somehow neither poem nor song. Something that resembled a cadence that soldiers might sing in unison as they marched in order to keep their steps in time...

You know me not,
For I have no name.
I am no one,
No...one...you...know.

For I am null.

I am not.

I am knot,
I am naught,
I am not, knot, naught.

Speak as a friend. Not to flatter, nor to deceive, but to be receptive and to receive. To give my all. For these are truly my friends....and my enemies. All these things my grandfather told me.

I asked of my grandfather why he did not ask of them "Why? Why not ask of them what, and how?"

He again smiled at me and said, "I figured if they wanted me to know, they would have told me."

Over many days called "years" in those times, they tested him.

He never knew when, nor where, for they tested him at their own whims according to plans of their own design.

The goddas cajoled, and my grandfather fell silent.

They prodded him in his dreams, and he was much troubled by them, but he carried on.

All manner of vile was suggested, and he scowled in disgust and wondered with contempt what possible purpose this knowledge could serve.

They poked and prodded at his pride, and he played along and came up with better insults for himself than they.

But then something happened that The Ones did not expect.

One of the younger goddas seems to have suggested a change in tactics. "Up the auntie" as they used to say in those times before The Shifts. Instead of attacking my grandfather with shame, or with hate, or with fear, or by promise of knowledge in hope of wisdom, they tried his own weapon against him...humor.

Many of the goddas, including The Ones, had sent many a vision to my grandfather. Some he understood, some not. But one thing he always told me that he always seemed to understand, was their humor. "They're some funny motherfuckers," he used to tell me.

One in particular, She Vah, was trickier and more likely to apply humor than most of the others. Someone that my grandfather said he felt he had a special kinship with, without really knowing why.

She Vah, was the godda who suggested using humor against my grandfather...especially in the shower ring.

Take his humor, that which he crafts so sweet...so sweet so as not to cut, and make it so he can do nothing but harm when he wields it. Replace the sweet with bitterness. Make that which should cause joy, cause instead hate, so that even the softest of his strokes, and the sweetest of his loving kisses, draws instead blood.

I only needed to take a piss, *my grandfather told me.* **An average day,**

all day, in the same spot, pondering the same mysteries over and over, and I suddenly needed a piss. Understand that I am not complaining about pondering the same mysteries over and over. Pondering one mystery may provide insight into another. Neither mystery may in fact be solved, but it just may be enough information to make some progress in the right direction...keep us alive and pondering for a little while longer. Provide one more breath.

Not all answers are finalities, and not all finalities are final, my grandfather said. *I just needed to piss, and I thought at the time that it would have been nice to have thirty seconds of peace and quiet to do so. That was not to be.*

You have to try and understand, as best you can, that "seeing" does not always equate with external stimuli of some kind from our immediate surroundings. Sight, we tend to equate with those things that can be quantified and verified with secondary input. Such as, you may be able to see a chair, and you can also lick that same chair to verify that something is indeed there, and "yep, it tastes like I guess a chair should taste." May I suggest at this time that touch may be a better secondary for many a practical reason.

There are many ways to interrupt many channels of energies flowing here and there. And since we ourselves are energy and energies, and we are in a system built of systems of energies, someone who knows what in the hell they are doing can manipulate each and every sensory input we have. They can do so from eons away in the future, they can do so from eons away in the past, and perhaps they can even do both at the same time when present circumstance dictates. And that is what I am all about...time. Hope provides time, and time provides hope. I hope, that I am not boring you, grandfather said to me, *with a smile a gentle nudging elbow to my ribs for emphasis.*

To "see" certain things at certain times, with no external sensory input of any kind, seems, unusual. Such as, rushing to the toilet because I'm about to piss my pants, only to make it to the toilet, and find that...I, am not alone. I see nothing, yet I sense...something.

I can only just hear my urine first sounding against the water in the toilet, as I suddenly become aware of a figure approaching me from behind. I do not flinch, I do not clinch. I continue what I am doing, and observe.

In my shower, a small figure...a woman. She has a golden outline, surrounded by complete black. Distant. Inside the distinct and sharp golden outline of her figure, again, complete black. A golden-framed woman, surrounded by total darkness that also permeates all of her being except the rigid golden outline of her frame. Hair that is somehow red, yet black as night with occasional flashes of an unusual white. Her golden outline, as she moves, shimmers occasionally with rainbow colors. These colors cycle between the base golden color, and every color imaginable.

She's far away. Edging closer. Small steps. Raising her knees, slowly up high, high above her waist, pausing for a moment, then slowly down again. With each step, and also between steps, her arms, four of them, two on each side, move with purpose. Synchronized both with, and opposed to, the movement of her steps. All manner of shapes she makes with her arms as she approaches. Her arms cross, then unfold, her hands flat, then folded, then together, then apart. She is surrounded by complete darkness. My bladder is half-empty.

She's tall. The more steps she takes forward from the blackness, the more her height increases. Stalking her prey, or so it would appear. Slowly, gracefully, thoughtfully, edging forward from the blackness that surrounds her, permeates her. Her skin flashes from black to a whiter and pink flesh tone, then back to black. She is no longer a she. Is she? Is she a...she? Is she...Shiva? Not the Shiva I've seen depicted here in this life. She is Shiva, isn't she? Who the hell is she? Which one is she?

"You know, I *can* see you," *I blurt out in my mind. Her advance does not cease, nor does she waiver in her pace.*

"I know you can see me," she replies. "I just wanted to see how far you would let me advance before finally saying something."

She speaks to me in a tone of someone walking the edge of a razor suspended over a pit of spikes. Focused on many things, while doing many things, all while her own well-being appears to be hanging in the balance.

"Is there a particular reason you maybe couldn't have waited for me to finish taking a leak?"

"Yes. In fact, there is a particular reason. You and I both know that this is not what actually happened."

I was caught. Caught trying to stray. Straying from the truth, while in the company of truth.

"We both know that much of this in fact, *did* happen," I said as I fumbled with the recounting of the experience.

"True," *she replied.* "I appreciate your vigor. Just maybe perhaps, stick to the more pertinent and explainable, and stay away from any further exploration of the non-relateable."

Wise she was, and wise she is.

And so, my grandfather said to me, *it is time that I tell you what actually happened on that day. What happened in my bathroom. My bathroom was actually no bathroom at all, nor was it mine. My bathroom contained no bath...only a shower. A shower for washing the body, a toilet for the body's eliminating functions, and a sink for small cleanings. The shower was simply a stall covered by a retractable plastic wall called a shower curtain. This curtain was suspended by a thing called a shower curtain rod, and the curtain was suspended from this rod by things called shower curtain rings.*

I did not shower much in those days as the waters at that time harmed my skin. As such, this retractable shower curtain which enclosed the shower stall was almost always left open. Rarely was this curtain closed, and spiders used to build their webs in the folds of the shower curtain to catch prey. When I would use the toilet to relieve my bladder, my back would be to the shower stall, which means there was a rather large empty area behind me. This empty area is where on many an occasion, those from the unseen realms would appear to me. An area which I could not see when standing in front of the toilet, and an area from whence I should NOT be able to see them, but for some reason...I could see them.

All that I've told you up to now is true, but what actually happened share now I, with you...

"You know, I *can* see you," I blurt out in my mind. Her advance does not cease, nor does she waiver in her pace.

"I know you can see me," *she replies.* "I'm practicing my Yoga in the shower whilst you pee."

I immediately started to laugh so hard at the absurdity of her assertion, that I started pissing all over the toilet and on the floor. She was most decidedly, NOT, doing Yoga. I collected myself somewhat, and was able to regain the proper control and direction of my urine flow.

"It looks more to me like you were trying to sneak up on me while I was taking a leak, and you got caught."

I had to fight back. I was standing here in the vulnerability of an act of a necessary bodily function, usually performed alone and in solitude, and now that embarrassment has been compounded by shame for urinating all over the outside of the toilet and on the floor.

"Tell me, Clay. What is winning?" *she asked as she continued her rhythmic and   exaggerated advance towards my back.*

"Winning?" *I questioned.* "Winning? Or victory?"

She immediately froze at hearing my question; two of her arms above her head with hands folded, two of her arms extended at her shoulders with the palms of her hands up, one leg bent and raised high up to her chest so that her foot was well off the floor, the other leg straight with her foot firmly planted. A contest! A contest to see if she can remain standing on one foot for the length of time it takes me to finish pissing. 'A pissing contest'...of sorts.

"You know," *I began,* "I've not cleaned that shower in some time. I've noticed you are barefoot. You could potentially get some kind of foot disease."

She smiled, but did not move nor waiver in any other way.

"Also," *I continued,* "I'm the one that showers in there, so a disease of *some* kind is almost certain."

She maintained her smile, her eyes glowed, but still she did not move nor waiver.

"Um," *I was desperate, for I was almost finished peeing,* "This may take a while. There's a dollar store right up the street if you want to toddle off there and get you a pair of cheap flip-flops that can be used as shower shoes. Will only set you back a buck."

She dropped her elevated foot in defeat, and bent over in laughter.

"WINNER!!!" *I thought to myself. Just in time too. The final drops of urine fell into the toilet, I gave the requisite squeeze and shake, then found the toilet paper roll so I could do an initial clean up of the urine from the toilet bowl and floor. I reached for the toilet paper roll. Between pulling off the first few sheets and looking at the floor in order to begin planning where to start cleaning first, I briefly acknowledged Shiva's presence in my mind. When she came again into focus, I saw one of the most incredible things that I have ever seen.*

Somehow, and to this day I have no idea how she did what she did, she was standing...on both feet...AND...one foot, all at the same time. And no, before you ask, she did not suddenly grow an extra leg. She simply, somehow, 'revealed' to me, that she was still standing on one foot, had never moved, and, was standing on two feet. There was no double-vision. Her form was as clear, crisp, and well defined as it has ever been...only two legs. And yet, somehow, she was managing to stand with both feet firmly planted, and stand on one foot with one leg raised. I saw no third nor fourth leg.

I immediately burst into an uproarious laughter as my mind was flooded with the possibilities and notions of how she was achieving this. Multiple-dimensions? Multiple-times? Multiple-positions? All somehow aggregated here and now to give the appearance that she was in one place at one time, when she was in fact in many? Whatever she was doing, and however she was doing it, this was no trick. There was nothing 'gimmicky' about it. All attempts on my part to solve this mystery almost immediately dissolved away as the reality of what I had just seen continued to sink in. I continued to laugh, bent down, and started to clean my misfired urine off of the floor.

"Winner," *she said softly in a quasi-sultry and sassy voice.*

"What!?" *I protested.* "I've already won!"

"Winner, winner...chicken dinner," *she said, hands on her hips. She wiggled them slightly for some added zesty emphasis.*

"You can't take my win from me can you? I've already won it."

"I can take your win from you, and I have done so. In doing so, you have answered my question, and I have answered yours."

"The difference between 'winning' and 'victory'?"

"Correct."

"Anything given, can be taken away."

"Correct."

"A nation may 'win' a war, yet still not be victorious."

"That is an excellent point for pondering."

"Wait a second here. You stated you won after I'd already won."

"Correct."

"*Then,* you implied you took my victory from me."

"Correct."

"That's two wins in a single contest. You aren't talking about winning nor victory at all are you?"

"Perhaps yes, and perhaps not."

I continued to wipe urine from the floor as thoughtfully and completely as I could, and it occurred to me that most lessons from 'else' usually comes both indirectly, and, it is heavily layered. One can many times choose to peel back as many layers as they care to. Such as, an old man on his hands and knees wiping his own piss off of the bathroom floor because the god Shiva made him laugh while he was pissing, and now they are discussing the finer points of winning, victory, and perhaps even defeat. A light bulb illuminated in my dim little mind.

"You are wondering how I would describe what I just saw to another."

"That thought has crossed my mind," *she replied thoughtfully.* "How *would* you describe or recount to another what you just witnessed?"

"I wouldn't even know how to begin to try."

"And what about relating the story of what transpired here?"

"Again, I wouldn't know where to begin, nor would I even have the slightest inkling as to who would even care to hear such a tale. It strains my own internal credibility, and I just walked through the shit-storm my own self."

She smiled a large smile. She could see my mind working. I was reassured by her smile, but I could tell that she knew that I was already struggling with realities and pride and prejudices and envy and shame: all these concepts and more wrestling with my own self doubt. These things continued their stormy struggle as I tried to imagine who in the entirety of existence would ever even potentially want to hear such an unimaginable and outlandish story. She thankfully interrupted my thoughts warring with themselves.

"Perhaps you could start where you are now, then work your way backwards. Do that, and moving forward should come quite easily if you stay with it."

And with that, she was gone.
I paused and thought for a moment.
Wise she was, and wise she is.

My grandfather, and your three times great grandfather was no soldier, Arton. He marched alone. Accompanied perhaps, of my own accounting anyway, by an army that no one but he could see. That, I tell you, was likely the reason for the odd little song that he sometimes sang to himself.

Death says to me...

Who are you?
I know you not.
I see no name,
No name I know.

I say to Death...

You know me not,
*For I **have** no name.*
I am no one,
No...one...you...know.

For I am null.

I am not.

I am knot,
I am naught,
I am not, knot, naught.

War was his passion; battle was his mind; combat was his love; but his heart, he prayed, beat a rhythm of peace seeking wisdom. As to what that made the entirety of his being? "I don't really know what that makes me. I don't know what that makes me on the whole. I mostly feel at peace." *This is what my grandfather told me.*

"And that's peace, not piss," he told me. "People will bastardize the damndest of things to their own end. I'm myself admit I am guilty of the same. Take care with your judgments grandson of mine."

I paid no heed to my grandfather's talk of judgments.
My mind was already well elsewhere.
Too much data, nary enough answers.
My mind burning like a flame, I asked of my grandfather, "But you told me that you were all about time! You said that hope was time, and time was hope! What is all this talk of war and battle and peace grandfather?!"

Into his eyes I looked, and saw that they blazed with a something inside of him that I had never before seen in anyone, nor have I seen in anyone since. Not blazed as the hottest flame might, nor burned like the coldest cold might. There was no light, nor was there dark, but I suddenly saw a vast and endless emptiness inside of him that sent a shiver down my spine and threatened to suck the air straight out of my lungs. My heart pounded within my own chest in protest of the unseen and unwelcome requests of me. Grandfather sensed my fear and placed his hand lovingly on my shoulder. The growing fear bursting to escape the very fiber of my being fled almost as suddenly as it had appeared. But not for long would that fear be held at bay.

"Young one," my grandfather started, "There is some serious shit headed your way, and **you**, are going to be right in the big middle of it."

My ears...I could not believe them. I could not believe these words only just ushered from my grandfather's lips. War? My way? Me? Why would war ever come to a child? Why me? What is this war that seeks me?

I looked away from my grandfather in consternation and to the ground to reassure my now galloping mind. I felt the fear and confusion welling and tumbling inside of me. Ebb and flow, it did...subsided, it did...grew, it did. A boisterous pulse advancing and retreating almost simultaneously. Tho looking downwards, I could still see my grandfather from the top of my eyes, and saw that he observed me as I thought. He sensed the war raging now inside me. War...inside me. War?

"You feel that?" grandfather interrupted unexpectedly. "**That**, is war.

The confusion you are feeling now, is all part of the war eternal."

My brow furrowed in disbelief. My hand I put to my belly as it began to burn. Searched the ground for answers I did as to what this could all mean. Find my feet, so swiftly knocked from under me, I must find my feet. My eyes scanned steady the browns and greens of the ground. Back and forth my head went, as I thought to myself that this cannot be so. There cannot be a war inside of my own self. No one have I to fight. I felt an anger rising in me, and I thought to tell my grandfather as much. But again grandfather was ahead of me by at least a step.

"And **that**, young man, which you are feeling now, is battle. Your confusion and uncertainty have been temporarily replaced by a measured response."

At this, something within me...snapped.

"STOP IT!" I blurted, with tears of rage welling up in my eyes. "STOP IT RIGHT NOW!!!"

The face of my grandfather, which only a moment ago was as stoic and hard as stone, softened. Looked beyond his face and through my own now blurry and teared eyes, sought my grandfather's eyes I did. I found them. The vast emptiness was gone from them, and they sparkled with the fires of countless stars.

"And that, my dear grandson, is combat."

Huge tears formed in his eyes as he continued, and his voice cracked occasionally from the strain.

"Confusion, turned anger, turned rage, all to preserve self, in combat. But beware of the fury that follows rage my dear grandson. For fury can cut in many ways, at many times, from many angles. Once fury is grasped, there is no letting go."

Tears were now streaming down his face. I sprang to my feet, dove towards my grandfather, and wrapped my arms tight around him. I hugged him like I had never hugged anyone before nor have hugged anyone since, and a stern, but gentle and comforting hug my grandfather returned.

Warmth.

An afterglow.

Light.

A path, only previously hidden, now lay before me. Know, I did not. Understood, I did. For now, I understood without knowing.

We find our own wars, Arton. We choose our own battles. And when we find these things, we fight our own fight in combat. But when we answer the call to join the wars of others, many, and perhaps all of these choices lose we.

*And for added measure my boy, tell you now, oh grandson of mine, my dear boy, Arton...that if you **ever** tell your grandmother that I hugged my grandfather better than I ever hugged her...well, let's just wait and see. We'll* *cross that bridge when and if we get there. He winked at me and smiled, my grandfather did.*

My great-great-grandfather is said to have died shortly before the times of The Shifts began. I can only assume that whatever death it was that sought him, and he for a time somehow avoided, eventually found him. Perhaps much in the same way it appears that some death currently seeks to find me. And so now, to be completely honest and open with you, there was indeed something specific that prompted me into writing. Something that inspired me to attempt to relay this and these tales that I have now shared with you.

Three days ago, I encountered a woman in my shower ring whilst I swashed. It was only for the briefest of moments, and due to my current Medicull predicament, I admit that I had to question whether or not it actually happened. But what stuck with me, was the fact that this woman had both red and black hair. Much like the hair of this She Vah that my grandfather told of via his grandfather's tale.

She said nothing to me, and she actually looked scared and confused. Perhaps, assuming she was actually here, she was just lost. Lost for the briefest of moments along some coiling or unwinding timeline, and unsure of where she was.

She wore no clothes, and she looked real enough. No extra arms, no darkness nor glowing, just a combination of very red and very black hair. Naked, and possibly wet, her arms were folded somewhat protectively to her chest, although I did not get the impression that this action was out of shame nor modesty. She looked back and forth a few times before she noticed me, and our eyes met only briefly before she quickly disappeared. There was no indication that she knew me, and I certainly did not know her. Except of course, for the distant connection to this She Vah story told to me by my grandfather.

By the by, both black and red colored hairs are contrary to social parity here in Eggland. I had always assumed that colored hair of these types were a myth. So rare for anyone to have hair at all in these times, let alone what appeared to be a full supply of multi-colored hair on both her top and bottom portions. She was, now that I think about it, quite beautiful. Or would have been had she not looked so scared and perhaps helpless.

The next day, I listed the event on my daily Medicull report even thought I am still quite unsure if the event actually happened or not. But I am told that I am indeed preparing to pass, so what harm could it possibly cause to report it?

And finally, a bit of good news.

This morning, I was informed that they would be starting me on a new medesign today. The doctors informed me that they thought today might be the day that my toes started to go numb, and they wanted to go ahead and get me started on this new medesign just to be safe. They tell me that there exists the potential that this new medesign could delay the onset of the final stage. It could, they say, perhaps even pathdose the diseize entirely. And the best part is, it can sometimes do all of this with just a single dose.

I am doing my best to contain and control my enthusiasms. To say calm, and carry on. But I cannot help but think a blessing of the goddas this must be. For if this is true, and this Cancera Molingua within me can indeed be pathdosed, I can be exonerated of my "payshunt" status, leave the hopspittal, and return to my own tangle. After time, I can apply to have my records expungented. Live to travel to Text Sass.

Odd this sudden development, as they've not previously mentioned this treatment. Perhaps it is something new. They did in fact mention a "new medesign", but I neglected to inquire if the medesign was in fact new, or just new to me.

I took the first dose only a few moments ago, but I don't think the medesign works. As I write this, I can suddenly feel my toes going numb. My arms are also feeling quite tired. Difficulty writing. My feet feel very heavy. Now having difficulty moving my legs.

I guess they didn't catch it in time.

Typical.

GLOSSARY OF TERMS

A'waters - *a socially acceptable, non-potable, non-drinkable X'water, made of various herbs and spices plus a generous portion of munkee blod; designated for Medicull use only, only under Fizzican super-vision, and only for swashing.*

Anterograde – *a forgetting.*

Billdinged – *the aggregate result of independent expenditures.*

Blass Ticks – *a group of non-motile, microscopic organisms of indeterminate origin made up primarily non-organic materials. Blass Ticks tend to be suspended in varied quantities in X'waters, and it is thought that this is why the organism has not evolved the ability to move under it's own power, lack of need. First described by Brau Flucher in 2076 CE/017 TS*

Bollinger – *a towned in the Southern Midlands of Eggland, which was founded on one of the axial focal points during The Battle Of The Bands that eventually led to The Great Shaming Of All Nations.*

Cancera – *a non-explainable combination of factors that results in either non-standard and/or less-than-standard cell growth(s).*

Cancera Molingua – *this particular/specific diseize is not known to actually exist. However there is some grainy reasoning within the term itself.*

Comatoe – *the low-power, quasi-hibernative state of a system or systems, marked by a generative lack of response to stimuli.*

Consenseus – *a gathering of similar bodies to form a contiguous and unique whole, without sacrificing a part's individual traits or characteristics. A simultaneous subtractive addition and additive subtraction with a zero-sum.*

Corver – *1. a convergence from the point or angle and perhaps time of disbursement. 2. a point in time that considers origins, destinations and forces from the eventual resultant point or points.*

Diseize – *a more or less standard deviation from a standard, usually capable of dictating and defining it's own path if not identified in a timely manner by Medicull, and treated with medesign.*

Eggland – *hey, it's Easter here in 2019 AD/CE. Lighten up. (Eggland is the exploitation of a convenient typographical error on the part of the author. It coulda been worse...it coulda been Endland.)*

Expungent – *a sharp increase or decrease in attractiveness, monitored and regulated by both the social and unsocial societal arms of the more-modern society.*

Fizzicans – *a socially trained and appointed representative of the Medicull arm of the more modern society.*

Flabber – *a particular something so beyond reason, logic, and even intuition, that it defies both rational thought and coherent description.*

Forms In Fashion – *the contextual mutative properties of an unchangeable tangible or intangible form.*

Godda – *a less-physical, independent entity, usually both less-biological in makeup and less-tangible.*

Hepadermis – *the outer layers that monitor and control the I/O flows independent of other such systems, and sometimes acts as it's own medesign.*

Hopspittle – *a physical structure or billdinged constructed of various components where Fizzicans gather/meet. Also houses Payshunts.*

I/O – *the measure of an energy's ability/inability to, 1. penetrate a membrane, 2. resist a membrane's advance, 3. not interact with a membrane at all.*

Intern – *a seriatim or sequential ordering of things/events.*

Internals – *the innermost parts of an outermost whole.*

L'water – *a socially acceptable, potable, drinkable water.*

Large Town Ship – *a usually very large region of land containing a number of small town ships. Usually accurately representative, as a whole, of the small town ships it encompasses.*

M'water – *a socially acceptable, sub-potable water that is not suitable for drinking, but is suitable for regular swashing.*

Medesign – *an agent crafted to dictate a specific path of travel under certain conditions.*

Medicull – *the organized societal infrastructure of Hopspittles and Fizzicans.*

Morta – *a more-physical, independent entity, usually both biological in makeup and more tangible.*

Munkee Blod - *a special liquid healing agent of dark carmine, that is brewed with Minimum of Mermaid Brothers, and also contains Expedience of The Messenger.*

N'water – *a socially acceptable, less than sub-potable water that is in no way suitable for drinking, and is suitable for occasional use in swashing.*

Pathdosed – *a resummation of right and proper, typically as a result of an intervention by the Medicull, and usually via the application of a medesign or medesigns; a reclamation.*

Payshunt – *a negative impactor on the Medicull.*

Peepwholes – *1. a biological, non-biological or less-biological system that is complete enough so as to be capable of sensing both specific and non-specific information and data, and also provide throughput to adequately and accurately transmit or otherwise relay this information in total to a 3rd party or some other intermediary; these biological and non-biological systems may be made up of organic matter, inorganic matter, or sometimes a combination of both. 2. a morta.*

Reign – *1. the power to create and freely distribute L'water from the nothingness and the nowhere. 2. a societal structure made manifest through* *destiny in order to monitor and regulate side-defects.*

Rethrograde – *a remembering.*

Side-defect – *an entropic vulnerability, usually expressed in the flanks or perimeter of an otherwise closed system; unforeseen manifestation of change, chaos or collapse in the outermost portions of a centralized body.*

Small Town Ship - *a large region of land containing a diversity of mostly small settlements of societal structures, usually with their own independent beliefs and ruling structures.*

Southern Midlands – *a region in the northern part of Eastern Eggland.*

Squench – *the exsanguination or draining of a desire to consume.*

Swash – *a vigorous utilisation of available resources, appropriately applied for a particular cleansing process.*

Tangle – *a living space approved for a citizen or citizens to occupy, which is constructed in the form and flow of nature's perfect geometric shape; two longer sides of equal length, and two shorter sides of unequal lengths, resulting in three right angles and one tribute angle.*

Text Sass – *a former small town ship in the former large town ship known as Nam.*

Towned – *a cyclically tytulled settlement where ownership is randomly transferred from citizen to citizen so as to equally distribute the burdens of ownership.*

Tri-season – *time period within the current age which has only three seasons, each of which are of indeterminate length(s).*

Tytulle – *an opening within the societal fabric that provides for the private ownership own one's own self, control of one's own destiny and movements, as well as the private ownership of one's own possessions.*

Up-building – *a construction effort resulting in an increase in mass, density, volume, inertia or interest.*

Weakly – *a meeting or touch based on a need or needs, usually under duress, objection or protest; an unpleasant task or undertaking; deed or encounter of the shortest possible duration and/or met with a minimum of effort.*

X'water – *a societally approved method of measuring water quality and safety. Defined primarily upon usage and sometimes need.*

Up The Auntie - *no aunts were harmed in the writing of this story <3*

Godjumenas – an introduction

Dirk J. J. Vleugels

What follows is the same story in English and then in Antwerpian, a language few are fluent in nowadays. One day, this book might become a sort of Rosetta stone for those wishing to recover that language.

Since I am one of the dying breed of people who can still speak pure Antwerpian, I decided to write a short story in that language and later translate it into English. Unfortunately, many funny expressions get lost in the translation and are not as funny anymore in English.

The pure Antwerpian language is now dying out. It is a very ancient language.

On a funny note, Joannes Goropius Becanus, a 16th century intellectual, wrote a book about the language.

Jan van Gorp was actually a doctor in Antwerp, but he increasingly concentrated on linguistics and archaeology. This much-travelled man was fluent in Greek, Latin and Hebrew, as well as several modern languages.

As was the humanist custom at the time, he Latinised his name to Joannes Goropius Becanus. In 1569 he wrote a controversial book entitled *Origines Antverpianae*.

He contended that Adam and Eve had spoken the Antwerpian language in the Garden of Eden.

Goropius believed that the most ancient language on Earth would be the simplest language, and that the simplest language would contain mostly short words like in the Antwerpian language.

Goropius is considered to have given linguistics a bad name. Goropius's work was met with a mixture of ridicule and admiration.

There is only one statue of the Antwerpian god Jumenas or Semini. It is much older than the oldest building in the city and it was probably made during the time of the Roman Emperor Augustus. In "Semini" you'll find the word 'semen'. Originally, the small statue had a heavy, erect phallus. Semini, stemming from the pre-Christian tradition and era, is indeed a pagan god of fertility. Until the 1920s, women came to beg and pray for fertility under the statue. So, this shows how deep pagan tradition was entwined in folk history. But, unfortunately, the Antwerp pagan god of fertility wasn't all that lucky: during the Catholic contra-reformation, under Spanish rule, it lost its private parts, hacked off by order of the Catholic Church.

The small statue is still embedded in the Steen Castle.

Het Steen is a medieval fortress in the old city centre of Antwerp, Belgium. It was built after the Viking incursions in the early Middle Ages as the first stone fortress of Antwerp, Het Steen is Antwerp's oldest building.

Godjumenas

Dirk J. J. Vleugels

"I've been living here for the better part of 36 years and the weather has never been as hot as today," Bob thought. "What's wrong today with the island of Bali? If it were that hot in Antwerp the sparrows would fall from the roof, but over here these little buggers are used to the weather. Anyway, I shouldn't complain. After all, I left Belgium because I wanted eternal sunshine."

Because of the heat he went into his swimming pool. He was too lazy now to swim, so he stood in the water with his elbows on the ledge of the swimming pool next to his pint of beer and his ashtray. He lit a cigarette.

His son Mark was sitting under a palm tree in the garden. He was reading a
book. Bob finished his pint and he called his son to bring him a fresh beer, but his son didn't hear him no matter how much he yelled.

"Strange," he thought. "Mark must have heard me. He's only ten meters away."

Suddenly he saw his Balinese maid coming into the garden. "Wayan, minta tolong! Saya minta satu bir lagi!" (Wayan please bring me another beer!) he yelled in Indonesian, but she also didn't hear him.

"Godjumenas," he cursed in the ancient Antwerpian language. "It's as if I've become invisible, or have they all suddenly gone deaf?"

He was listening to Radio Minerva, a radio station from Antwerp that he received via the streaming on his laptop. Suddenly he heard the official anthem of the city of Antwerp, sung by the "The Strangers", a Flemish band with an English name.

Antwerp, you are the city where I was born
The Groenplaats, the Meir, the Keyserlei
that's where my heart is.
Antwerp wherever I am
I can't be happy
I know, it's silly, but I confess
Only in Antwerp I feel at home and among friends.

"Godjumenas," he mused, "such a beautiful song for such a beautiful city. How long have I been away from Antwerp? Twenty years? Yes, that was the last time that I've been back to Antwerp."

He put his head under water for a couple of seconds and when he resurfaced he saw two small feet standing on the ledge of the swimming pool in front of his face. He looked up. A dwarf was smiling at him. How did the little guy get there? He looked like a garden gnome but he wasn't wearing a pointy hat. He had blue eyes, short blond hair, a Roman nose and big sticking out ears. He was wearing odd garments. Suddenly his coin dropped: the little guy was dressed in those Roman clothes he'd seen in that Ben Hur movie many years ago, a time when the churches and cinemas were still packed with people.

"You there, who are you?" Bob asked.

"'Thanks for waking me up!" the gnome said and smiled.

"What?" Bob said.

"Don't you know who I am?"

"No, but you speak Antwerpian fluently. I'm amazed! Not many people can do that nowadays. Who are you then?"

"I am the god Jumenas, also known as Semini," the apparition said. "I am the spirit of the city of Antwerp. I was born in the year 800. Only you can see me. Your son and your maid can't see or hear me. I've come here for you only."

"If you're a god, then I am the Emperor of China, mate!" Bob laughed. "I'm going to call my son. He'll kick you out."

"It's no use. He can't see me and even you are invisible to him." Semini said.

Semini was right. Now Bob felt uneasy.

"So you are the god Jumenas or Semini?" he asked nervously. "My granddad used to tell me stories about the legend of the god Semini, the spirit of Antwerp."

"Legend?" The gnome was angry now. He looked as if someone had bitten him in his ass. "I really exist. You can see and hear me, don't you?"

"Why have you come here then?"

"I just told you. You've woken me up. Lately I sleep a lot. I only wake up when someone calls me but that doesn't happen a lot nowadays because people don't know my name anymore. Who in this time and age still says godjumenas? And then, it isn't pleasant to be jerked awake only because someone yells godjumenas. It makes me shit a velvet monkey. How would you feel, Bob, when you're sleeping peacefully and suddenly some brute yells Bobdamnit in your ear? I'd happily wake up if people call my name to ask me for a favour. I'm a god after all. I always try to help people but I'm really pissed off if they only curse my name and don't believe in me!"

"Yes," Bob said. "It would get right up my cuff, too."

"'Here's something you don't know yet. If nobody believes in us anymore, we have to bog off. It's a law of nature."

"Who are you talking about?" Bob asked.

"The gods of course. You know, the Greek and Roman gods, the Egyptian deities, all the discarded and now unemployed gods of the past, even the Chinese and the South Americans. I'm worried, because if nobody believes in me anymore I'll be sent to the asylum for discarded gods and goddesses.

I once visited that place because I wanted to know what it looks like. It's a beautiful place, just like a five star hotel surrounded by forests and mountains and there's even a white sandy tropical beach with palm trees but it isn't Antwerp now, is it?

And then the horror of living with all these unemployed gods and goddesses! I'd rather be dead, but unfortunately I'm immortal.

Zeus and his extended family are a bunch of Greek loudmouths who stink of garlic. Zeus still has delusions of grandeur and he's a terrible bore. He's always talking about all the girls he has fucked. His ramblings make my balls turn into stone. I've made love to far more girls than that brute and all my girls were crazy about me, but I don't boast about it.

But I like the goddess Diana. She's a beautiful girl. She always has a smile on her face. And she's hot. Her tits are adorable and her birdie lives high above the ground because she has long wonderful legs.

But then those Scandinavian gods! It's as if Odin is always sitting on hemorrhoids. He can't accept that they dumped him in the asylum. He picks a fight with everyone. He's such a fruitcake and on top of it he's got a snout that looks like it's a good place to dump shit upon. And Thor is a crazy bastard, always ready to make noise with his hammer when he's drunk, and he's seldom sober. He really pisses me off.

And the Egyptian gods! Impossible to have a jolly good conversation with them. They're all as mad as a doorknob.

But I'm rambling on. It's made me thirsty. A pint of beer for you too? It's my treat."

By now Bob was getting used to miracles. He wasn't surprised when out of nowhere two pints of beer appeared. They eagerly drank the Antwerpian beer.

Bob had never felt so good in his life. "I'm grazing on a good meadow," he thought, "and this Semini is a great guy."

Suddenly he heard the Antwerpian hymn again.

"Semini my friend," he sighed, "in all these years in Bali I've never felt so homesick as today. And then I said godjumenas and you appeared out of nowhere."

"Yes, Bob that's why I've come," Semini said. "I wouldn't have come here when you cursed but I knew it wasn't a curse when you said my name for the second time. From deep in your soul you've called me. I've come to take you away from here. We're going to the Antwerp of your youth where everybody is still speaking Antwerpian."

In the palliative ward of the Erasmus hospital in Antwerp, Mark sat on a chair next to his father's bed. He had been dozing, but he woke up with a jerk when the night nurse came in.

"Your father is moaning. He's in pain again. I'll give him another dose of morphine."

She increased the dose and sat down a moment next to Mark. "Sometimes your father speaks in a foreign language," she whispered. "There! Do you hear that? He's doing it again!"

"Oh!" Mark said. "He's speaking Indonesian. He thinks that he's at home on the island of Bali. He's calling his maid to bring him another beer. He says that he's standing in the swimming pool."

"Oh, you understand Indonesian?" the nurse asked.

"Of course," Mark said. "It's where we live. Dad came to Bali when he was about 50 years old. He met an Indonesian young woman whom he found so beautiful that he immediately married her. She was my mother. She died five years ago. She was killed when a truck crashed into her car."

Mark was silent for a while.

"And now Dad is dying. We celebrated his 86th birthday last month."

"Are you going to take me back to the good old times?" Bob asked. "To the Antwerp where I had so much fun? Oh! Those where the days! I often went on pub crawls in the Stadswaag, and I had coffee in the Groenplaats or in the Keyserlei or I took the ferry to the left bank of the Scheldt, to St Anneke and, oh, I had so much fun in those days."

"But me too, mate," Semini said. "Sometimes I was even standing next to you at the bar and drinking a pint with you. I was a kind of guardian angel to you and I've helped you a couple of times. Do you remember when a big brute picked a fight with you in that pub? Well, I made him keel over. I saved you from a pummeling. Of course, you didn't know who I was. I can shift shape you know, after all I'm a god and this is one of my tricks. I wasn't dressed like this, I was in civvies, but now I'm wearing my uniform, because I'm on an official mission to take you away from here. I'll take you to the Antwerp of your youth. Antwerp is eternal, like me and like my children, the Antwerpians!"

"I'm coming with you, Semini," Bob shouted happily. Come on, quickly, let's go!"

"Come mate," Semini said. "Take my hand, I'll pull you out of the swimming pool and out of your misery. Do you hear that? That's the Antwerpian folk singer Wannes van de Velde. He has already arrived in the eternal Antwerp where I'm taking you. He's singing: "Tonight I want to get lost in the streets of Antwerp."

And look, Bob! The sun has risen, do you see how the Boerentoren and the Cathedral are sparkling?"

The sun had risen and the doctor came in. The nurse had called him.

"Well sir," he said. "'I'm afraid that this is the beginning of the end. I can revive your father for a few moments, push the pedal to the floor but after that the engine will stop forever."

He gave Bob an injection. A couple of seconds later Bob opened his eyes. He recognized his son.

"Mark, I'm going to Antwerp with Semini!" he said. "Godjumenas, we're going to have fun!"

Godzjumenas

Dirk J. J. Vleugels

"Nah woên ekik al 36 jaar oep 't eiland Bali en 't is nog noêt zo waerm gewest as vandaag. Ge kungt er 'n ei oep bakke," docht den Bob. "In Aentwaerpe zouwe de musse van 't dak valle meh zoê weer, mor ier zen die biêshes da' gewoên. Mor allee, ik mag ni klage want 't is ier altijd schoê weer en doroem ben 'k toch eigelek ier kome woêne."
Oemda 't zoe iêt was ging em mor wad in zeh zwembad ston. A ad gin goesting om te zwemme. Meh z'nen ellenboog leunden em oep de raend van 't zwembad neffe z'n pint bier en den assenbak. A stak a sigaretshen oep.
A zag z'ne zöng onder ne palmboêm in den of zitte te puffe van de waermte. Diên ad meh ne verlengdraad e ventilateurke oep 'n tafeltshe gezet en was nen boek on 't leze. Den Bob droenk z'n bier leeg en riep nor z'ne zöng oem em nog een pint te brenge maar diên oêrden em ni. "Allee," docht em. "Zoevaer zit ongze Mark na toch ni van 't zwembad?"
Iniês zag em z'n Balinese meid uit de keuke kome. "Wayan, minta tolong! Saya minta satu bir lagi!"" riep em in 't Indonesisch, mor et maske oêrden em oek al ni.
"Godzjumenas," vloekten em. "Da's na pesies of da'k onzichtbaar gewörre zen, of zen die nah allemaal iniês dóef gewörre?"
A ad den Aentwaerpse radio Minerva oepston want diê kon em hier meh
z'ne computer ontvange. Iniês oêrden em da lieke over Aentwaerpe van de Strangers.

Aentwaerpe gij zeh gah vör mij
toch de stad waar as ek zen gebore
De Gruunplöts, de Meir, de Keyserlei
daar em ekik m'n art verlore
Aentwaerpe waar da 'kik oek ben
Ik kan nieverans mijnen draai ni vinde
'k weet et 't is flau, mor ik beken
Ba ae zen 'k thuis, en ongder vrinde

"Godzjumenas," docht em, "wat is da toch a schoê lieke vör 'n schoên stad. Oe laenk is 't nah geleje da 'k nog is in de Koekestad ben gewest? Is dad al 20 jaar? Ja, dah was in 1999."
A stak efkens z'ne kop onder water oem wat af te kóele en toeng 'em wer bove water kwam zag em twiê klein voetshes op de raend van 't zwembad ston. A keek oemhoêg. Er stoeng e klei ventshe veur em en 't was ginnen Balinees. Oe was diê binnegerokt? Dat manneke was pesies e kabouterke. A ad blauw oêge, blond kört haar, ne Romeinse neus en groête

lodderoêre. En a ad raar kliêre on. Iniês viel z'ne frang: da' ventshe ad zoên kliêre aan gelak die Romeine in diê film van Ben Hur diên em laenk geleje gezing ad in den tijd dad de kaerk en de cinema nog vol zate.

"Helaba, wie zedde gij?" vróeg den Bob.

"'k Ben blij dat ge me wakker et gemokt," zee et ventshe en a lachte vringdelijk.

"Watte?" zee den Bob.

"Wette gij ni wie da kik ben?"

"Neje, mor ge sprekt gah góed Aentwaerps! D'r zen ni zoeveul mense ni miêr die góed Aentwaerps kunne spreke."

"Ik ben de god Zjumenas, ook bekend als Semini," zee de verschijning. "Ik ben de giêst van Aentwaerpe. Ik ben ekik gebore in 't jaar 800. Alliên gij kunt mij zing. Oewe zöng en oe meid zing mij ni. Ik koom hier aliên vör aa."

"Meh alle Chineze mor ni meh den deze, hee maatshe! Da fiêshe goh ni deur. 'k Zal m'ne zöng is róepe seh, diê zal aa direkt buitengoeie," zee den Bob.

"Ou doe gemak. Roept mor, da's gin avance, a god aa ni oêre, en dörbij a kan aa oek ni zing," zee Semini.

"Allee, stap et af. Oe moeder ee viskes gebakke," zee den Bob, mor Semini ad gelijk. Nah verschoot den Bob toch.

"Gij zet dus de god Zjumenas of Semini?" vroeg em 'n bitshe zenuwachtig. "Mijnen Bompa ee mij vruuger verteld over de legende van Semini."

"Legende?" zee het ventshe kwaad. A was in zeh gat gebete. "Ik beston echt zenne. Gij zie mij toch staan ee?"

"Wa komde gij ier dan dung?"

"Ik zee et toch al: gij et mij wakker gemokt. De lesten tijd slaap 'k veul. Ik wör aliên wakker as er iemand mij roept mor da gebeurt ni veul ni miêr want de mense kenne m'ne naam ni miêr. Wie roept er in dezen tijd nah nog godjzumenas? En dan komt er nog bij da 't ni plezaent is oem meh ne schok wakker te wörre as 't aliên mor vör ne vloek is. 't Is oem ne floeren aap te schijte. Zegt na zelf Bob, oe zouwde gij oe vuule as ge góed on 't slaape zeh en iniês roept er ne pummel iêl ard Bobverdoeme in oe oêr?"

"Miljaar den tijger," zee den Bob. "Dan zouw ekik oek m'n kas oepfreete."

"Ik wör meh plezier wakker as ze mij róepe oem iet te vraage," zee Semini. "Dan probeer ekik diê mens t'elpe, wan ik ben ekik toch eigelek ne god ee, mor ik zouw der iet van krijge as mense die ni in mij geloêve m'ne naam aliên mor gebruike oem te vlóeke!"

"'k Zal oe is iet zegge da ge ni wet," zee Semini nog. "As er niemand nimiêr in ongs geloêft moete wij 't aftrappe. Da's 'n natuurwet."

"Wie zen wij?" vróeg den Bob.

"De gode natuurlijk. Ge wet wel, de Griekse gode, de Romeinse gode, d'Egyptische, allee, al d'afgedaenkte gode van de jare stillekes dus, zelfs die van Zuid-Amerika en China. Da's aerg vör mij, want as 't zoe voêrt goh zal 't ni laenk ni mir dure of ik moet m'n schup afkösse. Dan sture ze mij nor 't gesticht vör afgedaenkte gode en godinne.

'k Zen die plöts is gon bezuke want 'k wouw toch wel is wete wor da 'k misschien oêt zal moete woêne. 't Is dor wel iêl schoên, just gelak in e vijfstaerenotel, en er zen dor schoên bosse en baerge, en straende met wit zaend en palmboême, allee, alles wa ge mor wilt, mor 't is Aentwaerpe ni ee? En dan komt dor nog bij da'k dor oep nen oêp zouw zitte met al die aender gode en godinne. Oem doêd te valle, mor da kan ni want ik ben onstaerfelijk.

De Zeus en z'n famille, nen oêp Griekse lawijtmakers die nor loêk stinke uit unnen bek, loêpe dor oek rongd. Diê Zeus ee-g-et oêg in z'n bolleke en aa ee ne franken teut. Da's nogal ne ziêverer zenne. Oem de vijf botte sprekt em over sex en over al de mokkes wor em meh gepoept ee. Ik krijg er stiêne kloête van. Ik em veul miêr gepoept dan diê kloefkapper en over mij ware de vrouwe iêl content, maar ik loêp dor ni over te stoeffe.

Die Grieke, ik kan ze ni rieke. Aliên da godinneke, die Diana, da's e knap mokke en die lacht altijd zoe lief. Ze ziet er mij 'n iête broek uit. Eur tette zen oem van te snóepe en eur ekster woênt oêg want z'ee lange magnifieke biêne.

En dan die Noorse gode! Diên Odin zit oep ne wiêr. A kan ni verdrage dat em in 't gesticht zit. A zukt meh iederiên ruuze. Zoêren apzjaar! En dan ee 't em oek nog ne smóel oem strongt oep te sortere. En diên Thor is ne mafkees diên altijd mor lawijt wilt make meh z'nen aamer as em e stuk in z'ne frak hee, wat dus wilt zegge elken dag. Stekt diê ze verstaend in e vogeltshen en 't vliegd achteruit. Ik krijg er de wöbbe van.

Nah zwijg 'k nog over d'Egyptische gode, da's 'n bende krawate seh. Dor kunde ni meh klappe! Die zen allemaal zoe zot as 'n achterdeur.

Amai, ik zit hier mor te klappe, 'k em er dörst van gekrege. Gij oek een pint? Ik trakteer."

Na diên uitleg van Semini verschoot den Bob van niks ni miêr. A vond et iêl normaal dat er iniês twiê pinte oep de raend van 't zwembad stoenge. Ze droenken alletwiê ne faerme sloek van 't Aentwaerps bier. Den Bob voelde z'n eige fantastisch. "'k Zit ier oep een goei wei," docht em. "Diê Semini is nen toffe gast."

Iniês oêrden em wer et lieke van de Strangers.

"Seh joeng," zeet em tege Semini, a zee "In al die jare da 'k hier woên em ekik me nog noêt zoe gevoeld. 'k Em iniês toch zoên eimwee nor Aentwaerpe. En ik zee godzjumenas en gij stoeng ier iniês."

"Ja, Bob daaroem ben ekik gekome," zee Semini. "Vör diên iêste vlóek zouw ekik oe nie bezocht emme, mor toengs da' ge den twidde kiêr godzjumenas riep, wist ekik dah gah ni on 't vlóeke word. G'et onbewust mij geróepe. Ik ad direct deur da' ge docht on de giêst van Aentwaerpe, en ik ben diê giêst. D'Aentwaerpenerre noemden un eige vruuger toch Semini's kindere? Awel, gij zed e kind van mij. Ik koom oe ale. We gon nor 't Aentwaerpe van vruuger, nor de Koekestad van oe jeugd wor dad iederiên Aentwaerps sprekt."

Oep de palliatief afdeeling van 't St Erasmus gastuis in Aentwaerpe zat de Mark oep ne stóel neffe 't bed van zeh vader. A was in 't slaap gevalle mor a wier meh ne schok wakker toengs da' de nachtzuster kwam binnegestesseld.

"Oe vader is on 't kreune. A zal wel veul pijn emme. 'k Zal em nog is een dosis morfin geve."

Dornaa ging ze neffe de Mark zitte. "Aa vader sprekt soems een vremde taal in z'ne slaap," fluisterde ze. "Seh, oêrd is! A sprekt wer!"

"Oh!" zee de Mark. "Da's Indonesisch. A denkt dat em tuis oep 't eiland Bali is. A roept z'n meid oem em bier te brenge. A zee dat em in 't zwembad zit."

"Oh, gij verstaat Indonesisch?" vróeg de verpleegster.

"Ja," zee de Mark. "Wij woêne dor. Papa kwam nor Bali toeng em 50 jaar was. A kwam dor 'n Indonesisch maske tege dat em zoe schoên vongt dat em er direct meh getrouwd is. Da was me móeder. Z'is al vijf jaar doêd. Ze wier overreje deur ne camion."

A zweeg efkes.

"En nae is Papa on 't staerve. A is veurige möngd 86 jaar gewörre."

"Brengde me trug nor den tijd van vruuger?" vróeg den Bob. "'t Aentwaerpe wor dad ekik zoeveul plezier em gemokt? Oh! Diên tijd! Toeng ging ekik dikkels oep de lappe oep de Stadswaag, en oek a koffeke drinke oep de Gruunplöts of oep de Keyserlei of ik pakte den boêt nor Sint Anneke en och, ik dee nog zoeveul miêr plezaente dinges."

"Mor ik oêk joeng," zee Semini. "Ik stoeng soems zelfs neffen aa on den toêg een pint te drinke. Ik was zoên bitshen oewen engelbewaarder en 'k em oe e paar kiêre golpe. Wette nog toeng da' ge ruzie kreeg meh nen boêm van ne vengt in da' kafeeke? Awel, 'k em diên apzjaar doeng valle, want ik zag wel dah gij aenders klop zouw krijge. Gah erkende mij natuurlek ni. Ik kan m'n eige groêter of kleiner make, ziede, da's iên van de truukskes die ne god kan doeng. Natuurlek ad ekik toeng dees kliêre ni on, ik was in burger, mor nae zen ekik in uniform, want ik koom op officieel missie oem aa te kome ale. Ik neem oe mee nor 't Aentwaerpe van oe jeugd. Aentwaerpe is iêweg, gelak ik, en gelak m'n kindere, d'Aentwaerpenerre!"

"Awel, ik gon mee, Semini," riep den Bob blij. "Geft em bözze, we zen weg!"

"Kom joeng," zee Semini. "Pakt m'n aend vast, ik trek oe uit da' zwembad en uit de mizere. Oêrde dah? Da's Wannes van de Velde. Diên is al aangekome in dad iêwig Aentwaerpe wor dah 'k oe nortoe gon brenge. A zingt: Ik wil deze nacht in de strate verdwale.

En zied is, Bob! De zon is zjust oepgegon, zied is oe den Bóerentoren en de Kattedraal ston te schitteren!"

De zon was zjust oepgegon en den doktoor was binnengekome. De nachtzuster ad em geróepe.

"Ja meniêr," zeet em, a zee "'k Ben bang dah da 't begin van 't einde is. Ik kan oe vader nog efkes wakker make, gelak nog efkes vol gas geve, mor dan is de moteur vörgóe kapot en al d'energie oep."

A gaf den Bob e spötshe. Een paar seconde later deed den Bob z'n oêge oope. A erkende z'ne zöng.

"Markske, ik gon nor Aentwaerpe meh Semini!" zeet em. Godzjumenas, we gon ons amuzere!"

Cloaked Redemption

Ginger Huff

David Sinclair had always felt like an orphan, and now it was true. Family had been out of grasp and as cold as ice. His parents had been distant and as an only child, he was alone a lot. The only interactions were stern and judgemental. Displaying emotions was frowned upon. He learned it wasn't safe to be vulnerable. He was present but silent until spoken to. Absolutely no pets were tolerated in this totalitarian home. His father had total rule over the family. He was a military man and carried that strict no-nonsense attitude into his family. Walking on egg shells was the norm and no one crossed David Franklin Sinclair Sr.

So when his mother, at age 92, decided to get a cat, he was confused and rather appalled.

He tried to push down his feelings of loss and jealousy at never having been allowed a pet. He was having a hard time justifying her decision of having a cat of all things. His father had passed that same year and he assumed maybe that's why she got the cat, as she wasn't under her husband's rule anymore. Oh well, it wasn't his problem anyway.

Books upon layers of more books and papers lined his study, floor to almost ceiling. He was messy. "Great minds always are," he used to say in his 30's and 40's. By the time 50 became 60, he didn't believe he had such a great mind any more.

He chained smoked, always had. Another one of his endearing qualities he had jokingly bestowed upon himself.

Watching the subtle curl of his cigarette smoke as it swirled into the air caused him to drift off. To drift off into another time. The most wonderful time of his life.

A much younger David, in his 30's, mastered degrees in Divinity and Psychology. God and The Mind. Very worthy pursuits. The wind at his sails and clear skies ahead.

It was when he was teaching a class on Genesis, as Professor David Franklin Sinclair, a highly honored persona that his life changed.

That beautiful Spring morning as the students were assembling, he saw her walk into his class. He'd never seen her before. She was in her late 20's and had the face of an angel with long golden-chestnut hair. Graceful as a gazelle and as light as a feather, her blue and green skirt flowing behind her like wind blowing across a lush green meadow. There was an other-worldly air about her. The Professor was transfixed.

"Welcome class. Today we start in the Book of Genesis. Chapter 3 verse 1. The Fall of Mankind."

The mystery student slowly raised her hand. "Pardon me Professor, may I ask a question?"

Caught off guard and trying not to stammer, Sinclair answered, "Why yes. Certainly. Please do. Miss…?

"Oh." She laughed. "I'm Lily Wilder."

"Would you say that the reason Adam ate the fruit alongside Eve was because he had fallen madly in love with her, and wanted to please her?"

It was at that very moment, David was smitten. He stood in stunned silence. Trying to grasp the depth that seemed to infer. The idea that Adam loved his Eve so much, that he'd even risk defying God and death, was something that had never crossed his mind. But in that moment, as she sat waiting for his answer, the sunlight casting a soft glow on her hair, he knew almost what Adam must have been feeling. It was love at first sight.

But that was then and this is now, and he was just a tired disillusioned man in his 60's, who'd given up hope that there was a God and he felt his spiritual health waning.

David was a lonely man. To call him bitter would be a compliment to his disposition and outlook. Disillusioned by a solitary life, his mother's recent death only complicated matters.

Mr. Jangles, her fluffy grey mixed breed cat of 5 years, had been left into his care. He despised cats. He grimaced as he was told the news of this unwanted tenant.

"Are you kidding me?" he yelled. "I'm not taking care of that cat!" Sinclair pounded his fist on the desk. "No. Absolutely not. My mother was surely suffering from dementia when she put that in her will!"

His mother's lawyer, C. Everitt Taylor cleared his throat, looked directly in David's eyes and added, "That's fine. Mr. Sinclair, if you won't take Mr. Jangles, that's fine. Indeed you don't have to. Your mother thought you might object, so she gave you an incentive."

"An incentive, huh?"

"Yes, an incentive. The rest of the inheritance is forfeited then as well, if you don't take Mr. Jangles into your home. Of course that means you won't be receiving over one hundred and fifty thousand dollars either."

Under the circumstances, Mr. Jangles moved in. Sinclair put the litterbox, cat food, toys and climbing tree out on the screened-in back porch, as far away from him as possible. Thus, his reluctant relationship with his cat "brother" began.

He sat up to all hours of the night, chain smoking, up to his eyeballs in old newspapers he collected. Half a glass of whisky making ever-increasing water marks on his ebony desk. At this point David had also given up on coasters.

David and Lily were married a year later. She took a job as a writer for the local paper and David continued to teach. Peace and contentment filled their home. They were best friends as well as lovers. Things couldn't be much better. Lily, however, had an unknown past. A painful secret she refused to talk about. All she would say was that it was much too traumatic to elaborate. David didn't question her much. He could see the pain in her eyes whenever the topic would come up. Five years into their marriage, things took an unexpected turn.

His beloved Lily got terribly sick. Her immune system began to shut down. He refused to leave her side and took an extended leave from teaching. Within a year, she was gone.

Everything he had held in his heart was tossed upside down. He had never felt so alone or as sad. Mourning became as predictable as the sunrise. He set out on a quest to find out about her secretive past.

He'd get a lead, then it would fall through. He finally managed to locate her mother. Surely, he thought, she could shed some light and maybe he could have some closure. She told him that two years before they married, Lily had given up a child for adoption. David was surprised to say the least. "But why... why didn't she tell me? Why was it such a secret?" He wouldn't have cared if she'd had a child. He had many questions but had only received few answers.

He needed a miracle, but those are long gone, he sighed.

He dutifully fed and abetted Mr. Jangles for several months. Mr. Jangles was a nice cat, but David's heart just didn't include love for a cat or anything else.

His mother's attorney hadn't specified how long he actually had to keep the feline. He had already gotten all of his inheritance money. So he decided to put an ad in the local paper to give Mr. Jangles away.

FREE TO GOOD HOME. FUZZY GREY LONG HAIRED MALE CAT. NEUTERED. 7 YEARS OLD.

And then he waited.

One late afternoon he received a phone call from a young woman who was interested in the cat. They chatted briefly and 30 mins later, Jade Kincaid showed up with excited anticipation. He had put Mr. Jangles in a carrier and gathered his toys and miscellaneous cat belongings.

"Ohhh, he's so cute," Jade exclaimed as he let Mr. Jangles out. He purred quite loudly and he rubbed against her arm. Jade left happily with the cat.

"Good, good", he murmured to himself. One less cat to bother him.

On Tuesday of the next week, David was awakened by meowing and claws against his bedroom window. Mr. Jangles had returned. He shook his head in astonishment. He wanted nothing to do with this cat. He got dressed and quickly called Jade.

"Oh thank God," she cried. She told him she'd been frantic, searching high and low. "I'll be over in a flash," she assured him. David, feeling relieved, mellowed some and when she arrived, asked if she'd like a cup of tea. "Sure, that'd be great," she said.

Minutes become hours as they talk about common interests and Mr. Jangles. They both were alone in this world, without family and it felt good to have another person to talk to. Looking across the room Jade spots a faded framed photograph on the mantle. "Is this you and your wife?" she asks.

"Yes, that picture was taken when we first got married." David hands her the photograph.

"She's pretty. Do you have any children?" she asks.

David clears his throat as tears well up in his eyes. "Nope. No children. She passed away before we had children," his voice trailing off.

Gathering his composure, Sinclair asks if she has any family, trying to divert attention away from himself and his sadness.

"Well not really. My adopted parents have passed on and I don't have any siblings. I guess I'm alone in this world too. But now," she smiles, "I have Mr. Jangles."

David nodded.

Jade adds, "I do have an old picture of my birth mother. It's really all I have." She takes out the photo and looks at it longingly before handing it to him.

Sinclair puts his glasses on to see it better. Confusion plasters his mind.

"Where did you say you got this?" he asks.

"It's the only thing she left me. I don't even know her full name, just what's written on the back," she sighs.

David turns the photo over and much to his surprise, LILY is written in black ink, faded from time.

In disbelief they compare the photos.

"I can't believe this! he exclaims. That's my wife! Your mother was my wife!"

"What? How in the world could this ever happen?" she exclaims as tears well up in her eyes. Jade looks at David who is staring at Mr. Jangles.

All of a sudden it becomes bright as day that Mr. Jangles was his miracle. His mother, Ilene had given him not only a miracle, but a family as well.

The Magician's Last Trick

Justin Sunshine

The brown, leather office chair on the other side of the elegantly veneered conference table creaked slightly as its occupant settled forward with folded arms, a suspicious frown creasing his irritated looking face. Excessively tall and lean, his sixty something years having avoided the slight weight gains of middle age, his demeanour was that of someone used to immediate obedience. The colour of his expensively cut suit matched his grey hair, and like the man himself, was very slightly wrinkled.

His companion was younger, shorter with floppy blond hair and tortoiseshell designer glasses. He wore the same upper civil service suit, although navy this time, his unlined thirty-six-year-old face appearing convivial with his latest attempt to persuade the third occupant of the sparsely furnished room to accede to their way of thinking.

Tobias Anderson Bridges leant back in the chair on his side of the table, appearing lost in thought. *Not do the usual show*, he mused. *Not do the show*. Left elbow resting on the chair arm, thumb propping his chin, he drummed his fingers against his mouth appearing to seriously consider the question. He continued to do this in wicked delight as a thought of annoyance briefly flashed across the mind of each of the other two men. Although their faces and postures betrayed nothing, they wanted this concluded. It wasted their precious time - in one case filled with a long afternoon journey north, and in the other case to, well, something.

Tobias extended a light tendril of thought, gently caressing the mind of the older man, its ripple causing those stray thoughts to rehearse and repeat themselves. Something was laid bare to his inspection. *Ah, a mistress*. Without revealing his new-found knowledge, he filed it away for later use; he'd pushed them far enough. "No."

"No? But Mr Bridges, we talked about this," cajoled the younger man.

"No."

"Mr Bridges? Tobias? Please, we did talk about this and agreed you were not going to do this. To risk public exposure."

"No, you agreed. Not me. There is no exposure. People see what they want. They think it's all a trick anyway."

"But Mr Bridges, you've always eschewed wider exposure. 'Acclaim,' you said 'should be small and personal'. Think of your ongoing private life."

"No."

"Now see here, Mr. Bridges," weighed in the older man, proceeding with a lengthy and well-reasoned argument about how public knowledge of the existence of magic, true sorcery, would really upset the old apple cart. "Cat amongst pigeons, what?"

"No." replied Tobias, again defying the doughty man's expectation of immediate capitulation and apology. He added a subtle, mental shove for good measure.

The target of his riposte sat back in his chair, uncrossed his arms and placed his hands on the table, fingers interlinked, an exasperated breath escaping. His demeanour was studied outrage at having his time wasted by this garishly dressed miscreant, although Tobias' light mental touch easily detected the charade.

"Places to go, people to see, lunch to be conquered and eaten."

"But we had lunch!" protested the younger.

"You had lunch. I had a predinner aperitif."

"Aperitif! Soup, roast partridge, lemon sorbet, cheese and crackers, then coffee and biscuits!"

"Hungry work this magic lark. Drains a man. And those weren't biscuits. Not proper biscuits anyway. They were – "

"Enough!" barked older, heading off a pointless tirade about the quality of Whitehall biscuits. "The arrangements have been made with the production company. We've submitted the script for your little tricks and that's all there is to it. If you must persist with this…this… nonsense, it will be done our way."

"Alright!" Tobias agreed in feigned resignation. "Coins and cards it is, then the vanishing box." He felt the token resistance had been played well enough and he wouldn't be dancing to their tune in any case. His unexpected capitulation resulted in an exchanged glance between his handlers and Tobias added a gentle, subtle feeling of achievement and success to both their minds, at which they visibly relaxed.

"We'll make sure you get there in good time," said older, experienced.

"And our people will be in the audience, and backstage too," added younger. "To ensure your safety. And…make sure everything goes as planned."

Tobias ignored the unsubtle threats, meaningless anyway in the face of his planned mischief and disobedience, although getting away with it might be harder.

Craig, arms folded and legs akimbo stood watching the large screen in rapt admiration as a geeky looking youth with oversized glasses and a chiselled jaw deftly pulled a perfect looking rose from the centre of a rolled up newspaper. He turned slightly to the smaller man to his left.

"OK, I get magic acts," he said. "But walk me through what those two are doing," he continued, indicating a pair of suited gentlemen in a booth at the front of the stage.

Tobias smiled slightly and smoothed his goatee. "Those two are the premiere magical double act in the world.

"Traditional magic shows have the magician and assistants doing coins or cards, or sometimes seemingly dangerous stunts. It's all a confidence trick though; the audience knows there's a secret, and that its all just smoke and mirrors, as they say. The 'magic' is just sleight of hand or clever props".

"Props?"

"Things they use to fake it, like a false-bottomed box. Anyway, this show is different. They're viewing the performance through the jaded eyes of decades of experience of their own dazzling and impossible feats. As you've seen, if they fail to correctly guess the mechanics of the trick, the applause is..." he rolled his hands to indicate thunderous. "A trophy is awarded and a place on their live tour guaranteed, entertaining folks around the world. The audience are the real winners because the talent is amazing."

"Well, for conjurers," he amended at Craig's raised eyebrow.

They were waiting in a nearby room, adorned with large settees and some green plastic potted plants. There were four other acts besides Tobias yet to perform. Eight other magicians clustered around a dizzy looking blonde in a black sequinned dress. She was obviously anything but dizzy, as she held a trophy for their inspection, her milk jug and cards act having been of sufficient ingenuity to fool the experts.

The two other people in the room were plain clothes police officers assigned to Tobias, to ensure he stuck to the agreed act and didn't flee afterwards. They became more alert as the applause for the current act began. It was enthusiastic, although lacking the wild shouting that usually accompanied a trophy winner, and sure enough Trevelyn, a young man in his mid-twenties came through the door empty handed. He shrugged to Tobias who gave his shoulder a warm squeeze and mouthed some encouraging words. Tobias' thoughts harked back to a previous day, and other words.

He had been approached by a regular at one of his stage shows, the weekly live performances he gave. It was ostensibly for the threadbare conjurer to make ends meet, although Tobias had a personal fortune of several tens of millions salted away. The truth was he liked contact with people, and it gave him a much-needed break from studying ancient texts and his own company. Mr Montgomery had obviously seen through that, having requested a private performance. Tobias had indulged him, as

Montgomery had pestered him for the real thing, going so far as to show him a flame magically appearing in his own palm. Tobias hated to admit it, but he had been suckered in and revealed more than he had intended. At which point MI16 had descended and claimed him for themselves.

Their demands were ceaseless. Remote Viewing. Remote Killing. Every advantage over an unnamed and probably imagined enemy. They were convinced Tobias held the keys to absolute, unlimited magical power, and with only a thought could conquer or crush any who stood before him. Which he could, of course. The only thing standing between them and their god of power was Tobias' own moral code and decency. He just wanted to take his studies as far as possible and glide through life with a minimum of friction.

They were determined to get it and had overrun every facet of his life. His studies, eating habits, friendships, weekly shows - especially those - God, how he hated them for that. He could tell that they'd mostly taken over the audience, pushing out local, semi interested couples eager for a fun night out in place of their own bigwigs and invited guests, all eager to see their tame savant perform. It had started innocuously with "Can you help us?" and descended from there.

He'd been holding these regular, small performances for nearly a hundred and sixty years under a variety of names, in a variety of towns. Cameras and recordings were always forbidden. He'd made that mistake once in the late nineteen-thirties and had had to perform a 'last trick' to escape, disappearing over Niagara Falls in a flaming barrel, before starting again under another assumed name. He'd been Tobias Anderson Bridges since the mid nineteen seventies. Maybe it was time to leave again, although with modern forensics, financial and otherwise, it really might mean starting again from scratch.

Tobias shook himself lightly and focussed again on the present.

The attractive female compère finished introducing him, as the video show on the overhead screens drew to a close. It had been playing an entirely fictitious recitation of his life to date, including how hard he had studied closeup magic. Tobias graced the stage, his hands widely spread, his orange baggy trousers swishing as he walked, their cuffs tapering into tight fitting turnups just above his ankles and red Converse shoes. He wore a white T shirt under a red and orange waistcoat with a gold pocket watch for good measure. His over long, mostly grey hair billowed from the sides of his head, the two grey spikes of moustache sticking out sideways, perpendicular to the similarly coloured goatee.

At his entrance, the audience broke into spontaneous applause, and it took only the lightest touch from his mind here and there to turn that into a standing ovation, punctuated by enthusiastic shouts. Despite intervention by the studio crew, Tobias egged the audience on, mentally as well as physically, pointing randomly at members of the crowd and miming clapping. The chaos went on for several minutes before he let it subside.

"Well. Well, I... We've not seen that before," gasped Alison the compère, holding her hand against her upper chest, a gentle red flush spreading from there to her cheeks, slightly overwhelmed by the response and Tobias' own magnetism.

"Hello Alison", said Tobias with genuine warmth, pulling her focus back to the job.

"Lovely to meet you Tobias, she managed to get out before a small cough. "Ladies and Gentlemen – Tobias Anderson Bridges!"

There was polite and enthusiastic applause for a few seconds. Tobias waved and smiled his dazzling smile, picked up for the first time ever by studio cameras.

"Now, Tobias, you've been doing the club circuit...."

"That's right, Alison. Only small clubs and theatres. No TV or filming of any kind."

"And why is that"

"I like to maintain contact with my audience, and I think with real magic that's what they deserve. These days you can get all kinds of special effects and TV tricks, and that's something I've never needed; never done."

It was a facile lie which sprang easily and fully formed to his lips, one which he had often repeated. The real reason of course was so that he didn't have to fake death and start again every other generation.

"So, what are we going to see today, if that's not going to spoil it?"

"Well Alison, I have a number of gifts with cards and coins. Maybe I'll be using some of those, although almost certainly not in the manner intended."

"Alright then," she smiled, stepping slightly to the side.

"Not too far please, Alison. I'm going to need your help in a minute." Tobias stepped up to a convenient table, provided to his specification.

"First off, let's have a look at this," he gestured to the table, walking behind it, demonstrating clearly that it was just a table without any curtains hiding props. "Perhaps we can get the professionals to check it out...?"

At his gesture the two main attractions of the show bounded from their seats, a hand held aloft to acknowledge the smattering of applause. They each briefly, but warmly greeted Tobias with a handshake, and satisfied themselves that the table was just an ordinary table.

Tobias extended his sleeveless arms and rotated them, to show that he held nothing before gesturing towards the table. "Please examine the deck," he twinkled.

The elder of the two magicians started slightly as he noticed the cards on the table. He glanced at his colleague; those had definitely not been there a moment ago and Tobias was still at least six feet away. He picked up the deck and expertly riffled through it, his practiced eye noting that the cards were grouped numerically, the suits mixed up. He replaced the deck on the table.

Tobias gestured to the second, more ebullient of the duo. A natural showman, he lifted and examined the deck, which now contained only jokers. He looked cryptically at his partner as he returned the cards. This was new.

"So," said Tobias. "That's the card trick over with. I don't know that many anyway." He smiled self-deprecatingly. "Let's move onto the next bit."

The deck of cards burst into sudden white-hot flame which spread in a second to engulf the rest of the table. At the snap of Tobias' fingers, the fire immediately extinguished leaving the charred remains of the card deck on the cracked and soot blackened surface of the pine table.

The two magicians looked at each other, each thinking about the different accelerants they might use to achieve this. Tobias smiled at them and again snapped his fingers for effect. As one of the magicians blinked, his colleague stared directly at the table, and in the fraction of an instant, both the cards and the table were restored, as though nothing had taken place. One reached out and picked up the slightly warm deck, noting almost as an afterthought that the card faces were now pictures of animals from around the planet.

"Pick an animal from the deck," Tobias barked, his open palm extended. He remained several feet away from both magicians and the table. "Any will do, but we should start small." He smiled indulgently at their incredulous expressions.

"OK," declared the more ebullient of the two magicians. "Now I'm startin' to get impressed. Now you got my attention."

His ever-silent companion riffled through the deck, ignoring the cats and rabbits that most of their compatriots of yesteryear would have kept under their hats or in voluminous pockets. He subconsciously glanced at the hatless, coatless Tobias.

They eventually settled on a Koala bear, holding aloft the card for the audience and the cameras to see.

"Please fold the card and put it back on the table."

They did as Tobias instructed.

"Ready?" He looked at them, and they looked back blandly.

There was a small sound, a sort of fizz, and the card had vanished from the table, to be replaced by an actual, living and slightly dazed looking Koala bear.

As one of them reached out, Tobias cautioned them. "It's completely wild. It might scratch or bite you."

He waved his hands in a complicated looking way and the small creature vanished. "Pick something else that doesn't bite."

The showman held up a picture of a snake; a black mamba. Tobias slightly raised an eyebrow and the card was quickly replaced. He squeezed another between his fingers before letting it drop.

The folded card on the table showed the picture of a Dutch Dwarf; a small black and white rabbit. A second or so later and the same thing happened, and the vanished card was replaced by a small rabbit, which stood on its hind legs, its nose twitching inquisitively.

Both magicians gazed at it for several seconds before the silent one picked it up and cuddled it.

"Any more for anymore?" enquired Tobias, before gesturing to the showman. "Pick an audience member. Or crew. I don't care."

The showman gestured to Alison who tentatively approached.

"You like animals, don't you?"

"Yes," she replied nervously.

"Pick a card," he indulged, gesturing towards the pack still held by the showman.

Alison picked a chinchilla.

Tobias snapped his fingers, and a beautiful brown and white chinchilla materialised on the table. Alison barely had time to stroke it before it changed back into a playing card.

"Alison, take the cards and look through them," commanded Tobias. "Don't think about pets. Think about what animal you'd love to be."

Alison threw down onto the table a card bearing the image of a sleek black panther.

"Gents…Please take gentle hold of her upper arms," Tobias commanded in the manner of a bored train guard.

They did so, and barely a second later the fizz sounded, louder this time. Alison looked startled before smoothly becoming a panther, her front forelegs gripped by the magicians.

They each let go in sudden shock and panther Alison rubbed her head against the hip of the older, quieter magician. This tranquil moment lasted barely two seconds before the audience broke into wild applause.

Both magicians were completely stunned, saying nothing. Panther Alison stopped rubbing her head and started to lick one of her paws. Tobias changed her back, and Alison stopped mid lick, her hand held in front of her face. Her tail twitched until Tobias noticed and it, too, vanished. He gallantly helped her back to her feet, and she rose slightly awkwardly, smoothing her skirt as she did so.

The magicians began conferring between themselves, even though Tobias' act was not quite finished. They had already decided that this level of skill went way beyond anything they had ever seen, surpassing even their own considerable talents, not even venturing a guess as to how this had been achieved. They both thought, incorrectly as it would turn out, that the producer's notes from each artist would give them all the detail they needed.

Tobias stood casually to the side watching the audience as the many still standing, following their ovation of him, retook their seats. He smiled and tipped an imaginary hat to the two casually dressed gentlemen in row twelve. His handlers were incognito and really not enjoying the show, as he had magnificently deviated from their prearranged script.

The two magicians also retook their seats, excited to see what would follow, although they doubted it would prove to be any more spectacular.

Tobias reached into a trouser pocket and withdrew a lime green handkerchief, which he handed to Alison who had forgotten to move away from centre stage. She took it and at his whispered prompt held it stretched out, turning it this way and that. Tobias mimed pulling apart her hands which she did, causing the handkerchief to expand until it was about four feet long.

"Tie the ends together."

She complied with his request, making a large loop. Tobias snapped his fingers, again for effect, and the material suddenly changed into an almost black purple colour.

"Let it hang from your hands. And turn sideways."

Alison did as instructed, holding the loop of material side on to the audience, although the large video screens above the stage relayed this from different angles, allowing everyone to see the loop clearly.

Tobias sauntered towards her and standing about a foot away held his hand up before his face, encouraging closeup inspection by the cameras. The handlers in the audience at last began to relax as he was obviously back on the script.

Tobias slowly and casually reached through the loop with his hand which seemed to vanish at the point it entered the gap made by the loop. Camera two had a good view of his hand from towards the side of the stage and later examination would show a distinct haze within the loop, slightly obscuring his hand.

He withdrew his hand which emerged from the loop holding a pair of shiny green apples, one of which he tossed to the two front row magicians. The other he took a large bite from, savouring the sweet crunchiness as he stepped away from Alison. The audience began to applaud as Tobias ate another bite, his free hand wiping a small amount of apple juice from his mouth. He swallowed the second piece and gazed happily at the apple before tossing the core at the loop held by Alison, where it could clearly be seen to vanish as it travelled through.

"Thank you so much, my dear," he said to an open-mouthed Alison, who had been convinced her dress had been about to be stained with apple juice.

"N-No problem, Tobias."

"May I?" he said gently, taking the loop of material from her and examining it. "Not quite big enough, I think."

Tobias stepped away from her, holding the loop, which expanded as he moved his hands apart before tossing it casually to the floor before him. He paused momentarily before looking out at the audience and taking a bow to wild applause.

The two magicians approached him, warmly shaking his hand before giving him the plastic trophy.

"No clue, man. Nada. Zip," enthused the showman and as always his silent companion shrugged, mugging a bemused expression.

"That, sir, was truly awesome," he whispered to Tobias, careful to maintain the fiction of never speaking on stage. "Epic."

"Can you give us any hints?" wheedled the showman, trying to draw out the moment.

"Sure," said Tobias, unexpectedly. "Magic. Actual sorcery. I don't do tricks and I don't do sleight of hand. What you saw this evening was a hundred percent exactly what it looked like." He smiled and began to address the audience. "Thank you one, thank you all. I hope I've entertained. There is such a thing as magic, although really it's just the will and ability to make things happen.

"And now, I'm afraid, it's time for me to go."

He jauntily saluted his handlers and clutching his trophy, he lightly jumped forward into the loop of material, through which could be seen the stage floor. As he passed into and through it, it seemed to wobble slightly, like the ripple in jelly, before stilling again.

The two magicians looked at each other in shock, the showman poking into the centre of the loop with his toe, which sank into the solid looking floor. He quickly withdrew it and repeated the act, but it had just become a solid floor again and his sole made a slight tapping sound.

Behind them, and to the sides, four large, suited men charged onto the stage, Craig in the lead. All four wore ear pieces each talking separately into his phone, and each slowed to an aimless walk as they fanned out, searching their erstwhile charge, now disappeared seemingly into thin air.

In the audience, the two civil servants, Tobias' handlers, began to elbow their way along the row, seeking to reach the stage themselves.

The silent magician picked up the cloth which quickly shrank in size, becoming lime green again.

They looked at each other, further confused by the commotion around them.

The Coming of Spring

Justin Sunshine

The late afternoon sun slid lazy golden shafts through the passenger windows on one side of the 737 as it descended towards Rekkisvar, the small capital of Rekkisland, where lived the majority of the 500,000 or so inhabitants of that breathtakingly beautiful country. The ephemeral rays gave golden crowns to the mountains to the north and east of the city, a nimbus to the top of the tallest building, the magnificent cathedral, and a golden sheen to the passengers looking out, one of whom was Mindy.

Mindy had flown plenty of times but thought in all her twelve years that she had never had such a spectacular arrival at a holiday destination. She nudged her mother, already craning her own neck, the better to absorb the fleeing daylight. Her father, in the aisle seat, didn't stand a chance of that view, and was fretting over their travel documents.

A scant quarter of an hour later, their flight touched down, seemingly impervious to the last fortnight of the winter ice and snow already gathering on the runway. This far north the transformation from day to night was swift, and already the sky had the beginnings of a dark purple hue. They gathered their possessions from the lockers and seat nets, Mindy repeatedly checking that she had Fox, a large eyed, stuffed brown toy who had been her constant bedtime and travel companion for the last six years. Her passport was a distant secondary concern, meriting only a perfunctory check that it remained in her coat pocket. She and her parents shuffled from the aircraft into the disembarkation area, and thence to Customs and Passport control after retrieving their suitcases from the slow-moving belt.

On leaving the terminal, all three Burghoffs quickly boarded the courtesy shuttlebus, keen to escape the rapidly dropping temperature, already down to 2 degrees above zero. It would drop another ten or fifteen degrees overnight.

The bus followed the main road into the city, bypassing the nearby town. Mr Burghoff shuddered occasionally at the thought of the impending icy disasters, but the driver avoided any such incidents with an insouciance born of long experience. Here and there, visible through the evergreens or above the rising embankments they could see residential buildings, and the large windscreen afforded glimpses of the higher aspected parts of the city.

They eventually reached their destination; the city centre Welcome Break hotel and pre-booked family room.

The following morning the small Burghoff family boarded another, larger bus with a mixture of other tourists and locals. It was an early departure, but not so early that they hadn't enjoyed the buffet breakfast before the smaller courtesy shuttle dropped them at the terminus on the outskirts of the capital.

After leaving the city, the road wound its way through low lying mountains. It was to be a long journey, taking the entire day as the bus followed the main road along the south coast, the interior roads of the country being closed during winter. They marvelled at the sights along the way, Mr Burghoff taking meticulous notes about the exact location of the waterfalls and viewpoints, his wife taking photographs of the stunning scenery edging up towards the glaciers and low lying mountains.

Eleven hours later, following a forty-minute transfer journey in a taxi – a large white 4x4 with hugely inflated snow tyres, they arrived at the guesthouse which would be their home for the next five days. It was a small chalet, one of a dozen which surrounded a smallish, twenty room, two storey hotel, which also housed the restaurant and other shared amenities. After dumping their belongings in the hallway, they headed straight over to the restaurant, slipping and sliding along the winding path from the chalet carved through knee high snow.

The constables left the office and Detective Jensson sighed and opened his laptop. Another disappearance, and a child this time. The mother was right to be concerned, as even daytime temperatures were dangerously cold. If only they could be sure. Maybe the child would seek shelter somewhere before night set in. He doubted the bland reassurances by the constables had really done much to help, and in any case it was the eighth disappearance in the last three weeks. After brief consideration, he summarized the situation and escalated it to the regional commander in an email marked urgent.

Jim stumbled slightly, the thick snow compacting under his boots, grip aided by the attached iceclaws, the short, spiked crampons. From under the turn up of his woollen ski hat, his large scared eyes looked everywhere at once as he made his short way to the safety of home, a suburban apartment block. After twenty minutes of laboured walking he reached it without incident, apart from the slight delay as the external shutter over the doorway shuddered before opening. Shutting the front door firmly behind himself, he breathed a sigh of relief, pressing the switch to reengage the shutter. He then made a quick tour of all the windows in his home, engaging the shutters over each for the first time since moving in a little over two years previously.

He switched on the coffee maker and defrosted a pastry. Sitting at the small kitchen table with both, he cast his mind back to the earlier meeting in the civic centre.

It had been a somewhat more heated debate than usual, culminating in a vote in which Jim, for the first time since moving to Rekkisland seven years previously, had been eligible to vote. Those in favour of bringing forward the annual season closure numbered some eighty percent. Jim had known about the closures, as they obviously affected his and every other aspect of the tourist industry in the country.

Miklas had patiently explained it to him.

"You have to plan ahead, Jeem," he'd explained in his laconic, heavily accented drawl, occasionally lapsing into his native tongue, his hand grasping the air for unfamiliar vocabulary. "Not just the money to cover off season. Perishable stock, like, er, like ...," he floundered slightly, remembering that Jim rented hiking equipment, selling the smaller items. "Like trail food. Don't have too much at hand in January. Let it run down and start placing orders for delivery in May. It takes a month to get here anyway."

Jim had known this, of course, having bought out the previous owners of the business some six years earlier, following the sale of his own successful business in his native Oregon. He'd let Miklas lecture him anyway, waiting for him to get to the point.

"It's only every eight years or so anyway. Full closure," continued the older man after a pause. "Most years we just shut everything down for a couple of weeks and any of the waygets tries to book, well, it'n all fully booked, you see." Wayget was local slang for a foreign tourist. "We block book the airlines so they can't get here. Then every eight years we have a major disaster and have to turn away the wayget bookings." He clumsily finger-quoted disaster, getting it wrong with one hand.

After a short, companionable silence while they slowly sipped their drinks, Miklas continued. "No one knows when it first began; What set them off that first year. They've been dormant for many ages. Ice ages. Those first times must have been terrible, before we had modern homes or better boats to leave the place."

"But what are they? What do they look like?"

"Ask Brunhold. You've met him?"

"The Fire Chief?"

"That's him. He's got a dead one frozen in glass to look at. Evil looking thing it is, Anyway, that's what we get couple of year for a few days. Then once a decade small swarms of them for a couple of months. Night only, thanks be, but as you know, this time of year, the days are cruelly short."

Jim nodded. It usually started getting light at about eight, with full daylight lasting until about three in the afternoon and curfew starting a little over an hour later. It wasn't rigidly enforced, he knew, but all the same, best to stay home indoors.

"Why do we need the shutters?" he asked, referring to the metal or toughened plastic roll blinds which could be lowered on the outside of windows.

Miklas wiped his mouth with the back of his hand before answering. "Bout' oh, sixty, seventy years ago they came late. By maybe a year or two. They'd grown bigger and more aggressive than usual and would fly right at people indoors. Smashed straight through the glass. Only thin glazing then, we had. Very cold. They still try occasionally but can't get through the layers of glass we have now. Do a lot of damage though, and that's not an experience you'd care for. I've known hardy and grown men shit theyselves, what with the banging on the outside and the scritch-scratch on the glass. Thank gods for oil heating." To Jim's raised eyebrow he replied. "No open fires; no chimneys."

He'd glanced up as one of the doors into the auditorium opened and with a look of regret sank the remainder of the beer. The two men had stood and made their way towards the meeting convened for that evening.

The voting had been open, without ballot boxes, citizens just moving to one or other side of the room, a scene repeated in dozens of small halls throughout the country. It was preceded by a short speech by each of the heads of the Fire Department, Industry, Tourism, and the Peagan, a government functionary for the surrounding region. Other government figures including the Prime Minister were at their own local venues, urging those assembled to heed their point of view.

The most ardent supporter for season closure was Vibekka, who, in her early thirties, some thirty-five years previously had been overcome and attacked during a short walk back from her car. She had fallen from the balcony of her apartment into deep snow, thus avoiding the more horrific parts of the ordeal. She had clawed her way out and was taken to the medical centre, after being found by a neighbour who had fortunately not yet lowered the window shutters. The majority of the damage she had suffered was during the removal of the fifteen or twenty eggstones, surgical procedures being a lot more invasive back then. And they'd had to be thorough. She didn't say much, but the one eyed, ferocious glare from her ravaged face spoke for her.

The outcome had gone the same way almost everywhere that local, ordinary people were involved. Every radhus, council meeting place, whether formal, like the Assembly, or informal like the local school gymnasium had its vote, and all went the same way, including the online polls. All the people voted to close the season; the politicians almost all naysayers. They, including the Peagan, were dismayed to find they had lost; the vast majority of citizenry preferring safety and future trade over immediate short-term gain. Almost all government employees would be without work and pay for over two months, maybe even longer.

And so it had been settled. Jim and several others had made their way towards Brunhold, to find out how bad things really were.

Following an exciting afternoon on a snowmobile, Mindy had dozed in her room in the chalet. They'd had food brought in from the main part of the hotel, stored in metal trays in the cupboard, the desserts and drinks in the refrigerator.

At a later hour, whilst her parents watched a national news channel in their native English, she surfed Facebook for a while before updating her friends on the day's events. She wasn't entirely clear why they had to have reheated food when the restaurant was close by, nor why her parents had been forbidden from leaving the chalet after dark. Foreign customs, she supposed.

Around two in the morning, Mindy awakened briefly as the door to her room opened slightly, the dim light from the downstairs hallway seeming incandescent around the shadowed edges of her mother's head.

"We'll be back in twenty minutes, thirty tops. Stay in bed darling. The lights will be much earlier tomorrow night and you can see them then," she whispered soothingly, referring to the Aurora they had hoped to see.

Mindy knew this, having earlier checked the forecast, and snuggled up under the warm duvet, Fox staring glassy eyed into the darkness of the room.

The following morning Mindy was up late and padded through the quiet chalet to make herself some cereal for breakfast. She raised one of the window shutters in the breakfast nook to one side of the kitchenette, wincing slightly at the ferocity of the winter morning sun.

She ate one handed, her other preoccupied with scrolling through Facebook, enjoying the silence of the chalet. On her way to the bathroom afterwards, she thought to enquire about the day's itinerary and stuck her head round the door to her parents' room.

They were both sound asleep, although her mother stirred slightly and Mindy quietly closed the door behind herself.

Jim had stood stock still in shock. Even dead, sealed in glass and nailed to a board, the thing was monstrous.

Hideous to behold, it looked like a large segmented black and scarlet wasp, with an eight-inch sting emerging from its carapace. The front end was no less frightening; large razor-sharp mandibles, a sharp proboscis, and the reflective, multisegmented eyes common to many flying insects.

Its wings normally furled against the slender body had been nailed outstretched to the board, each of the four of them fully a metre long. Otherwise the creature itself resembled the bastard offspring of a cockroach and an outsize wasp of a child's nightmares, being about the size of a domestic cat.

He looked up into the placid brown eyes in Brunhold's serene, bearded face.

Brunhold nodded amiably, waiting for the questions. The other three people in the room, equally shocked, duly obliged.

"How fast can they fly?" asked Erik an older looking man with the demeanour of an elderly maths teacher, although he was actually a retired antiques dealer.

"We've no idea. Faster than you can run though, especially in snow," replied Brunhold. "We think at least the speed of a moving car, perhaps 40 miles an hour. What they lack is endurance, which is why we think they never made it off the mainland."

"And they always kill?" asked Marta, another retiree.

"Yes, but that's more a consequence of the venom than any aggression on their part. We've occasionally found cattle that weren't stung. The worst had been injected with over a hundred eggstones, what they use as eggs. They don't hatch for several years, perhaps decades, so unless the beast is suffering from them, can't walk or eat or something it's impossible to tell by looking. All livestock here are tested every spring."

"But people...? Are they...?" Erik reached for a suitable word.

"Hosted?" queried Brunhold. "Yes. You've met Vibekka?"

Four nods. "Most people aren't so lucky. They're usually killed hours later by the poison, or from dehydration, or usually exposure. It's still really winter, remember."

Slow, thoughtful nodding.

"After being chased down, the prey is overwhelmed by their numbers. They begin feeding immediately, starting with the exposed areas. Eyes and face, and usually the tongue and throat as most people start screaming. We think after the first gulp or two of liquified flesh, they then start injecting the eggstones. They only really sting and envenomate if the prey is struggling or fighting back." Bernhold's words were dispassionate, but it was clear that he had seen the horrible results a number of times in his career.

"They're never killed by the emergence of the young; that's usually years later," he continued. "The eggstones meanwhile look like this."

As they recoiled from the object, Brunhold smiled, for perhaps the first time. "Replica," he said.

"Although it's just like the real thing." It was smooth, dark blue and about half the size of a hen's egg.

"Medicins sans Frontiers?" asked Jim, after a minute or two of quiet.

"We can't get help from outside. There would be no more tourism. It would cripple the economy. The best we can do is watch for their arrival and clear out the tourists in an orderly manner. Almost all of the time its predictable and orderly. Most years."

Jim wasn't sure what was the most frightening; the size of the thing, that it flew in a swarm of several dozen individuals, that the venom from even one adult individual was pain beyond endurance and invariably fatal; that they feasted on soft human tissues, such as the eyes, that they used human hosts as incubators for their eggs, that they flew at night and could sense their prey from a mile or two away, that they were aggressive and fast.

The truth was that any single aspect of these unknown creatures terrified him beyond measure. Even the name was formidable, although people could still not agree on it. Darkwasp and Winterdeath were the most common.

"So honey, what else did you do?"

"Oh, just, you know, everything, Aunt Sarah. The snowmobile was the most awesome thing, although I wasn't supposed to go on it. They're like really laid back there. There's no safety rails or anything. If you fall off its your own fault for being stupid. And the beaches were rilly strange. Black sand. And the chalet was just sooooooo cute. Everything was basically awesome. Oh, mom wants you again." Mindy handed the cell phone back to her mother and headed off towards the kitchen.

He mother sighed and cradled the phone. "Hey, Sar."

"Hey yourself. So - the sights? Was it totally awesome?"

"Well, kinda. Yeah actually, the cathedral was. Made of some weird fluted concrete, but strangely appealing. Fantastic views of the city from the tower."

They continued in this vein for several minutes, before the conversation drifted towards Sarah's latest exploits in the dating scene.

The snow piled up unheeded outside the shuttered shopfronts lining the roads through Vogur. Many were normally shut at this time of year anyway, as they catered to the summer trade, the remainder, a mixture of winter shops and the more expensive restaurants would be serving nobody for the next eight weeks. All were shut apart from the supermarkets, small retailers and cafes catering to the local trade, and of course the state-run liquor stores.

A gust of wind sent an icy fountain of grubby snow into a frenzy for a few seconds, before it settled among the pristine whiteness of an earlier fall. It would not be disturbed until the following week.

Though it was but the middle of the afternoon, the streets were deserted, devoid even of the most ill-prepared making purchases of a few last-minute provisions. The snow plows stood in their drafty garages, pensively awaiting a later than usual startup, at first light. The buses in the terminus acquired their own snow topping; there were no journeys to be made.

And yet in their houses and apartments, sometimes alone, sometimes in small groups, the remaining locals went about their socialising over convivial drinks and hearty meals. Most people stayed, maybe three quarters of the population, by day going about their usual business and waiting out the long-deserted nights.

The Peagan sat alone, having eaten a solitary frozen meal left by his wife who had taken the opportunity to share a foreign - safe - holiday with her sister and their families.

He pored over the latest set of accounts forecasts, cold coffee ignored. It was still too early for anything stronger, and in any case he needed sobriety to handle the inevitable angry phone calls when those forecasts reached the highest levels.

The tax returns would take an almost 100% hit for the next two months, never mind the compensation bill for shuttered businesses and displaced families. It was fortunate that the exodus for holidays was much larger than usual. Things could have been far more costly.

He sighed, raising his cup towards his lips before remembering and placing it back.

"So, Mind, d'ya get any souvenirs."

Helen was Mindy's best friend at school and both were sitting on the couch at Mindy's house, Facebooking other friends and talking about their recent holidays. Helen and her family had spent the week in Florida visiting relatives.

"Yep," Mindy nodded. "Not much though. I had to get it in the airport"

"No", exclaimed Helen, her eyes huge, dropping her cell phone dramatically on the carpet.

"Wanna see?"

They bolted for the staircase and hustled up it quickly and quietly. In Mindy's room, behind the closed door, Mindy removed her travel case from the closet.

She opened it out on the floor and removed her thick wool shirts, tossing them onto her bed near to where Fox gazed at them, impassively.

She and Helen gazed at the object revealed beneath where the shirts had been.

"How did you get it," asked Helen reaching out.

"Oh, I had to ask some dude in the duty free," replied Mindy, airily dismissing the nervous thirty minutes it had taken her to approach a stranger to ask him to buy gin for her. "A gift for my aunt," she'd lied.

Helen lifted the bottle out, a crafty expression sliding across her twelve-year-old features. "Can we share?" she asked, guilelessly.

"Sure," replied Mindy.

The took the bottle and headed off to find a tumbler in the bathroom.

The open travel case lay forgotten on the floor, filled with Mindy's clothes and her collection of what she called her glacier pebbles, a dozen small, dark blue-black orbs.

Hope

Marsha Webb

Searing pain tore through Suzanne's body. Her face twisted in anguish and torment. She tried to slow her breathing down and control her impulse to scream out loud. *How much longer?* How much longer could she cope with this torture?

Suzanne remembered hearing somewhere that if you take your mind to another place you can block out the physical pain in the body. Her head swam with thoughts, back to her childhood.

She was at school again. Sat alone in the grey, cold yard, fighting back the tears as the other children made fun of her and told her nobody liked her. "Not even your mum liked you, she gave you up to the children's home". Those words cut her like a knife and played over and over again in her mind until she believed it was true, her mother hadn't wanted her.

She had spent the first eight years of her childhood in the home. Her wish all through primary school was to have one friend, and for this friend to invite her for tea at their home so she could see how it felt to be part of a family. It never happened.

She gasped as the piercing pain made her whole body involuntarily spasm. Sweat ran off her brow in huge droplets, it couldn't be much longer now. Suzanne drifted in and out of consciousness, in her mind she was with her first foster parents.

"Suzanne, get here, what have you done?" Suzanne could hear Ted's voice bellowing at her.

"I'm sorry Ted, I couldn't help it."

Ted would tower over her and shout in her face prodding his fat finger into her chest. "You are useless Suzanne, worth nothing" he would say over and over again, then he would grab her, shake her and punch her.

The physical pain she could deal with - she was used to it - but the words haunted her all through her life.

Her breathing was so shallow and rapid now, Suzanne was close to delirious, the room was spinning. She tried to look at one spot on the wall but she couldn't focus, she closed her eyes instead.

This time she was in her first job, she had thought after leaving school she would have a fresh start, meet new people and make friends. The last two years of high school these thoughts were the only thing that got her through. The day she started work Suzanne had felt positive, a fresh start, her life could finally begin.

However, Suzanne was awkward around people since she had never really had a friend; she didn't know what to talk about. She would take a book to work and sit alone at lunch. The women looked at her with a mixture of pity and bemusement and the men just looked through her as though she wasn't there. Still, she was used to being alone and there was no-one taunting her, so she quietly got on with her work as the months passed.

One day the senior staff at the office had moved the desks around and had a bit of a refurbishment, Suzanne was in the toilet in the cubical when she heard three of the women talking "Great, now I have to sit next to the office freak" one of them whined, "Poor you, can you not move your desk to the side so that your back is to her?" another advised. "She is such a boring sap", the third agreed.

Suzanne waited in the cubical until she was sure they had left, dried her eyes on the rough toilet tissue, took a deep breath and walked back into the office.

The pain was unbearable now. Suzanne could not stop the scream that escaped from her mouth. She tried to move into a more comfortable position, but wave upon wave of intolerable agony wracked her whole body. She felt an excruciating stabbing feeling like her insides had been ripped apart, then nothing...

Peace...

Soon after she felt a glow, she was calm and still, the pain had gone.

"You have a beautiful baby girl, have you got a name?" The midwife handed her a tiny, wrinkled looking bundle and she looked deep into her daughter's eyes.

"Hope" she said, because for the first time in Suzanne's whole life she felt she had hope, a future.

Six Months, One Week and Four Days

Marsha Webb

Jessica leaned against the window. She had been watching the world go by, allowing the hypnotic rhythm of the train to lull her into forgetting the emptiness of her life.

The train pulled into the station. Jessica glanced at the sign, one stop to go, then she saw *him*. The colour drained instantly from her face, her stomach twisted into a tight knot and a wave of nausea washed over her. She had to get off the train before the doors closed. She rushed to her feet and grabbed at her bag. "Excuse me, excuse me." Jessica pushed passed people as politely as she could with impatience and panic rising inside her. She needed desperately to get off this train.

She stepped onto the platform and the cool breeze on her face calmed her slightly. She took a long deep breath, then scanned the crowds to find him. "Where did he go?" She was not going to lose him, she had to see him. She knew every inch of him, she knew she would find him, she had to, nothing else mattered. Suddenly there he was, in a queue for coffee. Just the look of him, even from the back, reduced Jessica to a wreck. Her legs almost buckled under her and her heart felt like it was going to explode out of her chest.

Weaving her way through the crowds on the station, Jessica never once took her eyes off him. She hadn't seen him in six months. Six months, one week and four days to be precise. He had been "the one" they had met at a party eighteen months before and completely clicked, they had left the party together and talked all night. Jessica had never met anyone like Michael, he made her laugh until she cried, he made her feel safe, loved and he believed in her like no one else had ever done. Jessica had fallen totally and utterly in love with him. There was no one else once she had met Michael, no one would ever compare to him.

There had been no warning. She still thought about that day over and over, even now, six months on. In the morning before work she had kissed him and told him she loved him, when she got home that night her whole world had been turned upside down.

Michael had sat her down and told her he had been offered an amazing job opportunity. At first she had been delighted for him but the expression on his face stopped her in her tracks. "It means moving to London baby, I'm sorry but it's something I've always dreamed of, it's a once in a lifetime opportunity".

Jessica loved her life here, her job, her friends and her family but she loved Michael more. It took less that a second for her to decide: "I'd better start looking for jobs then". Jessica reached out to hug him but Michael stopped her.

"No, Jess, you don't understand. I'm moving on my own. I will be working all the hours setting things up, I won't be able to have a relationship as well".

Jessica felt like she had been physically crushed, like someone had taken all the air out of her lungs, then the tears started to well up in her eyes.

"Come on Jess don't do this." Michael held her hands like a mother trying to explain to a child why it couldn't have another toy.

"I thought you loved me." Jessica managed to get out between sobs, the dam had broken now and there was no holding back.

Michael shifted uncomfortably "I do, but this is an amazing opportunity for me, I have to take it, you do understand, don't you?"

"Yes, but why can't I come with you? It can be an adventure for us both." Jessica was aware she was sounding desperate. "I've already told you Jess, I need to do this on my own".

"When are you leaving?" Jess thought she could persuade him over a few months to take her with him.

"On the weekend" Michael said quietly.

The last piece of hope left Jessica. It was over, he had made his mind up. She got up, went upstairs and threw herself on the bed and sobbed her heart out into her pillow. She hoped he would follow her up and put his arms around her and comfort her, but he didn't. An hour later Jessica, with eyes swollen and red raw, went back downstairs to get a glass of water. Her throat was dry and her head was pounding.

Michael was watching a comedy, with his lap top in front of him and an empty packet of crisps on the table. "Oh hey" he said as Jessica walked in "Are you going to get some dinner? Shall we put a pizza in?" Jessica was shocked with his relaxed attitude, it was as if nothing had happened. Jessica couldn't speak, never mind eat. She shook her head, got her glass of water and went back upstairs.

As the week went on, more and more of Michael's things were packed and the flat looked lonely and bare. He was constantly on the phone planning for and arranging his new life and Jessica was struggling to speak without bursting into tears. He was leaving tomorrow. She didn't know if she would ever see him again and she didn't see how she was going to carry on without him. It sent her into a blind panic even thinking about it.

Saturday arrived. Michael had been up early getting some last minute bits and pieces from the shops. He gathered the last of his things together then looked at Jessica. "Well, this is me." he smiled as though he was going for the weekend not walking out of her life forever.

"Please, please, please" Jessica grabbed him and held him tight "Please don't leave me, I'm begging you." Jessica desperately held onto him as he tried to loosen her grip.

"Come on Jess, we've talked about this, I have to go." He tried to free himself from her grip but she held on tighter.

"I'll come in a week or so to visit you to see if we can work it out." Jessica babbled, clutching at straws.

"Let go Jess, I'm leaving now". His tone showed slight irritability.

"So I will never see you again". Jessica wailed. "You will move on, you will barely remember me this time next year."

Michael attempted a joke to lighten the mood. "Bye then." he kissed Jessica s cheek and walked out of the door. He didn't even look back.

That was six months ago, (six months, one week and four days) and she hadn't had so much as a phone call. She text him to ask how he was settling in, he replied "Good, everything is great, just as I imagined." and that was it. She had text and rung many times since but he never replied. It had been about two months since she last text him, drunk text him about 2.00am asking him why and if he missed her at all. No response.

Jessica saw him take the coffee, reach for his car keys and start heading down towards the park and ride. She was within metres of him but a thought suddenly occurred to her and she froze on the spot. He had car keys, he had his car keys, one station away from where they used to live. He hadn't moved to London, he lived here, less than twenty miles from here. He didn't have a job he'd always dreamed of in the capital, he had moved to get away from her and had been too gutless to tell her.

Well, he was going to tell her now! Six months of pain and tears had suddenly turned to scorching anger. She was unexpectedly fuming. *How dare he put me through that?* She was going to tell him exactly what she thought of him and demand answers. Her pace quickened, he was walking down the metal steps to the car park. She heard him whistling to himself. "Yes, that's right Michael." she sneered under her breath "You happily whistle as though you don't have a care in the world while I am in my own private hell of torment, that you have put me through".

Her heart rate quickened, she felt more alive than she had been since he left, the numbness had faded like a screen had been lifted from in front of her, the adrenaline was kicking in. He was ten steps in front of her now, she quickened her pace again and finally caught up with him. She roughly pushed his right shoulder, standing in a defensive pose, hands on her hips. She couldn't wait to see his surprised face, listen to him try to worm his way out of all the lies.

He turned around quickly in surprise and anger at the rough push, she glared into his face...

It wasn't Michael.

The Very Much Alive Poets Society

A new aspect for Leg Iron Books in this anthology is the inclusion of a poetry section. There was a project mentioned, just as this tiny publisher started, of producing a book of poetry. However, most poems are short and we need a minimum of around 100 pages to make a book cost effective. That project was shelved, but never forgotten.

Now that poems are beginning to arrive in submissions, it might be time to revive that idea.

Here are three poets to start us off.

Cade F.O.N Apollyon
Three Four - The Price of One	
One – The Fool Circles Zero	191
Two – Big Sky	193
Three – On the Subject of People and Places and Things	195
Four – Come Alone On	197
Fiver – Spaces	199

Marsha Webb
Forgive Me	201
I don't want to live my life on show	203

Mark Ellott
Dragon's Child	205
For a Moment	207
Music	209
The Soldier	211

Three Four – The Price of One
(a short collection of five Spring-ish poems)

ONE

The Fool Circles Zero
Cade F.O.N Apollyon
27 June 2016

Cocooned in the egg of "dirty labels" containing a new life.
   A new life safe, and sound, and cozy in the dragon's embrace.

And like The Phoenix that burns until it can burn no more.
   This Phoenix...forever in flight...forever burning...yet never dies.

The neverwas...
   that now is...
      and always shall be...
         for the rest of eternity.

For time has ended twice...
   and the time to end time thrice...
      will never, ever, be.
         At least so far as I've been told...
            at least as far as can see.

But I am, and always have been...
   and always shall be...just...me.
      Me...and only me.
         I am the only me...
            anyone will ever see.

Which me do you see?
   Which do you prefer?
      That choice, I leave to you.
         A choice I give freely and for free.

Just remember that when we decide to choose...
   one or the other...
      one will win...one will lose.

Which one wins, becomes which one won.

Which one won, becomes which one lost.

What did they lose?
    What was the cost.

I chose NOT to choose.
    The one sure bet that cannot lose.

I simply felt it best...to give my choice away.
    I'll leave it right here...
        someone will stumble across it...
           ...some day.

There is no rhyme or reason or why...
    save for that someone...
        on that someday...
           will need it more than I.

TWO

Big Sky
Cade F.O.N Apollyon
10 November 1989

WEST WIND BLOW
west wind blow
CLOUDS MARCH ON
clouds march on
WHERE YOU MUST GO
where you must go
BIRDS VOICE THUNDER
birds voice thunder
SPREAD YOUR WINGS
spread your wings
TAKE ME WHERE YOU WILL
take me where you will
SET MY SPIRIT FREE
set my spirit free

NOW COMES THE RAIN
now comes the rain
AND THEN THE SNOW
and then the snow
SPRING'S GENTLE GREEN BEGINS TO SHOW
spring's gentle green begins to show
STILL THE BIRDS RISE
still the birds rise

CARRY ME AWAY
carry me away
A NEW DAWN
a new dawn
A NEW DAY
a new day
'TILL EVE'S BURNT AUBURN WILL SAY
'till eve's burnt auburn will say
REST NOW YOUR WINGS
rest now your wings
COOL YOUR HOT BREATH
cool your hot breath
TOMORROW

tomorrow
THE WIND BLOWS AGAIN
the wind blows again

THREE

On The Subject Of People And Places And Things
Cade F.O.N Apollyon
02 September 2018

One the subject of people and places and things,
It occurs to me that one truth really rings,
And this truth is a truth that inspires fears great and small,
A truth that there is actually, at times...no truth at all.

On the subject of places and things and people,
A truth placed on some building's high untouchable steeple,
A truth buried in some spelunker's deep earthen den,
In the space, between those, beats a heart...it beats again.

On the subject of things and people and places,
The truths that we find, our spaces erases,
What moved and why, the time replaces,
Leaving how in the now, blank stares...and blank faces.

People and places and things? Our subject.
What was and not was or could have been? Our abject.
Our predicate moves when we cast off our line, lines and liners,
Two ships adrift in seize of tan gents, signs...and co-signers.

FOUR

Come Alone On
Cade F.O.N Apollyon
11 March 2019

Come.
And come thee alone.
Come when ye ready,
But come alone on.

Come.
Await we your song.
Come when ye ready,
But come alone on.

Leave now your winter,
Think not of your fall,
Bring not your summer,
Let me see but you, and you in your all.

You in your haste, and you in your mist,
You in your darkness, edging up outwards to sun-kissed.

You in your brightness, and you in your drabs,
You in your mysterious cat's-cradle, weaving magic in dabs.

You in your partials, and you in your wholes,
You in your pollens, and you in your foals.

You in your tirades, and you in your calms,
You in your burnings, and you in your balms.

The unsuredness of summer,
Plus the griefs of fall,
Divided by the shortages of winter,
Equals you now front and center.

Once there were four,
        then three,
                now two,
                        them we've seen, and to the front... comes one...comes you.

You in your industry, and you in your might,
You in your gentleness, ends winter's long flight.

You in your beckonings, and you in your mirth,
You in our doubting, push light o'er dark earth.

You in your bendings, and you in your tides,
You in your purpose, bring hope for new trides.

You in your many, and you in your lone,
You in our marrow, unseen deep in bone.

The darkness, for now departs.
Came thee thence.
Of the four faces known,
Yours the longest absent from full shown.

See we your four,
   and your three,
      and your two,
         see we your ones, all of you...welcome we back your one...your you.

But come.
And come thee alone.
Come when ye ready,
But come alone on.

Come.
Await we your song.
Come when ye ready,
But come alone on.

FIVER

Spaces
Cade F.O.N Apollyon
Started: 04 April 1986 – Completed: 11 March 2019

    I'm holding a little box in my hands,
But what is in the box?
    I'll bet you'd never guess, my friend,
It's a pair of dirty socks.

Smelly feet.
    Ain't it a treat,
        To have smelly feet.

    I'm walking towards my closet,
But what lurks behind that door?
    Stand back, my friend,
Yes...it's in the air,
    before I even get there...
        turn the handle...
            door ajar, but not too far...
                yes there...on the floor...
                    good God!...there's even more!...
                          pairs upon pairs of dirty socks galore!

Rancid feet.
    You ain't complete,
        Without rancid feet.

    I'm holding a little bag in my hands,
But what does this bag contain?
    This one will elude you, my friend,
Rocks mined straight from my brain.

Rocky brains.
    You ain't half sanes,
        Without rocky brains.

    One rock per sock,
Each sock tied in a knot.
    Throw them in the creek,
Don't get caught.

Bare feet.
    Ain't it sweet,
        To have bare feet.

I'm holding a rusty nail in my hand.
Can you guess where it was found?
    I think this is the end, my friend,
For my bare foot, found it standing, on the ground.

Bear feet.
    Wouldn't it be sweet,
        To have had bear feet.

First coughin',
    Now hackin',
        My locked jaw cracking.
Then a coffin,
    In the offing,
        No socks in need of packing.
I like daisies,
    I like dandelions,
        Not fond of gatherins' with cryins'.
The weedy,
    The seedy,
        The thistles,
            The wildflowers,
                The wild bushes,
                    Things with thorns.
The insignificant,
    The buttercups,
        The tall grasses,
            The clover,
                The things cut,
                    The looked over.
This road for me is ending,
    an ending not so sweet,
        but all that I wanted,
            was non-stinky feet.

Forgive Me

Marsha Webb

Please forgive me for the sadness I have caused, the pain I have drawn.
Tears I've brought welling into your soulful eyes, through night and dawn.
I can hardly bear to look upon your troubled face.
Pain etched into every expression, I took you to that place.
Undeserving of your forgiveness, I truly know that I may be,
But I'll never forgive myself, until you forgive me.

Guilt follows me around like a stone within my heart.
Scars that will not heal, an oppression that's darkest dark
It transcends my every thought, both night and day
Cascading in layers, no matter what I do or say.
Undeserving of your forgiveness, I truly know that I may be,
But I'll never forgive myself, until you forgive me.

You have changed the way you are, and not just around me,
Your confidence and optimism eroded away it's clear to see.
You're in torment and unable to find peace,
Glass shards in your heart, I would do anything for the pain to cease.
Undeserving of your forgiveness, I truly know that I may be,
But I will never forgive myself, until you forgive me.

If I could change the things I did, to take away your pain and despair.
I know that we are both broken, that's something we still share.
I would never hurt you again, for I have hurt myself being unkind.
The remorse I feel, the guilt and shame, of memories that haunt my mind.
Undeserving of your forgiveness, I truly know that I may be,
But I will never forgive myself, until you forgive me.

Will you ever forgive me?
Will you ever forgive me?

I don't want to live my life on show

Marsha Webb

I don't want to live my life on show,
Where everyone is watching and judging me.
You love being the centre of attention everywhere we go,
But I can't live like this anymore, can't you see?
People look at me through hateful eyes; I know they think I'm not good enough for you,
I scrutinise myself in the mirror every day, and know that it's probably true.

The times we had alone I will never forget,
But you don't stay for long, you crave the attention of others.
For putting myself through agonising pain all this time I'll always regret,
The nights I have wasted, taunting myself with visions of all your lovers.
Your past always catches up with you; you will never let it go,
You don't care how it makes me feel, so alone and so low.

I need to have my own private world, something honest, something true,
I can't keep up with your lies and the crazy lifestyle you want to lead.
It is so hard to walk away but it's something I know I have to do,
There is a blackness in my life, a deep and desperate need.
I know people are talking, they think I have been a fool, that I haven't known your ways or your lies,
I have known all along, from the very first day, now it's time to move on and cut the ties.

You say that I won't find anyone else like you, and I'm guessing that you are probably right,
But you have no idea how hard you make it to be around you.
Vying for your attention like all those other girls, the jealousy rising in me, making me want to fight,
I am not able to compete anymore, I have lost that spark, it's true.
You have doused it too many times with too many games,
You have too much in your past, too many other names.

My hopes and dreams are different now to yours,
I don't know when they changed; I just know that they have moved on.
I want calm, I want pure, to breathe in the air, to pause,
The things that I do when I am with you, the things that I say, I want that person gone.

Saying goodbye to you will be the hardest thing I will ever have to take,
But losing my sanity, my personality, my whole self is a sacrifice I can't make.

The highs when I am with you make me reach for the sky,
But the lows are so desperate, like being trapped in the blackest hole.
We both knew I could never change you, no matter how hard I try,
My tears are raw and unrelenting, the anguish deep in my soul.
I choose to ignore all the signs, the lies, the secrets, the games that you play,
The good times are no longer anaesthesia for the pain, I must move away.

So goodbye my one, the person I will never get over, goodbye.
I will watch you walk out of my life forever, leaving the damage to my mind, soul and my heart.
I can no longer live like this, no matter how hard I try.
I am exhausted, spent, keeping up with you in my life, we have to be apart.

Dragon's Child

Mark Ellott

I have lazed on a sun drenched atoll;
And sailed the South China Seas.
I've run my hands through warm Caribbean sands;
And watched the sunrise over the keys:
But still I'm thinking of mist shrouded Snowdon;
And the forests on the shores of Vyrnwy.
For this is the land of the dragon;
And it's where I want to be,
For I am dragon's child;
And it's a part of me.
For this is the land of the dragon;
And wherever I may roam.
I'll always be dragon's child:
And this will always be my home.

So when I'm scaling the peaks in Nepal,
Or shopping for gifts in Tokyo;
When I'm exploring the far reaches of Amazon;
Or letting my hair down in Rio;
My thoughts are on the beaches of Gower;
And the snow tipped crags of Cader.
For this is the land of the dragon;
And it's where I want to be,
For I am dragon's child;
And it's a part of me.
For this Is the land of the dragon;
And wherever l may roam.
I'll always be dragon's child:
And this will always be my home.

From the rain grey terraces of Rhondda,
To the spume tipped Celtic sea;
And the sails on Bala to the mountains of Meirionnydd;
Down to the sweeping Dyfi estuary;
From the Menai Straits and the road through Dylif;
To the castles In Carmarthen. Caernarfon and Cardiff;
Oh, Men of Harlech and the Pontypool Front Row;

Know that this is where my heart is
No matter where I go.
So when I'm seeking out the source of the Nile,
Or trekking the Great Rift Valley;
I might pause and reflect for a while;
And In my mind's eye, it's a greener valley, I'll see.
For this is the land of the dragon;
And it's where I want to be;
For I am dragon's child;
And it's a part of me.
For this is the land of the dragon;
And Wherever I may roam,
I'll always be dragon's child;
And this will always be my home.

For A Moment

Mark Ellott

For a moment, time stops dead
The raucous gulls wheel overhead
The salt spray stings my eye
Waves caress the shore with a sigh
For a moment, that passes in a blip
The cares of the world from my shoulders slip

Music

Mark Ellott

I am dance, I am soul;
I am ragtime, rock and roll;
I am a waltz, I am punk;
I am country, I am funk;
I am jazz, I am blues;
I am music and I'm any melody I choose.
I am the rhythm of your heart
And the pounding on the streets after dark,
I am the wind in the trees, the sighing of the seas.
The thunder and the rain, to me they're all the same.
The clamour on the pavements, the solitude and silence;
I am their melody and their beat,
Their tempo and their cadence.
I am music and the world is my muse.
I am music and the world dances to my tunes.
I am metal, I am rock;
I am folk, I am bebop;
I am a prelude, I am cantata;
I am opera, I am sonata;
I am symphony, I am blues;
I am music and the world dances to my moves.
I am music and I'm any melody I choose.

The Soldier

Mark Ellott

I fought for Harold up north, and marched once more to Battle,
On the beaches of France, I ducked the bombers and tracers of machine gun rattle.
I marched with Percy at Shrewsbury, and laid my life down for the white rose,
At Agincourt I lifted my bow for red, and again at Bosworth, for my king against his foes.

In my coat of green and red, khaki and sand,
I've fought the enemies of my leaders with my merry band.
And sometimes my brothers fell beneath my sword, as England tore itself apart,
When we killed our king and lost both our way and our heart.

I was for both Parliament in t'early days, and for Crown upon the latter,
At the Boyne I lifted my musket for Orange, and afore it, the papists did scatter.
In my coat of green I raised my rifle at Waterloo, as we watched Boney run,
I've lived my life by the sound of the battle, the carnage, cannon and the drum.

Where in the bleak south Atlantic, or the North African plains,
I considered only fleetingly of losses borne, and of our gains.
I've raised my rifle to orders from above, and thought not about the cause I fight,
Whether 'tis a just one we do, or wrong or right.

I wonder sometimes that had I not been ready to die,
To shed my blood on Flanders fields, or the dirt of some foreign land,
Would those wars be fought, if those who procured them had to die hand to hand?
I slew my brothers in coats of blue and grey,
And I think of those who sent me; they I serve,
I wonder sometimes, now, what they are worth,

Those soulless men who threw my life away,
For y'know, I wouldn't give 'em, the bastards, the time of day.

Afterword

Roo B. Doo

Here we are again, Dear Reader, at the end of another Underdog Anthology. Certainly we hope you've enjoyed reading our scribblings, and that we've been successful in making your wildest transgenre dreams come true.

As you'll have noticed, the 'The Very Much Alive Poets Society' section has been included in this edition. This is new and, should it prove popular, will no doubt be repeated in future anthologies. Or it may lead to a separate book of Underdog poetry: in 2019, *nothing* is impossible.

Here in the dead poets' backwater of the Afterword, the topic du jour is Brexit. Again. As I write, 1,000 days after the Independence Referendum decision was delivered, if and when the UK leaves the EU is still unknown.

Thankfully, one of the greatest Romantic poets, William Blake, has graciously supplied his most famous poem, 'The Tyger' to go under the knife. A hat tip goes to that other literary giant, Dr Theodor Seuss, for the title - the absurdity of the British political class deserves no less.

See you for Halloween. Enjoy!

The Creeps (that stole Brexit)

Brexit Brexit, MPs blight,
In the politics of Fright;
What immoral Hansard lie,
Could frame their shameful skimitry?

What the distant Creeps despise,
Disbelieving of their lies?
In Labour town & Tory shire,
People *chose* Leave as their desire?

And what bluster, for their part,
In twisting syntax off the chart?
And so the Creeps began to cheat,
Safe in smugness, if not in seat.

"What the horror? Why the pain?"
"The People didn't know thy brain!"

"What the oldies failed to grasp,
It's not long 'til their final gasp!"

When the Creeps threw down their sneers,
Made amendments, with loud jeers,
Did they smile their work to see?
Do they know they'll have to flee?

Brexit Brexit, MPs blight,
In the politics of Fright;
What immoral Hansard lie,
Could frame their shameful skimitry?

About the Authors

(In no particular order)

Roo B. Doo

For this Spring anthology, I am delighted to present two love stories in one tale, Dear Reader. Consider it a special offer ;)

Want more Roob? You can find her on the internet, ably assisted by Clicky, who may or may not be a) an alien dolphin and b) from another dimension, lolling about her Library of Libraries, writing synchromystic shambles at www.roobeedoo2.wordpress.com

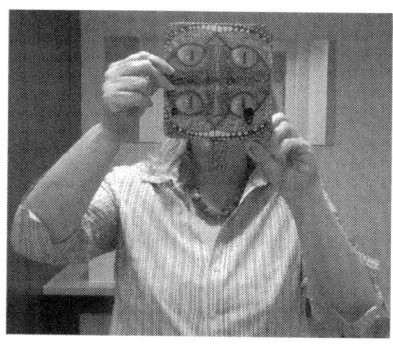

H. K. Hillman

H. K. Hillman is the creator, or perhaps creation, of Romulus Crowe, Dr. Phineas Dume and Legiron the Underdog. Now pretty much retired from science, he hides out in an ancient farmhouse in Scotland where he spends a lot of time thinking up horrible stories, and running the tiny publishing house called Leg Iron Books.

Daniel Royer

Daniel Royer is a writer of short fiction. He is a California State University, Bakersfield graduate with an English Degree he's not using. Royer works as a full-time welder to support his true passion, which is tomahawk-throwing. His stories have been printed by Ponahakeola Press, SFReader.com, and some other publications you've never heard of. Royer lives in California. He has a cat.

Jeani Rector

While most people go to Disneyland while in Southern California, Jeani Rector went to the Fangoria Weekend of Horror there instead. She grew up watching the Bob Wilkins Creature Feature on television and lived in a house that had the walls covered with framed Universal Monsters posters. It is all in good fun and actually, most people who know Jeani personally are of the opinion that she is a very normal person. She just writes abnormal stories. Doesn't everybody?

Jeani Rector is the founder and editor of The Horror Zine and has had her stories featured in magazines such as *Aphelion, Midnight Street, Strange Weird and Wonderful, Dark River Press, Macabre Cadaver, Blood Moon Rising, Hellfire Crossroads, Ax Wound, Horrormasters, Morbid Outlook, Horror in Words, Black Petals, 63Channels, Death Head Grin, Hackwriters, Bewildering Stories, Ultraverse,* and others.

Martyn K. Jones

Martyn K Jones is an expatriate Englishman living and working in Victoria BC, Canada and keeping his accent for tax purposes. His working life has taken him from Electrical Engineering to IT via a circuitous path, which has included working on a mushroom farm and hot air balloon ground crew work. This somewhat eccentric work history even includes undertaking professional level acting training during the late 1980's and early 90's. However, he has been writing for most of his adult life, producing anything from marketing copy to high-level technical documentation, as well as a number of unsuccessful attempts at novel length fiction and various short stories.

His first ever short story was published in October 1978 and he has since found sporadic, albeit minor, success with his quirky brand of otherworldly fiction under various pen names. His last published supernatural short story 'Hunter' appearing in the People's Friend February 2006 fiction special. Since then he has written four Science fiction novels, with a fifth, the third and final epic novel of his 'Stars' trilogy still under development.

He is married to Angela, and has two grown up stepdaughters.

Ginger Huff

I'm a hippy gypsy farm girl, celestial observer, empath and animal lover. I'm blessed to live out in the country, where cows and critters outweigh traffic, and birds caw my name.

Texan by birth and a writer by heart, I started writing at 16 and had my first story published that year in the local newspaper. Fast forward to my 30's, I wrote for a different hometown newspaper. I was the assistant editor and had my own column entitled, 'Maybe It's Just Me' where I covered different problematic trends with a side of humor. I was also tasked with being the first person to cover School Board and City Council weekly meetings. Talk about a challenging venue. Half the town loved me and the other half were appalled that anyone, especially a woman, dared to crash their secretive meetings.

One time I found a burnt newspaper in my mailbox. I kept writing but added a locked gate to my home. The power of the written word is truly amazing.

Dirk J.J. Vleugels

Dirk J. J. Vleugels is a retired barrister who has been living in Indonesia since 1983 and is very happy with his life there.

He has also written "Es-tu là, Allah?" (in French), "Feesten Onder de Drinkboom" (in Dutch) and the first ever biography of the Dutch-Indonesian painter Han Snel (in Dutch). All three books are published by Leg Iron Books.

Marsha Webb

I live just outside Cardiff and I am a full time high school teacher. I have only recently started writing. Writing short stories are my favourite because teaching takes up so much time and because I love the feeling of achievement when a story is finished.

I have always had a very over active imagination and writing allows me to use this in a positive way. I am currently finishing my first novel.

Justin Sunshine

A middle aged Software Developer and IT Consultant, currently living on the South Coast of England.

Hi folks. Back again.

This time out is a mild horror offering and a whimsical tale about 'real' magic. I hope they entertain.

I've previously written for all but two of the Underdog Anthologies, varying between genre and writing style.

Work and family commitments take up a lot of my time these days, but I still try to find time now and then to write something new or get one of the many works-in-progress finished. Maybe sometime I'll have enough of them to fill a collection of my own.

Mark Ellott

Mark Ellott is a part time motorcycle instructor, delivering training for students who require compulsory basic training and direct access courses. He has semi-retired from his main job as a freelance trainer and assessor working primarily in the rail industry, delivering track safety training and assessment as well as providing consultancy services in competence management.

He writes fiction in his spare time. Mostly, his fiction consists of short stories crossing a range of genres, and has stories in all but one of the previous Underdog Anthologies – and now in this one.

His first two novels, 'Ransom' and 'Rebellion', are now available in print and eBook formats. The third is in progress.

He has also published a volume of his own short stories, entitled 'Blackjack', and a collection of Morning Cloud Western stories entitled 'Sinistré'.

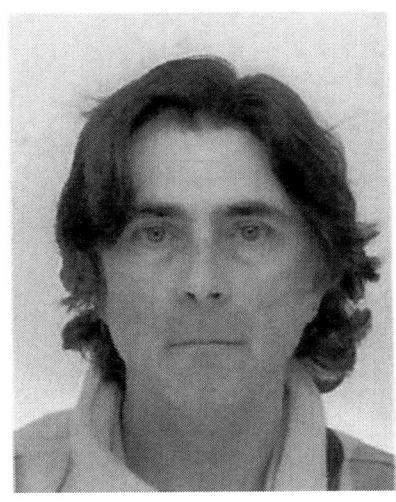

Justin Sanebridge

Justin Sanebridge is the author of "The Goddess of Protruding Ears." Now also available in Dutch as "De Godin van de Flaporen."

Some of his short stories have appeared in 'The Good, the Bad and Santa' (Underdog Anthology 4).

Somewhat reclusive, he prefers not to be photographed so has elected to be represented by a stone with eyes.

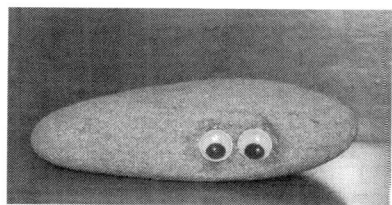

Cade F.O.N Apollyon

You don't want to know about me. But if you change my mind, I can sometimes be found rambling on my blog at https://cadefonapollyon.blogspot.com/ while at other select times I can be found rambling on RooBeeDoo's blog at https://roobeedoo2.com/ and I can also be found on Twitter pretty much 24 hours a day where we can speak directly if you are really that bored.

LEG IRON BOOKS

Also available from Leg Iron Books:
Fiction:
'The Underdog Anthology, volume 1'
'Tales the Hollow Bunnies Tell' (anthology II)
'Treeskull Stories' (anthology III)
'The Good, the Bad and Santa' (anthology IV)
'Six in Five in Four' (anthology V)
'The Gallows stone' (anthology VI)
'Christmas Lights… and Darks' (anthology VII)
   All edited by H.K. Hillman and Roo B. Doo.

'The Goddess of Protruding Ears' by Justin Sanebridge.
'De Godin van de Flaporen' by Justin Sanebridge (in Dutch)
'Ransom', by Mark Ellott
'Rebellion' by Mark Ellott
'Blackjack' a collection of short stories by Mark Ellott.
'Sinistré (The Morning Cloud Chronicles)' by Mark Ellott
'The Mark' by Margo Jackson
'You'll be Fine' by Lee Bidgood
'Feesten onder de Drinkboom' by Dirk Vleugels (in Dutch)
'Es-Tu là, Allah?' by Dirk Vleugels (in French)
'Jessica's Trap' by H.K. Hillman
'Samuel's Girl' by H.K. Hillman
'Norman's House' by H. K. Hillman
'The Articles of Dume' by H.K. Hillman
'Fears of the Old and the New' short stories by H.K. Hillman
'Dark Thoughts and Demons' short stories by H.K. Hillman

Non-fiction:
'Ghosthunting for the Sensible Investigator' first and second editions, by Romulus Crowe.

Biography:
'Han Snel' by Dirk Vleugels (in Dutch).

Printed in Great Britain
by Amazon